AUCKLANDERS

AUCKLANDERS

Murray Edmond

Press

Published by 99% Press, 2023
an imprint of Lasavia Publishing Ltd.
Auckland, New Zealand
www.lasaviapublishing.com

'RSA' was first published in Landfall 243, March 2022.

ISBN: 978-1-991083-03-6

To Joanna Forsberg for listening with love
and critiquing with insight and honesty

Special thanks and much gratitude for feedback on
specific stories from Tom Bishop, Rod Edmond and
Lisa Samuels.

CONTENTS

1

CROSS-EYED PIRATE

When the magistrate asked me to make a submission to the court on behalf of my father, at the time he was up on the indecent exposure and disturbing the peace charges, what I ended up writing down needed a good editing before it could be submitted. My father was never an easy man to live with or to deal with. The plain fact is, he didn't want to be easy. And he had no intention of ever trying to be. If he hadn't insisted, when the police arrested him, that he be 'taken before a judge and processed by the law,' as he put it in his funny old Dutchie English, there wouldn't have been a trial. The police didn't want it. The judge tried to get it over with. But Dad, being Dad, made sure it was a process.

What follows is not what I gave the magistrate. Nor is it my first draft, the one that had to be edited. The fact was that first draft contained a fair slice of blaming. Most of which was pretty justified. Dad treated Mum like shit. (That's the kind of thing I didn't pass along to His Honour.) He's always been an arrogant son of a bitch who thought the world shone out of his arsehole (again omitted). He's never listened to anyone else. He thinks he is the most tolerant man in the world, but, truth to tell, he's just as intolerant as most of the rest of us. He is *interesting*. I'll grant him that. I can see why Mum would have fallen in love with him. And, to be fair to her, she only did it once. I grew up mostly with Mum. I would come down from Hokianga to Auckland for the school holidays to stay with Dad. Dad would drag me off to weird parties. I'd go to the Art School with him, where he used to teach, and that was kind of cool. I could play with some of the gear, the cameras, the lights and the computers. And Dad did always let you do what you wanted. But he was only interested in what he was doing. Or what young student he fancied might give him her time of night. But that became increasingly rare. Enough of that. I wrote that so you could know the kind of thing I didn't forward to the Court.

What follows is version three – a bit of draft one, some of draft two, and a lot of draft three. I'm not going to pause to interrupt myself any longer to explain which bits came from where.

I've been living out the back of 18 Bryce Street for the past three years, while Dad has occupied the actual on-site dwelling. The sleep-out is self-contained, it's warm and dry (unlike the crumbling villa itself), and it costs me nothing. Dad was never a skinflint. He never wanted people's money or tried to rip them off. And the really good thing has been that it has allowed me to get my own start-up going, Manu Murray Techno-Solutions, and now the business is humming along. I took on two staff a year ago and they have been the bomb. In fact, it's time to call a halt to the exponential growth of the last year and take stock of where we are at. But it's all basically good. So, thank you, Dad. I won't say you owed me, but you did.

Dad turned seventy last year. I'm not sure he's still the man he was. He falls asleep in the old rocker on the back porch now, and then pretends he hasn't. That rocker was where he used to sit and play his guitar and sing his Dylan songs. I do remember that, before Mum and I left for up North. He could play okay, a bit of Māori strum, some Robert Johnson slide, all rather clumsy, but passable. The rocker was also where he used to sit and fire off his air rifle. He'd set up a line of Wattie's Baked Beans cans along the framing of the back fence, and, gently oscillating in the chair, with the gun tucked into his shoulder, he'd let rip. Pow! Ping! Gotcha! Mum would be furious. 'Jan! Stop that! There are children in the next property!' Of course, he only did it to make her mad. 'I missed them' he'd call back. 'Fuck you!' she would say, and grab me and say, 'Come on, we're going up to the shops.' We could hear Dad laughing as we walked up the street.

We'd go to the shops and the swings in the park and get an

ice cream and as we came back we'd hear Dad's raucous Dylan whine singing at the top of his lungs:

See the cross-eyed pirates sitting
Perched in the sun
Shooting tin cans
With a sawed-off shotgun
And the neighbours they clap
And they cheer with each blast

Mum would be holding my hand too tight. 'It's okay, Davey,' she would say. I don't know why she called me Davey, or who Davey was. My name was Manu and mostly she called me that except when she was mad and, I guess, a bit scared too. Maybe Davey was a big strong man who was walking beside her and would stride up the front steps, through the house, out onto the back porch and say to Jan: 'Cut the crap.' It wasn't as though he was violent. He didn't hit people. And he wasn't a drinker. Never touched a drop. Some people say that's suspicious in itself. No, he intimidated. I mean, he didn't hit people, but he did fire his air rifle at the back fence when there were children – and, indeed, adults – just behind the fence. It was all a big joke to him. But he scared people.

Kids would run away when they saw him. He'd lost an eye when he was a kid himself, to an infection that hadn't been picked up properly and should have. But he didn't complain. Instead he always wore a patch and played the pirate to the hilt. His hair was long and straggly and pulled into an untidy ponytail with a tiny sword on a ribbon hanging off the end. He wore – still wears – a colourful scarf around his head. His preference has always been for a bare chest and some leather garment, waistcoat in summer, jacket in winter, tight pink trousers, big boots. He doesn't design himself to be missed. And he'd often have his Kris, the dagger with the wavy blade, tucked into a belt at his waist. The Kris was a relic from his parents when they'd fled Indonesia after the Second World War. Yes, he was (not so much now) a big man with a lot of swagger. And as Mum realized pretty quick, one or two young women at the Art School each year were likely to fall for his act. After all, she had herself. But she was the one who became hapū.

Mum's name is Angela Murray. She'd come to Art School from up North, and she'd been a bit of a star pupil. Design and sculpture were her thing. They still are. She has a little gallery on the Hokianga, sells heaps out of the gallery shop to tourists. I think I picked up my business sense from Mum. Not from Dad, for sure. Business was part of the large range of things in the world that he despised. I heard him once, when he was popping the Wattie's cans, muttering under his breath: 'Business – bang! Bourgeois – bang! Banks – bang!' He could make you laugh. But it was impossible for Mum. When I was six, she picked me up and walked out. We went to Wellington, then to Hawkes Bay, then to Dunedin, but finally we went up North.

Dad had been singing 'Farewell Angelina' for a few years by the time we escaped, just to rark Mum up. He doesn't sing it anymore. In fact, he doesn't play the guitar. It's still in his room. Used to hang off the wall, but now the guitar has been stuffed on top of the wardrobe. I don't know what happened to the air rifle. Maybe the police came and took it for safe-keeping. The police were another of those Wattie' cans in Dad's mind, though they probably weren't aware of it. Things are definitely mellower than they once were. But he still has the Kris. Well, at least he did.

I remember the street, back when I was there for those years, still had big Polynesian families living there. I know now that was changing fast. Of course, we were a half-Polynesian family, but I don't think anyone thought of us like that. We didn't belong to either side of the great divide. Probably we were an example for both sides of the kind of disaster best avoided. I reckon that those who were in the process of moving in and 'taking over,' so to speak, were pretty hopeful that Dad would soon be gone. He was alert to that unstated, but bloody obvious, desire, and nothing could have made him more determined to stay. He has never done anything to the house. The front verandah now falls away on one side and hangs pendulously in the air. Buggered if I know what's holding it up. On the other side, the verandah is stacked with junk – old bikes, chairs, sofas, the fridge from twenty years ago, shoes, tarpaulins, pots for pot-plants, pots for cooking. Mum makes great sculptures out of junk – ah, out of recycle – and I did suggest to Dad recently that I could get the lot shipped up to Mum to use. 'Don't you touch it!' he said, and added, 'It's beautiful.' Cheeky old bugger. So, the neighbours no longer clap and cheer. Instead they stare and glare. 'It's doing so much damage to their property values!' Dad hoots. WTF can you do? (That wasn't for the judge!)

I was at work when the first incident happened. One of the many things that enrages Dad is Halloween. I would think that American culture in general and Halloween in particular would each earn a Wattie's can to shoot down.

'It's not even Christian. All Saints' Day! All Hallows Eve! Bloody pumpernickel! It's a pre-Christian festival. It's pagan.'

As he launched himself into one of his 'raves,' as even he called them in his calmer moments, he would acquire a rather heavy Dutch accent. Jan himself was only one year old, when he arrived in New Zealand, so this 'accent' was part of his 'I'm a crazy European' act. He would refer to his 'Dutchie English' and ally himself with the civilized world of Europe (which, at other times, he would spit upon in disgust as a nest of imperialist racist poppycocks). But it is all contrived, as he has grown up only in Aotearoa speaking English, though he would have listened to his parents speaking Dutch at home and would have been able to follow what they said. But he doesn't actually speak a word of Dutch and I doubt he would understand a word of it now either. And on he would rave, every year, as October drew to an end:

'The Day of the Dead! Opposite Walpurgisnacht on the Calendar! Pain and life versus harvest and death! Listen to bloody Stravinsky! And these kids come round the streets looking like they are doing a Hollywood audition. Five-year-olds! Not the children – I mean, the films. Hollywood films are made for five-year-olds! Before those wishy-washy Christians came marching into Europe, children were sacrificed to the goddess of fertility. What do these pumpkin-headed, pumpkin-eating popinjays know about that?'

'Dad, no one knows what you're talking about.'

'That's my point! Trick treat – twick and tweat. Tweet tweet tweet. So this is it? The climactic moment in the whole evolutionary enterprise? Twick or tweet?'

I was heading off to the office. Halloween was happening that afternoon. The parade of tiny no-necks and protective parents, loaded down with gear from the two-dollar shops. Or, sometimes, masterpieces of kitsch that their mothers had sewn. And begging bags. The moment I said what I said, I felt the regret rise up in me. Saying anything to Dad has always been more than a provocation. It's a bloody invitation:

'Dad, I won't be home till late. Just leave it, eh? Let them go, Ignore the door. Don't answer. They'll go away. Anyway, they'll be too scared to come to our door. The haunted house. I reckon that's what I'd call it If I were a kid.'

I could see the glint in Dad's eye as I left.

The children came of course. They'd never come to the house much before. Maybe it was a dare: dare you to go into that house. So, the knock came. And Jan van Beek was ready and waiting. He'd sought out, from the old suitcase, the one with the shipping labels still sticking on it, his parents treasured mask of Rangda. In Bali, if you look it up in Wikipedia, as I had to do, you find that Rangda is 'the demon queen of the Leyaks,' an army of witches she leads. Her mask has fangs, goggle eyes, and a sticking-out tongue, with long, unkempt hair. And, of course, she eats children. What could be better?

He was wearing the mask with his chest bare, his old pink trou and bare feet, with the Kris in hand and he'd snuck down the side of the house, where he lurked, waiting, so he could trap the snotty little bourgeoises and terrify the living daylights out of them. When he heard the knocking, he let out a blood-curdling holler, and came dancing round the side of the house, hopping from foot to foot like a crazed, wind-up toy. There was a unified shriek from the bunch of kids as well as the one parent accompanying them. Panic broke out. Some of the kids rushed to the far end of the verandah where the flooring hung swaying in space. Several jumped. No one actually broke a leg. That might have been lucky. But it didn't happen. The parent, a mum, then panicked also, and jumped off the end after the kids and twisted (but did not break) her ankle. The twisted ankle would be something that was noted in future dealings. Seeing that the wretched trick-and-treaters had eluded him, Dad turned to run back down the front steps, which he had bounced up with remarkable agility for a man of seventy, but in the process of turning, with the heavy mask obscuring his vision, he tripped on the top step and plummeted down the three further steps. He landed hard on the concrete pad at the bottom. But the worst was that the Kris twisted in his hand as he fell and he managed to stab himself in his buttock. It was deep enough to really hurt. That gave rise to a second blood-curdler, which filled the neighbourhood.

I wish someone had had the presence of mind to have their cellphone out and film the whole thing. I think Mum and I could have shared the moment. The ambulance came. When I got to the hospital he was lying on his side with his arm around Rangda. I didn't see the Kris.

He grinned and asked me to, 'Take her home and put her to bed' – referring to Rangda – because 'she's done a good day's work.' Irascible, intractable, he was grinning from ear to ear. Maybe the painkillers had kicked in.

I took Rangda home. Because I have everything I need in the sleepout, I haven't spent much time in the house the last three years. Jan is pretty much holed up in the back bedroom, next to the kitchen and the toilet. I took Rangda inside, found her suitcase and bid her good night. Almost got the feeling she had a glint in her eye too. It was ages since I'd been in the rest of the house.

Theodore Hook invented the postcard. I know that Dad had changed his name by deed poll to Captain Theodore Hook not so long ago. I had chosen to ignore it. He was still Jan van Beek of 18 Bryce Street for me. He explained that he was turning himself into a work of art. I gave him my cheeky look and said, 'But, Dad, you've been a work of art for years. Everyone knows that.' Across the lintel of door that led to the villa's central passageway elegant calligraphy spelt out: THE WORLD OF CAPTAIN THEODORE

HOOK, DELTIOLOGIST. And then something that I reckoned must have been in Latin: NIHIL CONGERO, but it was beyond me. I pushed through the door and quickly realized every available surface, walls and ceilings and even the floor, was plastered with postcards. We all knew he had been working on his 'Postcard Project' for god knows how many years. 'It'll finish me before I finish it,' was one of his standard pronouncements. I tiptoed – that was the effect this had on me – into what had been my room when I came to stay. It was the same in there, as in the hallway. I think that's when I realized things were a little more advanced with Dad than I had realized. I tiptoed slowly backwards and squeezed the door silently shut behind me.

He came back from the hospital after two days. He seemed in high spirits. Energised even further by his time there. The neighbours must have been watching us and watching the house, because one day, not long after Dad had returned from the hospital, when I was coming back from work and was going to head round the back, up the side path, to the sleepout, a bunch of locals suddenly materialized. I didn't really know any of them. I mean that's what it's like living here now. But they seemed to know each other. They were the local neighbourhood committee apparently. There were even a couple of children with them, god knows why. They didn't seem to know who I was either. They thought I was a boarder. When I told them I was Mr van Beek's son I could see they didn't believe me. That ratty old long-haired Dutchie – and this smart young Māori in his collar and tie. It didn't take me more than a couple of minutes talking to them to notice I'd begun to feel like Dad: they just want me out, don't they? Well, bugger them!

I listened, standing there with my brief case in hand. They were concerned. 'I hear you,' I said. About what happened at Halloween. 'I know,' I said, 'I understand. But he's okay. He had to have a dozen stitches, but it's all healing up fine.'

But, no. That wasn't what they were concerned about.

'Helen MacInnes badly sprained her ankle in the incident,' a voice piped up.

'I'm sorry to hear that,' I responded.

'She could have broken her leg,' the same voice persisted, 'and she's got two children to bring up and her husband's in Thailand.'

I turned my attention back to the whole group: 'So what is the concern?'

They were concerned about the neighbourhood, they told me.

'It's a very nice neighbourhood,' I said.

'That's exactly the problem,' one of them said.

I knew I needed to stay calm and polite, but I also felt an overwhelming desire to say, 'Grow up!' and turn on my heel and walk away. I said: 'It would probably help if you explained what you mean.'

One of them said, 'What do you think we mean?'

Fortunately or unfortunately, I was saved by what happened next. The front door flew open and slammed against the wall. The gaudy passageway of postcards stood fully revealed. And in the doorway stood Dad. Stark naked. He was still hobbling from the stitches, but that didn't stop him from lurching from foot to foot, screaming, 'Bugger off! Bugger off!' and then charging out, leaning on a stick, but also waving the stick around, threatening the neighbourhood committee. Who duly buggered off. The police arrived remarkably quickly. I was still holding my brief case. Dad was sitting on the front steps, still stark bollocky. He was explaining to me how you never want to let the bastards get the better of you.

The officers were polite. When two members of the neighbourhood committee came to tell them how to do their job, they said they'd come and interview them soon and asked them to go away. They asked Dad to go inside. He insisted on being arrested. They said, okay, but go and get dressed first. He did. I had about fifty emails to go and write. But I kept my head. I explained. They said they'd drop him home soon. As he was getting into the car, Dad held out his hand. I took it and we shook.

'Well done,' he said. 'You did well.' He winked.

RSA

She used to come in every Friday. And stare. Just stare. I took to standing back. And calling out the orders louder – Ham! Chicken roll! Goulash! – from the back of the kitchen then running forward and dumping the plate on the stainless-steel bench as fast as I could then running back.

Fred said: 'What's biting your balls?' Prick.

I asked him if I could swap days and have Fridays off.

'You nuts? – it's our biggest day!' Prick. 'I can't get any proper workers any more, 'cept you, you dumb bastard.' He was trying to be nice to me. Prick. Fred struggles with his emotions. It's on account of being so fat he has to sit down to cook.

The kitchen's okay. I don't mind the kitchen, even with Fred in it. I hate that stuff up front. Everyone stares. It's probably the scar. You can sort of see that they're staring by not staring if you know what I mean. And they've probably noticed me with a funny little smile on my face. Probably think I'm friendly or something. At least they know Fred's not friendly. You see there's all those old guns hanging on the walls beside the Queen and the Māori warriors and why I'm smiling is because I'm thinking about me taking one of those old 303s and blasting a whacking great culvert in their skulls while they're slopping up their trifle and pink striped ice cream and the frigging canned peaches. Also, the scar makes me look like I'm smiling when I'm not.

Excuse my Swahili but it's important not to struggle with your emotions which is why I've been clean now for twenty years working with Fred but that doesn't answer why she was the worst of the starers. It wasn't just the scar. And anyway, it's faded no matter how you look at it. The thing is you wonder if it's someone who's connected to something you don't remember from the past. Because I don't remember that much from those times. The worst one yes of course, because I had to go over and over that with the lawyer so it's stuck now in my brain. But that's nothing to do with her. She looked like she was about seventy-five years old, thin, grey, green, purple, like a little feather floating in the stratosphere. Staring. Nothing to do with me. But it freaked me. People should just get on with it and stop making stuff up. That's what I've done.

So, it was in the car park. Takes ages to clean up on Fridays then I get two hours off then I've got to come back and run the whole shebang in the evening 'cos Fred has to go home and watch his porno movies. The weekly wank. I ask you. I was taking my apron off beside the Honda when I heard: 'Can I ask you something?' It was her. Waving a kind of cloth bag. Her teeth weren't all there which is something I hadn't noticed before. I just wanted to get in the car and drive away, but I'm not like that.

'You see, you remind me of someone.'

'I know' I said, 'George Clooney, it happens all the time.' I was trying to be friendly, but she didn't know who George Clooney was.

'Something happened to me a long time ago,' she said.

I almost said, 'Me too,' but I didn't because I could see that she wasn't quite following what she was trying to say. Nor was I for that matter.

'I think you might be my son,' she said.

'I'm sorry,' I laughed. Well, I really was. She had this idea that I was the right age even if she didn't know what age I was and that would have made me one of the last eggs in her body, ha ha. And then there was the scar. It was in the right place and all that. And the way it had faded would be just about right, she thought. I was looking all around the car park, which was pretty empty now and I spotted Fred shuffling out the back door and I waved and he gave me the fingers. So I told her, 'No, I got the scar in a big fight when I was a teenager after I got out of the boys' home, so, nah, it couldn't be that.' That wasn't strictly true really, because I did have the scar from when I was very young and of course that was how I got identified and they caught me. But she didn't need to know that stuff.Her face looked disappointed. But also kind of relieved. I've noticed that, how those two things go together. That's what Fred can't sort out for himself. His disappointment could be a relief, if only he'd stop struggling with his emotions.

'Sorry I've got to shoot through,' I said to her. 'Nice to meet you.' I wanted to say 'Mum' but I didn't because I've learned that cheek doesn't get you anywhere.

The thing is that she doesn't come in now anymore on Fridays, but I can't help thinking that if she did she wouldn't be staring and that would be a lot better for me going up to the counter with the hams and chickens and stuff. Maybe she died. Just like that. People do. More amazing is that Fred hasn't karked it yet.

I said to him just yesterday, 'Why aren't you dead, you prick?'

'Wanking keeps you healthy,' he said, 'You should try it.'

If she was there but not staring, then that would be better, if it was like that. It's kind of disappointing that she isn't there anymore, even if she is dead. Say she just walked in? Might sort of be a relief. Not that I'm looking out for her.

NO OFFENCE

He called me in the afternoon. Told me the boss had called him in in the morning. Told him to finish his afternoon run, then take his severance and piss off. Apparently undelivered items, namely batteries, had failed to be delivered after being packed in his van. Nor had they come back to the depot. Where were they? That was something he couldn't rightly say. That was that. No find, no job. Curtains. Yet again. Another job gone.

I said I was sorry. Well, shit, I was mad, but I wasn't going to say that. I said, 'Are you going to be home tonight?'

He said, 'Why not?'

I said, 'Sometimes you don't come home when things go wrong.'

He said, 'When?'

I said, 'It doesn't matter.'

Then he said, 'Can you come and get me?'

I said, 'What do you mean? I've just gone for a run and I've got to go on the late shift tonight.'

He said, 'No, I mean now.'

'Now? It's the middle of the afternoon. Just come home tonight and we can get some takeaways and then I go to work.'

I could hear him getting antsy in the silence. I'd woken up early from my night shift. I felt I needed coffee. Walked down to the van that sells coffee at the corner of the carpark. I was just in tracksuit and jandals, but the coffee smelt good and I needed some cash, there was nothing in my purse, so I headed for the ATM down the road by MacDonald's. Must have looked like a homeless. It was midday, everyone was pressing on up and down the street going places, doing stuff, running for a quick lunch.

'I'm at the end of the motorway,' he said.

He'd said nothing for so long I thought he'd got cut off. I was thinking, how does he think we're going to manage? I said, 'What motorway? Where?'

'Southern,' he said.

'That's thirty Ks, Bryce,' I said. 'What are you doing down there? Aren't you meant to be at work?'

'I am at work,' he said. 'I'm just leaving.'

'You're not making any sense, Bryce.' There was another one of those silences. I can always see how he's shuffling round in those silences, that inane grin. I know he thinks he looks like he's 'on to something' but he doesn't seem to realise he looks like a startled sheep. Where shall I run to now?

When I got to the bank I put my card in and pressed the buttons. Fifty bucks. I'd just take that out and keep it safe. In case of an emergency. Sometimes I press the buttons and nothing comes out, because Mister Somebody has been busy needing it. Just fold it away and it'll be there, in case. Then out they came – one, two, three, four fifties. Jesus, are they going to stop? Two more! And that was it. I looked down to see if anyone had changed the buttons to magic ones, but they seemed completely normal. I looked around. No one was looking at me. No one had noticed me. I folded the purple notes in three and stuffed them into my pocket. Walked quickly away, finished the coffee, dumped the takeaway cup, and headed home. By the time I got there I knew what I should have done.

Thing is, Indie, Bryce said bursting back into life, I called them up at the depot and told them, stuff it, if they want their van and their precious deliveries then they will find it all at the end of the motorway.

And you want me to come and get you, do you, Bryce? Can you, Indie? Just because you want to play some smartarse trick and make an even bigger stuff-up to the stuff-up you've already made? Is that right, Bryce? There was an even louder silence. When I got back to the flat, I tried to phone the bank. But you can't phone the particular branch just like that. All you get is a list of buttons to press, none of which apply to you. I found a service email on an old account. So, I wrote to that. Explaining what had happened. I mean I had to tell them the truth. Meanwhile I carefully put the notes away in that old handbag at the back of the wardrobe from when I was working at the hospital up north, years ago, when I just started. They'd be safe there.

'Bryce, what say I can't come? What are you going to do when they arrive to collect their van and see you sitting on the side of the road? Where are you going to run to? Bryce, I want to finish my run. Can you hear me?' Silence.

I cooked eggs. I was really hungry. Three patients had woken up on the ward last night. Pain relief wasn't working. God knows. We couldn't give them any more. With wholemeal toast. I love that. And I made another coffee. Always do before I run. Nobody's drug-testing me. Dumped the plate in the sink and went back to the computer: We apologise for our error. We are pleased to inform you that the situation has been rectified and the missing $300 dollars has been restored to your bank account. I read it again. I went back to my email. No, I had told them what happened. Someone couldn't read. I'd invested fifty dollars at midday and had a six hundred dollar return by 1pm.

'Indie, you can't leave me here.'

'Get in the van, Bryce, and drive it back to the depot.'

'I already told them to shove their van.'

'Get in the van, Bryce.'

'I threw the fucking keys down a manhole.'

'You what?'

Silence.

'Yes, Bryce, I heard you. What actually happened to the batteries, Bryce?'

I went into my internet banking. There it was. Three hundred extra dollars from nowhere. From nobody. For nothing. Thank you for nothing. Thank you for everything. I went into the wardrobe to check if the notes were still there. Actually, that handbag doesn't look too bad. Almost retro. Perhaps some things were meant to be. Same as some things weren't meant to be.

'So, you loaned the batteries to a mate? And do you think that mate has still got them, Bryce? Yes, I'd say it was unlikely. What do you mean there's a fence? Where? Oh, by the motorway. I thought you might have meant the other kind of fence,' then I said it: 'No offence.'

He went off his nut. You've been treating me like blah blah.

When he'd run out of abuse, I asked him, 'What about the fence? What? You're going to climb over it? You need to get off the motorway. That's what I'm saying, I know it's illegal to be on a motorway. What's behind the fence? It's someone's house!'

It was then that I got the thought. 'Tell you what, Bryce, you do that. I'll finish my run. I'll ring you back and find out where you are.' I actually could hear the siren in the distance just before I rung off.

I turned and ran back, fast as I could to the flat. The flat's for you, Bryce, all for you. Remember, we put it in your name, like you wanted? It's amazing how much you can stuff into a Mazda 323 in an hour. Mia would be home. She'd let me stay. We would be on the same shift at midnight. That handbag looked snug there on the front seat beside me, stuffed full of purple folding stuff, as I drove out. Just about as retro as the Mazda. But I'd be keeping them both.

SUIT YOURSELF

1

The gym teacher, Mr Ryle, used to parade up and down the edge of the swimming pool with his cane in his hand. It was girls in first, then girls out and boys in. While Vile Ryle was trying to explain something, prior to our 'boys in' moment, he spotted Gregor talking to the boy next to him

'Pilich – what are you gasbagging about?'

'The new Jethro Tull album, sir.'

'Can you think of any reason why I shouldn't cane you, Pilich?'

'Suit yourself, sir.'

'You cheeky little – get up here! I'll show you what happens to gasbaggers who answer me back.'

'You asked me, sir.'

'Right! I was going to give you two, but now you're getting four.'

I tried to say something: 'Sir, please, sir, that's not really fair, sir.'

'Do you want your turn as well, Winters?'

Well, I shut up then and watched, as we all did, the spectacle of Gregor being given four thumping whacks with the cane in his swimming togs in front of the whole class under the mid-morning Auckland February sun. The bruising lasted for two weeks.

His hair was chestnut red and his skin was a little brown, and he was everything the word 'weedy' conjured up, a little wisp of an urchin. The kids used to call him 'Gypsy.'

I asked him if he was okay about that.

'But I am,' he said.

'What?' I asked.

'Gypsy,' he said. 'My Mum says her father was half Gypsy, but he was exterminated.'

'Exterminated? How do you mean?'

'In the war. The Gypsies were exterminated.'

I had to say I didn't know there were any Gypsies in the war. It didn't make much sense to me.

The thing about Gregor was, which saved him really, that he could play anything, any instrument you gave him. His Dad, who was a maths teacher at our school, used to play the violin. I heard him when I went around to Gregor's house. But no one ever seemed to have taught Gregor music. He just did it. This earned him some respect. Mostly he liked to play bass. And since we were always trying to put a band together, Gregor was a precious cog in the wheel of our schemes. We had to look after him.

We had to look after him, because he wasn't very good at doing that for himself. Gregor could behave like a Zen teacher without knowing he was doing that. In Geography class, when he was fifteen, the teacher asked him a question one day.

'Well, Pilich, are you going to answer the question?'

'I'm thinking, sir.'

'Oh, how long will you be?'

'Not sure, sir.'

'Oh, very well, we will just look out the window at the playing field and wait for you then.'

'Thank you, sir.'

He was immune to sarcasm. There was a long pause. The geography teacher waved his hands in the air to indicate we were all dealing with a hopeless case, as if he and the rest of us were sharing a well-guarded secret at Gregor's expense. Some of the class giggled.

'Aww, look, I just saw that blade of grass grow,' the teacher's heavy sarcasm drew a few sniggers this time. 'How are we going, Pilich?'

'Still thinking, sir.'

'Well why don't you go and do that sitting outside the headmaster's office?'

Gregor quietly left the room.

He lived with his mother and father in a little house in Mount Roskill in a dead-end street. In our final year at school, we finally formed our band. We called ourselves Ran and Dom, which was a fairly accurate description. Gregor said I could be the drummer and all I had to do was stick with him. But I couldn't. He was way too good. When I said I wouldn't be able to keep going with the band, because I had study to do, he just smiled. Never said a critical word.

If I went around to his house, I never saw his father, though I had been in his maths class in the fifth form. The kids, of course, treated Mr Pilich with derision. His heavy mid-European accent, his patches of fluffy white hair and his bowties set him up for such treatment. 'Please, sir, Mister Pilich, I've got an ITCH – can I go to the toilet and take a PILL for it?' At Gregor's place, the only sign of Mr Pilich was a vigorous quaver of the violin as he rattled out string settings of Liszt's Hungarian Rhapsodies behind closed doors. Gregor's mother was the sweetest woman. But, then, one day we came into the kitchen to get some milk from the fridge and there she was standing in the corner crying. She waved her hands and said something in Czech, and Gregor pulled me back out. He never said anything. But I didn't go round there again.

At school I asked him how the band was going.

He said he didn't know, that he'd been kicked out of the band.

'What!" He smiled. 'They didn't want me. I guess my playing was too good. I showed them up – so they kicked me out.'

'Suit yourself, I said.'

'And is it still, 'Ran and Dom'?'

'Nah, they're calling themselves 'The Equalisers'." he laughed then, which he didn't do much. 'It all started when the others wanted to change the name. I said I didn't mind. Then they asked me if I had any ideas. Then we had an argument. Then they kicked me out. I 'had no idea of' the kind of music that would be successful, so I was 'a drag on the band' – that's what they said. So, before I left, I said, 'The Equalisers' would be a good new name. And they jumped on it, yeah, yeah, yeah.'

'Dildoes,' I said.

2

Gregor never seems to have connected with the world at any point. I suppose I was a bit opposite. My Dad was a carrier, with his own truck, and Mum worked for the post office in the sorting, so I wanted to get on and get connected. I knew what it was like not to be much connected. The University of Otago was just starting up its four-year Bachelor of Surveying in the new year, when I left school, so I applied and was accepted and went to Dunedin to live the student life for four years. Mostly I did my study and worked on the weekends and in the evenings and, supplemented by holiday jobs at the meatworks back in Auckland. I came out with a degree and a good tranche of savings. Inevitably Gregor disappeared from my mind. When I returned to Auckland, I enrolled at the University for a Bachelor of Commerce, which, with cross-crediting from my first degree, I completed in two years. At that point I went looking for a job. The business world was lively and restless and frustrated and people like me were welcomed. I signed on as an Assistant Project Manager for a major construction job in the city and after three years of keeping my head down and working hard I was promoted to project manager for a new investment, I had got myself married and even had a first child on the way. And my luck just kept growing, as the Fourth Labour Government swept aside regulations and money began to slosh around like goldfish in an earthquake. I was never tempted to buy fraudulent rubbish on the stock market, but I found myself flying to Wellington often, for meetings at Head Office and even to represent the company in lobbying meetings with this or that minister.

It was on one of my trips that I bumped into Gregor again. I was wearing a smart new coat, three hundred dollars worth, for which I felt a little embarrassed. It was too hot for Auckland, but would be fine when I stepped out into the Wellington southerly. However, at the Downtown kiosk, where the Airporter bus left to take you out to Mangere to the Airport, I was sweating as I searched the magazine and newspaper racks for *The National Business Review.*

An impish kind of voice piped up with the old chestnut: 'Can I help you?'

'Ah, *National Business Review*, ah, do you have –'

'Hullo, Richard.' That caught me by surprise. Gregor was grinning. 'How's the drumming?'

'My god! What are you – are you working here?'

'Welcome to the Downtown Kiosk.'

'Good to see you.' Well, I really felt it was. Here he was. Bright and chirpy as ever, a little rounder than before. 'Looks like life's treating you –'

'And you,' he said.

'Are you?'

'Yes,' he said, 'a three-year-old daughter, and an unknown on the way.'

'Coincidence,' I said, 'A four-year-old and yes, another one on the way. Where are you living?'

'We are sharing with the other members of the True Light Gathering.'

Actually, at that point, I hadn't heard of the True Light Gathering, though they were notorious latter on. I tried to be friendly, asking how his father was these days. Well, Mr Pilich the maths teacher had died from medical misadventure. 'And your mother?"

'Not good. She's in the psychiatric ward.'

I remembered then that his mother and father had come from Czechoslovakia sometime after the war. Kids at school had said his father had been in the Hitler Youth, but it was very likely his father had been a Young Communist Pioneer and then had managed to scramble out when his loyalty creds ran out in the dark days of the show trials. But that was just my surmise. I looked at Gregor, who was looking back at me, not smiling, taking a good look at what I had made of myself. My Mum and Dad were still in Hillsborough, still keeping things going, still saying 'can't complain' to each other. The bus was leaving soon. I needed to pay for my *National Business Review*. I held out my hand to Gregor, to say good-bye and how nice it was to see him, but he said, 'No, we don't do handshaking in the True

Light Gathering.' What they did was hugging. He threw his arms around me before I could back away and held me, almost vice-like, surprising in his strength. Everyone does it now, but grown men still weren't doing that very often then.

I managed to murmur, as I walked away, 'Are you still playing the old bass?'

'I play for the Gathering band,' he said, 'all our energies must go to the work of the Gathering.'

3

'No, luck, eh?'

That was the next time I heard Gregor's voice. Must have been at least ten years later. Hadn't been such good times for me. My marriage had gone. Well, I did something stupid, that's true. 'That's that,' she said, 'Enough's enough.' Then she added, 'You prick,' for good measure. The funny thing was that Gregor would have known her, Julie Rollins; she had been in the next class up at high school. After Otago, when I came back to Auckland, I stayed with Mum and Dad for a year and had bumped into Julie at the local library where she worked. Now I think about it, I took an easy choice, then got bored with it. So, my bad. Of course, when you get set free in your thirties and you have a bit of cash to throw around, well, you find there is a field and you become a player. That was exactly what was going on when I heard Gregor's voice in my ear: 'No luck, eh?'

There'd been a conference for a day, which the newly named 'Business School' had organized. Totally effing boring. I'd hooked up with this lady whom I knew worked for a rival firm, and we'd left the final session in mutual agreement that academics know nothing about the real world, agreed to have dinner, then kept going, on to this nightclub, a place I knew a bit already, very low key really.

'I thought you were going to be in like Flynn.'

'Jesus, Gregor, where the fuck did you come from?'

The hair was going grey, and he was definitely a lot rounder now, and his eyes, once a rather entrancing greenish hue, were big and round and faded, like two dilated drains. He didn't look so good.

'I'm the DJ. I was trying to put on the right music for you – then suddenly she up and left. What did you do, Dick?'

'She suddenly says, 'Well, that's been nice, and good luck with your next big project, I enjoyed hearing all about that, but I've got a husband at home waiting for me and my dinner will be getting all dried up in the warming oven."

'Done like a dinner.'

'Ha, ha.'

'You remember my Dad?'

'Old Itchy!'

'That's the one. When he came here, he didn't speak any English and he used to teach himself a phrase a day. Done like a dinner. In the pink. In like Flynn. Then he'd go and try them out – and nobody knew what he was talking about!'

'Good to see you. Have you got a few minutes?'

'Half-hour break.'

'Great.'

We began to have a man-to-man. I explained my happy marriage to him. He explained that his wife was in America with the kids and the Guru of the True Light Gathering. There was symmetry in our self-pity. He hadn't known about Julie Rollins. In fact, he couldn't remember who she was. He was wearing a Velvet Underground t-shirt and track pants and jandals. I was amazed they let him out amongst the public. Even in the half-light of the club, I could see the dog hairs sticking to the shapeless cotton pants. It was all a little awkward, truth to tell, with me in my suit. And there was something about him: not just that he'd sniffed something chemical while spinning his discs, as the wide-open eyes were telling me.

While we were sharing our mutual male misery, he leaned into me and said; 'I don't really mind about the marriage. You see, I found out she was an alien.'

'Well, of course,' I laughed: 'I know what you mean!'

He nodded meaningfully: 'Manifestations of Mithras.'

'Sorry,' I said, 'I don't follow.'

'The aliens were here before. And now they're coming again.'

'Really.'

'In ones and twos. Infiltrating. Sometimes I hear their messages in the music. I'm becoming more attuned.'

I didn't stay much longer. He told me he was living in a room in a boarding house in Mt Eden, that he had, as I already knew, a dog, and he was very, very happy. I didn't ask if the dog was an alien too.

4

Who was it that said, 'Life is a joyride'? Lou Reed, maybe? I had become Mister New. New job – I was in management now – new house, new wife, new kids. You get to fifty and it all looks different. I was taking the twins, who were five now, to the Museum on a Sunday, being the kind of father I hadn't been so good at before. Nice to have a second chance and do it right. You smile, the world smiles, and so on.

Getting through those heavy rotating doors at the Museum with two random five- year-olds in hand meant I had my head down, making sure no small ones were crushed in the making of this excursion, so I didn't look up until I was in the foyer, with all its marble and bad acoustics. I spotted Gregor standing by a pillar. He was in his uniform: security guard. His hair was brushed and combed back – what was left of it – and he was doing his best to pull the waistline in and look like a man who knew what he was doing. You see it all the time in management. It makes you even a little forgiving. Just then the haka performance started up and I saw Gregor almost snap to attention and turn his head in the direction of the shell trumpet's blast.

'Come on,' I said to Felice and India, 'Let's go this way.' I was going to spend my time avoiding Gregor.

I succeeded. Five-year-olds don't last long at anything so once we'd swung around a few displays and been to see the beehive in the Weird and Wonderful Section, we were out again, to catch the sou'wester as it rattled the top of the hill. We took off towards the car down in the carpark by the duckpond – let's go visit the ducks. And shit, walking up the bloody path straight towards us came Gregor. I thought, hold off, maybe he won't recognize me.

But no such luck.

'Dick! Dick! Are they grand kids?'

After the True Light experience, I would have thought that hugging was no longer such a drawcard. I let him hug me. I guess it was mainly camphor I smelled, from the uniform, which he would have put on when he got to the Museum, then taken off and hung up when he left. But there was also another smell – thank god for the camphor. Silverfish, mice, weevils – museums must be in a state of constant fumigation.

'I'm late,' he said. 'Afternoon tea break.'

'You better get going.'

'I think they're going to sack me anyway. Sometimes I go up to people and say, "Can I show you to the Egyptians?" Some people think it's funny, but I was told there have been complaints. Your job is security! Yes, sir! I said.' And he clicked his heels, saluted and suddenly started to dance in a little circle, clapping his hands and singing some old lines of Bob Dylan's: 'She wears an Egyptian ring, that sparkles before she sings . . . '

Felice and India loved it and they started to dance around too. Then India grabbed my hand and started yelling, 'Come on, Daddy, dance!'

And Felice joined in: 'Dance, Daddy, dance.'

I managed a few skips and said we needed to get to see the ducks before they flew away.

Gregor looked at me and said: 'How true.'

'Well, see you around, old mate.'

'Just before you go,' he said, 'there's something I need to tell you.'

My heart sank.

'I'm not living where I used to.'

'Oh,' I said. 'But you've got somewhere?'

'It's a hostel place.'

'That's nice. Got some company.'

'That's what I wanted to tell you. The man who lives over the back fence –'

'Look, we've really got to get going – '

'Won't take a minute. He's a big chap. He built a gallows in his back garden. I was watching him build it, looking over the back fence. So, I said to him: "Who's it for?" And he said, 'You." So that's the thing, I'm going to have to move out. In case you're wanting to get in touch with me.'

'But I don't know where you're living now anyway.'

'Oh,' he said. 'Oh.'

And he just stood there. The kids wanted to get going, so we took off. The ducks were still there, of course.

5

My wife often drags me along to hear the Auckland Philharmonic Orchestra. It's okay. I'd never been to listen to music like that before, my concert going life had been a bit more participatory. She'd arranged a baby sitter, not that long, maybe a year or two, after the meeting with Gregor outside the Museum in the Domain, and we'd parked in the underground carpark. We were a little early and the evening in Aotea Square was quite mild, so we took a stroll round the circuit of Aotea Square. Just as we came by the statue of Lord Auckland, a great hunk of bronze that no one notices, we heard someone singing.

'It's that old Janis Joplin song,' my wife said, 'You'd know that one, it's from your time.'

'O Lord won't you buy me . . . '

Janis never got the backing track down before she died, so that's how it's come down to us, the acapella version. But someone was making a fair fist of picking it out on a guitar.

'What's he singing?' my wife asked.

'How do you mean?'

'Those aren't the words, are they?'

'Oh Lord won't you buy me . . .'

'A Noozifora Tree? What's a Noozifora Tree? I've never heard of a Noozifora Tree.'

But I could hear what Gregor was singing: 'a noose for a tree'.

'It's just some crazy. Let's go get a drink before the concert.'

'Look at him – he's singing to the statue.'

'Leave him alone.'

'No, I want to see.' And she walked over to where I could see

Gregor was standing looking up at Lord Auckland, picking away on a beat-up old guitar and singing his pleading heart out to the cold, unmoving Lord: 'Oh Lord won't you buy me a noose for a tree.'

I'd stayed way back. 'Come on,' I called.

Nora – did I mention my wife's name was Nora? – walked back: 'Far away in never -never land,' she said as she took my arm.

6

I had to go to court as a witness the next morning. That was why I took the bike ride that Sunday afternoon: to clear my head. I would be meeting our lawyer at 8.30am and he would brief me. There had been a challenge to the status of the land, some kind of historical Treaty claim thing had been raised, and I was simply there as a technical witness to the difficulty of demolishing the structure now it was half-built. The lawyer said it was all a matter of lining up the ducks. But I've never enjoyed this sort of abstract waffle that interferes with the business of getting the job done, which is always what benefits everyone in the end. I said to Nora I'd be gone for a couple of hours, put on my lycra and helmet, and took off. There're some boardwalks, once you get off the North-western motorway that are fun to bounce over on a mountain bike.

The wind was blowing, the sky was thickening up, and there wasn't anyone around. It took me an hour to get to my farthest point and I was looking forward to the challenge of turning around and seeing if I still had it in me to cycle back in the same time I had cycled out. I stopped on the boardwalk in amongst the mangroves and unhitched my water flask and took a good long gurgle.

'Dick! Dick!'

That voice. I swiveled my head, because my goggles made it hard to see peripherally. Nope. Couldn't tell where the voice was coming from. Then I saw a couple of bright points of light. Two eyes were looking at me through the empty corner-glass of an old car door that had been propped up against a hoary old mangrove. Then the full figure stepped out, still crouching, a woolen beanie yanked down over his skull, a heavy old overcoat and those ridiculous gloves with no fingers, but I had no doubt who I was looking at.

'Nice of you to pay a call.' His voice had some of the old lilt and sparkle from when he was at school and used to say, 'Suit yourself' to the teachers.

'Is it you?'

'Never been more me.'

'What are you doing here?' As if I didn't already know.

'I live here.'

'You mean –'

'You came to my front door. Welcome.'

I was lost to know what to say. To tell the truth, it was all starting to feel like a bad stage play. You know what I mean, the slowing down of the action, the bad costumes, the exaggerated gestures.

'Come here,' he said, 'Don't be frightened.'

'I'm not frightened.'

'Course you're not. It's only me. Sorry I said that.'

I got off the bike and wheeled a few paces towards him.

'Look,' he said and he pointed up at the thickening cloud. 'Do you see it? Don't worry, your goggles will protect you. Good thinking.'

'What am I meant to see?'

'The hole in the sky.'

'You mean those clouds?'

'Yeah. That's where they'll come from.'

'Who?' I asked.

'It's so good to see you!'

He shouted and suddenly sprang at me. His arms gripped me tightly as he flung himself on me. I lost control of the bike, staggered backwards as the bike crashed down, but kept my footing. And, regaining my balance, I threw him off me with one big push.

'Jesus, Gregor, what in Christ's name are you doing?'

He seemed to fly through the air for a moment and then land with a nasty thud as his head hit the edge of the boardwalk.

'What are you on about, man?'

But he didn't answer. He just lay there. I had no idea he was going to do that. He'd just sprung at me. I checked his pulse. It was going. His breathing. A bit rough, but that was probably normal. Behind the old car door there were the remains of three well-used sleeping bags and a couple of big black polythene bags and some smaller ones. I made him comfortable there, with one of the sleeping bags over him and his head resting on one of the small bags, for a pillow. He still hadn't opened his eyes when I saw what the time was and that I'd better get back to Nora. This was his place, after all. The bike seemed to be in good working order and there wasn't really any sign of anything having happened, so I hopped back on the bike and set out to see if I could get back in the same time as my outward journey.

HORSE AND RIDER

The Sensei turned the fitting-out of the new meditation centre into a group exercise that was typical of his approach to everything: let the mind of the sangha decide what is best for the sangha. 'Who am I but your humble and affectionate servant?' was one of his favourite responses to foolish questions. 'How long will it take me to get enlightened?' a new member had asked on joining up. 'Who am I but your humble and affectionate servant?' was Sensei's reply. Then he smiled and winked and added: 'Yours sincerely.'

During a teaching session he had declared himself to be a service provider. 'You come here with your urgent emails and you send them through me out into the universe of stars and neurons and goats and algae and radio waves.' He glared at everyone seated round the zendo for a long time with disconcerting vigour and a palpable silence. Then suddenly clapped his hands so loudly that some people visibly jumped in their seated positions. Sensei laughed with happiness. 'And here we all sit, waiting for an answer!' He could hardly keep himself from falling out of his rock-steady sitting posture he was laughing so hard.

It had been this vigorous, erratic, yet decidedly tender style of teaching that had meant the size of the sangha group began to increase rapidly. People arrived, they felt included, they wanted to contribute. And the new centre followed, with its fund-raising and its working bees and its necessary payments to professional builders, plumbers, and electricians. Everyone's suggestions had been included as far as possible and it had been remarkable how far most wishes had at least been acknowledged. The only thing approximating a disagreement occurred when it came to one of the last aspects of the interior decoration of the zendo, the carpet to cover the floor. A small group clustered around the idea of a visionary colour, a sort of heavenly lilac, soft, not intrusive, but uplifting. Another group opposed this, feeling that a dark, deep grey, something somber yet steady, like the silences of outer space, would allow the meditators to zone in on the confrontational depths of their practice. This opposition precipitated a third interest group in the politics of enlightenment, this time bidding for a kind of infinite blue that might stretch away in all directions, so that when the sangha members were seated on their cushions, they might feel as if they were lotus flowers floating on a still pond. At this point, before more groups formed, such as the honey-coloured carpet constituency that might remind us of our industrious collaboration in the pursuit of truth just as a hive of bees knows itself to be one and many at the same time, Sensei intervened with a surprisingly heavy hand. The hand went up – for silence. And the hand came down for emphasis.

'Above all else,' Sensei pronounced, 'the carpet must be boring! Boring and neutral. As near to nothing as it is possible to get.'

You could see this last phrase, which had become dangerously close to an aphorism, tickled Sensei's funny bone, but he studiously repressed his laughter this time. Sensei held up a sample carpet square. It was neither quite fawn nor brown nor beige, and its odd non-colour was beset by a barely perceptible 'fleck' of something else that rendered it void of any single dominating tone. As you looked at it, it seemed to come and go, but mostly go. Any dominance of any kind was broken up into a meaningless scattering of bits and pieces. It was really nothing at all to look at. Incredibly boring. No one liked it. It seemed to breathe disappointment, to emanate a lack of emanation.

But Sensei liked it a lot. 'I spent a long time looking for this. There's not much of it left in stock. Very popular. We must buy it up before it's all gone.'

Nobody disagreed with him – well, nobody dared to, to tell the truth – but also there was really so little to disagree with, it was no strain to let it pass. Then the carpet-layers came and laid the carpet and the floor was at last there, the zendo was open for business, and the business of resting non-looking, but all-seeing eyes on this boring and neutral surface morning after morning, evening after evening, began in earnest. The sangha sat and rested their many eyes on the carpet, but their singular mind was not with the carpet but, so to speak, with another. And the new centre continued to attract more members. It wasn't simply that meditation had become a fad, a degraded version of what was actually possible, but that real seekers came having heard of the teaching and the practice and also the inclusivity that was allowed. As in some places, as at some times, there seemed to be a moment when a happy confluence had arrived. Sensei had a good notion of what all this meant and would often remark, 'Remember nothing stays the same.'

There was always a round of green tea and biscuits and a quiet conversation period after each sitting session for those who could stay a little longer. After this, everyone would disperse. The first mention of the horse and the rider happened at one of these after-sitting round-tables. There were only seven or eight people there, when one of the long-standing members of the sangha, an accountant by trade, asked if anyone had recently been sitting down at the end corner of the room, near the door that led to the toilets and to the room where the robes and cushions were stored. No one had. Hmm, he murmured, maybe it's just me. His cautious approach to everything was a source of gentle amusement to everyone, even himself. His name was Frank and Sensei delighted in saying, 'You're Frank because you're never frank!' There was nothing malicious in this and Frank was rather proud of being 'Never Frank.'

'I don't know,' said Frank.

'You never do!' laughed Sensei.

Frank explained. Towards the end of the sitting session that evening, he could have sworn that he had seen, in the Sensei's beloved boring carpet, the image of a horse and rider.

'Was it Princess Anne?' roared Sensei, who was old enough to remember who she was.

'Mark Todd,' piped up the small, wiry Polish carpenter Tadeusz. He had delighted in accumulating encyclopedic information about New Zealand since arriving two years previously.

Though Frank smiled, he looked troubled. 'I don't know,' he repeated. 'I went and checked again, after the sitting, but I couldn't see anything. But I did see it – I think – I mean, I'm not the sort of person –'

'That's where you always sit, isn't it?'

Alexandra was right. She taught Classics at a local high school. She must have been the youngest classics teacher in the city, maybe in the world. Though she looked like she was fifteen, she was at least twenty-two. Attractive buck teeth, eyes shining through small round spectacles, a skin like ivory.

'That's the reason,' she went on, 'no one else has sat there for ages. Would you like to swap? I can't come to another sitting till next week, but then, if you're here, let's swap. If you're not, I'll grab your posie. I'd like to meet your horse and rider. Sounds like the Vandal hordes invading decadent Rome!'

'Where do you sit?' asked Frank.

'Anywhere,' said Alexandra.

'Oh,' said Frank, deeply confused.

Sensei said that people could sit in whatever position they liked, as long as the general arrangement of the room was always observed: facing the wall, a metre or more away, eyes on the carpet, everyone's backs towards the centre, where Sensei himself sat. He also said, it didn't matter what people thought they saw – or heard for that matter – none of it meant anything. If you heard Mr Whippy music in your head, ignore it. If the face of your long-lost lover floated up before your eyes, ignore it. He, Sensei, at least, wasn't interested.

But Alexandra couldn't resist. She sat in Frank's old place several times over the following two weeks. But nothing. 'Nothing is good' Sensei roared. Everything made sense to him. But Alexandra was disappointed. Not only was the carpet boring, her own life was somewhat tedious. She couldn't rid herself of the feeling that, even though she had just begun her first teaching job, all the other teachers were dull, even stupid, as well as old and, yes, some of them were even smelly. A horse and rider offered an attractive alternative.

Some said Sensei was a Georgian. He was a very hairy man, even with his shaven head and clean-cut face. A dark and swarthy man. The black hair tumbled up from the neckline of his grey robe. He was not an evasive person, but he almost never talked about himself. Naturally this led to speculation about who he was in the sense of where he had come from. Another version was that his grandfather had been Georgian. He certainly didn't sound like a Georgian would sound, if he were really a Georgian. Most of the sangha realized and accepted that this was another thing that didn't matter. Then Rex, who taught maths at the university, a beanpole of a man in his fifties who rarely spoke, one day opened his mouth and silenced everyone by claiming he had grown up in Ōtāhuhu with Sensei and had gone to school with him. He said that, back then, he was called George. That certainly brought things down to earth. No one had witnessed any interaction between Rex and Sensei that might indicate a shared past, a passing word about the old days, for instance. But again, that would make perfect sense – another of those things that were not important. It was uncanny, Alexandra had once said, round the post-sitting table, how, if you took the 'I' away from Sensei, you were left with the word 'sense' in English. As a language scholar, she well knew this was magic gobbledygook, but still it fascinated her, a little in the same way that the prospect of the horse and the rider attracted her. How restless she felt, and most of all when she was sitting in meditation. She sat there, utterly still, all the while pacing back and forward, back and forward, like a fevered horse.

'The trouble with places like this,' said Missy, a rigorous, upright woman perhaps in her forties, stern yet strikingly beautiful, 'is that people spend their time here looking at each other, not at the carpet.'

She was clearing the cups, causing some round the table to gulp their tea and hold out their empty for her to collect, as if they were being helpful by giving her more to do.

'Take it to the sink yourself,' she said to them.

She was already sweeping the biscuits' crumbs away with the dish-rag, bending and twisting herself across the table while delicately observing the limits of intrusion into personal space.

'It would be best if we all did our meditating on our own and only came to see Sensei when we needed, one to one. But no one's got the guts to do that. We need each other to ramp up to the next level, otherwise we'd all be stuck, staring in horror at our grubby navels, wondering, What next?'

Her hands were in the sink, frothing up the detergent, rinsing the cups, arranging them on the rack as neatly as the sitters in the zendo itself. Missy didn't mind if she did all the work. She even said she liked it – because she didn't much like the way most other people did the day-to-day stuff. She ran her own business, PR, promotions, candidate selections, and the word was that she could run background checks if you needed. She wasn't so much 'Jill of all trades and mistress of none' as someone who thought that the only way to get to the fun was to sweep aside the nonsense. Sensei almost never spoke to her. And she hardly ever spoke to him. It was as if they were running separate enterprises in the same premises with the same staff. Sometimes Sensei could be caught glancing hard at Missy, with a look on his face that asked, 'Why are you doing that, Missy?' But he never said anything. Two knights, jumping all over the board, never landing on each other.

'Anyway, we're here. And that's our carpet.'

There was a long pause, because no one was ever sure if Missy had finished.

Then Rex spoke: 'I think I saw it.'

'What?'

'Them. I mean, them.'

'You saw what?'

'The horse. And the rider.'

'When?'

'Tonight.'

'In the carpet?'

'But you weren't sitting where Frank was sitting.'

'No.'

'Don't tell Alexandra. She'll be pissed off.'

'What did you see, Rex?'

'Just as I said – the horse and the rider.'

'Can you – you know – elaborate?'

'No. Not really. Just as I said. I saw them.' Rex so rarely spoke, there was a desperate hope that he would continue. But he didn't. 'Anyway, I've got to be going,' he said.

And Rex left. If it had felt odd that Frank should have seen 'them,' it really was distinctly unlikely that Rex, the mysterious mathematician, also would. Alexandra, of course, everyone would have expected.

'Alexandra was trying to see them. That's why she couldn't.'

'What is that meant to mean? If you don't try to meditate, then you will find you are meditating?'

'Where was Rex sitting?'

'Where the old door was that got blocked off. '

'Miles from Frank- land.'

'Maybe it's something in the carpet?'

'Easy to blame the carpet.'

'Has Frank seen it again?'

'He hasn't been sitting in the same place.'

'That's right, I haven't. I like moving round.'

'But Rex wasn't either . . . '

At that moment Sensei came in from the office and stood in the doorway. Missy had her back to him, wiping down the bench, so she didn't see he was there when she started speaking.

'I've seen them too,' she said. 'But not in here. Not in the carpet. None of you know my friend Kurt. Well, he's had a brain tumour for the last six months. Very aggressive.'

Before she turned to face everyone, Sensei had slipped back into the office, though he could surely hear what was said, since Missy was addressing the whole room.

'He's been up on the family farm the last few weeks, since they said there was nothing to be done. I went up to see him ten days ago. He died just the other night. Lovely man, Much older than me. When I was there, he could still walk. We walked together, just a short stroll, but you could see what an effort it was, putting one foot after another. We got as far as the duckpond. The ducks came out to see us, and sure enough, Kurt had brought a handful of goodies to scatter on the ground. He gave me some. We sat there on a log, while the ducks squabbled around our feet. I can't remember what we talked about. Probably the ducks. I had to help him back to the house. He was just buggered. So, yeah, I saw them there, Kurt the horse and Death the rider.'

Missy's point about the horse and rider in the carpet versus Kurt being ridden hard was immediately clear. That sudden contrast made everyone look at each other in a different way. Tadeusz remembered Goethe's poem, 'Der Erlkonig,' and even began to recite it in German, 'Mein Vater, mein Vater . . . ' but no one else knew it, let alone who Goethe was, so Tadeusz's point drained away to nothing.

However, Alexandra had not been there that evening. She had not heard of Rex's sighting of the horse and rider, nor of Missy's sobering reinvention of the image in a more concrete reality. School was painful, middle-aged teachers teased her in the staffroom, behaving like six-year old boys. Nobody in the school thought that Classics should be taught any longer and her job was clearly perceived as blocking more worthy candidates in more relevant subject areas. The students mocked her enthusiasm for her work and she overheard one saying to another that she was an 'unco.' She tried sitting at home, morning and evening, by herself, achieving exactly what Missy had accused all in sundry of being incapable of. Her meditative sitting was fierce, intense, relentless. She knew it was too harsh. But she also knew that she was good at it. Between these contradictory poles of doing it badly and being good at it, she vacillated wildly back and forth. She became the restless pendulum of her own being. Eventually she called Sensei and requested a private session to see him, to seek some guidance. Of course, of course, he said.

Alexandra was not an officially accepted student of the Sensei, merely an attendee at regular sessions. Normally such members of the sangha were not given those notorious riddles known as koans to beat their minds against. And what Sensei gave her to think about was not a traditional koan at all; rather something he'd invented, probably after listening to Missy from his office with the door open: 'Who is the rider, who is the horse?' It was a koan built for a young Classics teacher: Quis eques? Quis equus? Sensei's strategy was probably worth the risk. He knew he could have sat and listened to Alexandra for an hour and a half and offered her sage advice about enduring the slings and arrows and calming troubled waters and focusing on the breath, but he was inclined to try something that might stop the pendulum swinging back and forward.

'What am I meant to do about it?'

'Do? What?'

'The questions.'

'Think about them.'

'Is that all?'

'Not too hard.'

'How often?'

'All the time.'

'Even when I'm asleep?'

'I think that's enough. I'll see you next time we are at the zendo together.'

'Do you want me to have an answer?'

'If you like. Why not? Hope so! But if you haven't . . . so what?'

He closed the door. She had to leave. It was raining. The wind brought the rain crossways so that half of her was soaking and half was dry by the time she reached her car. Of course, she was already thinking. Trying not to think too hard. But that was hard itself. She drove home already imagining she was riding a horse through the stormy night. Once in bed, she felt the old wooden villa shake on its piles when a strong gust struck. She did fall asleep. And then she dreamt. She was the horse. On her back sat a proud Georgian horseman, dressed in a long garment like a kimono, with a shining white Astrakhan hat on his head, waving a sabre in the air. The horseman raised himself so he was standing on her shoulders as she galloped round and round the school playing fields. Then he bent down, placed the hand that was not carrying the sabre on her head, and lifted himself into a one-handed handstand. She was going faster and faster, so fast that together they took off into the air, lifted, floated, flew . . .

Alexandra didn't go to the zendo until the following week. She had set her jaw at school against the under-miners, led with her nose and swept the view around her with disdain as she went about her work. At least that felt like it established some less violable territory around her, insisting, come and sneer, if you dare. She also felt she had an answer. Nothing as trite as 'the teacher is the rider, I am the horse.' That was simply the silly game that dreams played. The point was really about being bound (as in 'earthbound') and taking off (as in flight) and not being held back. The horse and the rider had to work together. They were one, naturally, not two. There was no them.

She arrived almost as the bell for sitting sounded, only just in time to take her place. So, it wasn't until the end of the first round of sitting, when they were doing their kinhin walking, that she was noticed Sensei wasn't there. She had to wait till the end of the whole session to ask where he was. It was Missy she asked, because Missy always knew everything.

'Didn't you read the internet newsletter?'

'I saw it had come, but I haven't got round to reading . . .'

'He's gone away.'

'Away? Where?'

'Apparently, he's gone to learn horse riding.'

'Horse riding?'

'Correct.'

'Jesus!'

'Or someone.'

This really did feel like the continuation of her dream.

'Is he coming back?'

'I believe so. '

'When?'

'Six months he said. It isn't easy, so he said, to learn to ride a horse, though god knows I used to ride them as a child all the time.'

'I guess he never did. Perhaps it's more difficult when you're older. What's going to happen to the zendo?'

'We carry on.'

'Together?'

'Of course.'

'I had something to tell him.'

'Tell him when he gets back. Meanwhile, Sensei asked me to keep things moving. I won't be doing any talks or private sessions. But I'll be running the sittings, keeping the time.'

'You will?'

'Yes.'

'It's a bit of a shock.'

'Me being in charge? Nothing to fear. I'm not going anywhere. I won't bite you.'

'No, I mean Sensei . . . just . . .'

The sangha shuffled along by itself. Numbers certainly fell, there was no shining light. But Missy kept all the surfaces scrubbed and the cushions piled neatly and she treated everyone with an even hand. Frank went back to his old position. There were no more visions of the horse and rider. There were no sudden enlightenments. A certain pervasive ordinariness set in, the way that once a change of season has established itself, all you can do is look forward to the long haul, believing that change will never come. They all sat round facing the walls, but there was no Sensei sitting in the centre, facing the image of Kuan Yin, the goddess of compassion.

This state of affairs began to eat away at Alexandra's mind. She had found her answer, but there was no one to give the answer to. She knew she was right, but knowing that and having no one to say to her, yes, well done, you have it, that was a more refined form of frustration than not being able to find the answer. She grew suspicious of the fact that there was no news about Sensei, no messages from him, nothing. She didn't really believe it.

Missy was like a wall: 'Let the man do what he's got to do – isn't that why we are all here?'

Alexandra wanted to say, 'No, that's not why I'm here,' but she let it go.

She tried approaching Rex, on the basis that he might know more than he let on, given the apocryphal shared schooldays, but all he said was, 'We don't have a personal relationship,' and that left her unsure if he was referring to Sensei and himself or Alexandra and himself. From now on she attended almost every sitting she could. She sat upright, centered, sure of herself, knowing herself to be both the horse and the rider, wondering if anyone else knew this. At the after-sitting sessions she stayed to the end, hopeful of hearing something. She felt the gradual subsidence of energy that had begun with Sensei's departure was rendering these sessions desultory. Then one evening Frank suddenly blurted:

'I don't know if it's just me, but I'm feeling a little, well, how would you say – '

'Desolate?' said Tadeusz. His English improved week by week.

'Hmm, yes, probably that's it – desolate.'

'It's natural. It's grief,' Missy pronounced. 'It will pass.'

'What say it doesn't?' Alexandra spoke up: 'What then?'

'Then we go on grieving.'

'I saw him yesterday. While I was at the work.' Tadeusz seemed to have changed tack completely.

'You saw who?'

'Sensei.'

'When?'

'I say, yesterday. At the work.'

'Your work?'

'Of course! I don't go to other people's work! Even crazy Poles are not that crazy!'

'Where?' Alexandra felt hot around her neck. She put her hand up quickly, and, yes, tiny drops of sweat.

'I was on the job for the horse school. They have the broken fence there. Up on the road to Mahurangi. I was fixing the fence all the morning. Who comes out to say 'Dzien dobry' but Sensei himself. There's a big Wild West Rodeo show practicing there. They have cowboys – and Russian Cossacks too! I laughed. Russian Cossacks! On the road to Mahurangi. Silly costumes. I never see Russian Cossacks like that!'

'Cossacks?' Alexandra asked.

'Yes, Cossacks! Silly white furry hats. Fake swords. Cheap

kimonos from the Japanese two-dollar shop! And no Russians! I said hullo in Russian, but nobody knows what I say. Cowboys and Cossacks – what a joke! But good riders. I think some from South America, from Australia.'

'How is he?' Missy asked, and Alexandra could hear the slightest nervousness in her voice.

'He is living there.'

'At the horse place?'

'Yes. But he's not staying.'

'No? Is he coming back?'

'No, no, he's going with the Cowboys and the Cossacks. He tells me that. He has decided to start again. Start again, that was what he said. What is 'start again?' Those riders, they are all thirty years younger than him. He is crazy.'

The silence arrived while everyone took in the news. Alexandra noticed that both Rex and Missy had adopted knowing looks. Tadeusz broke the silence, shaking his head and repeating, "Crazy, crazy . . .' softly to himself.

'So, what is this place where he is called, then?' Alexandra asked.

'Ah, something Māori, now, um, yes, 'Hō – hō - hio – '

'Hō-iho – it's the word for horse.'

'Okay, yes, Hō-iho – ah – Wana - wana – '

'Wānanga. It's just the word for school. The Horse School.'

The next day was Saturday and Alexandra set out early, driving through the city, onto the motorway, and headed north. She had switched on her GPS, which would be useful once she turned off the main road, because Te Wānanga Hōiho seemed to be at the end of a dead-end country road. Two ambulances screamed past her, sirens on. An enormous articulated truck and trailer outfit drove up behind and settled a few metres behind her, eventually pulling out and sounding the horn loudly as it passed her. The riders in their cars wove in and out of lanes, without signals, and without sounding their horns. They suddenly appeared passing you on the inside and shot away. But she kept her head calm and straight and didn't let the impulses of the weekend interrupt her focus.

The entrance to the school was announced with a large pseudo-rustic wooden gateway in dark brown wood into which had been burned the name Wānanga Hōiho, though stylistically something like Mariposa Ranch would not have looked out of place. Then she saw, as she bumped along the gravel track to the dusty cul-de-sac, that, inside the gate, two ambulances were stopped, their red lights flashing as they revolved. Alexandra felt her neck begin to burn again, and her throat tightened as she brought the car to a halt. How could she not know without knowing, so to speak, that she had arrived too late?

There was quite a crowd of people standing round the gateway. Alexandra got out of the car. Immediately she began to walk, stones invaded her sandals. A man, who was coming out of the gateway waved at her and pointed. What did he want? He was shouting something. 'Your door! Your door!' She turned. He was right, she had left her car door open. She ran back across the cul-de-sac, just as another car came driving in. The car tooted at her as it had to brake to avoid her. She waved a sorry to the driver. But the driver was already parking and getting out.

Crossing the cul-de-sac for a second time, she found a place between two men, who were standing watching, from where she could see through the gate. A barn-like structure with its double doors open seemed to be the focus of the small crowd's attention. Nothing happened for several minutes. She glanced around in the morning sunlight to see if there were any faces she recognized. But, no one. The arrival of the two ambulance teams, each with a body on a stretcher, heading for their respective vehicles, brought the crowd forward, so that the same man, who had an Australian accent, the one who had waved at her about her car door, told everyone to keep back. The stretchers were loaded, and the drivers went to their seats, while the other ambulance person stayed in back. Alexandra took that as what might be a good sign. It gave her courage to look over at the man beside her and ask:

'What happened?'

'Weren't you here?'

'No. I just arrived.'

'Accident.'

'Oh. Bad?'

'Not sure.'

Then the Australian man began ordering everyone back as the ambulances started up and backed and turned to leave through the gateway. Sirens were switched on. Alexandra thought that might be a good sign too. After all, you needed some hope in order to hurry. The members of the crowd turned towards each other, after the ambulances had gone, and some went quickly back through the barn structure.

She straggled to the gate. More stones. Balancing on one leg, she took off her sandal and shook the stones out. Crossing back to her car, she took more care, keeping her eyes on her feet as she went. She put her hand on the door handle and glanced quickly back to the gateway, in case, well, in case she had missed anything. But the gate was deserted. Opening the door, she was about to get back into her car, when she heard:

'Did you think it was me?'

At first, she couldn't see where his voice had come from, but at last, there he was, standing in the shade of the big macrocarpa tree. She closed the car door once more.

'Come here,' he said. And she went over, into the deep shadow. Once her eyes adjusted, she saw he was smiling at her and nodding: 'You found me. I should have known I could not hide. No, no, it is good to see you. I think they will be all right. They fell. It's a very tricky manoeuvre they were doing. The horse is meant to stand still, you see. The rider sits on the horse. But then – another rider mounts the horse and performs a one-handed handstand on the other rider's head! Would you believe it? Impossible, you would say, except I have seen it. But not today. Bad luck? Who knows? But I don't think it's too bad. Maybe a broken arm. Maybe a dislocated shoulder. Good luck? Who knows? The horse moved, I was told. Why wouldn't it? And you, you are just standing there. Come here.'

Alexandra stepped across to Sensei. His brown hands reached out to her pale face and he rested them on her cheeks. She felt her neck and her throat relax, the breath come back into her.

He put his arms around her and pulled her to him. He smelt of horse, nothing but horse. Her arms went round him. She had never held him before. After some time, he let go, and she did too, and his hands went back to her cheeks and he kissed her on her forehead.

'So, you have the answer.'

'Yes, I worked it out – '

'Don't tell me. I can see you did. That's it! You're right.'

'Are you – going away?'

'Yes. I have a job. I needed a job. I needed to begin again. Just like you. You're just beginning. So, I won't be riding much, though I can do it now. "Maybe you would have been a natural – if you'd started years ago!" That's what the chief of the Cossacks said to me. Too late for that. But I help look after the horses. I get a ride-on part as the old drunk in their comedy riding section. And – listen to this – I'm the cook! Now I have to learn to cook! I didn't tell them!' And there he was, laughing in the old way.

'What about the zendo? The sangha?'

'Good luck! You need to learn how to cook. Now's your opportunity.'

The laughter would not stop for him. Alexandra went over and took his hands in hers. She kissed him on both cheeks.

'Send me an email and I'll send you some recipes,' she said.

She turned and walked to the car, got in and drove away. Even with the windows open, the car smelled of horse. Nothing but horse.

2

HER NAME LIKE A SUMMONS

That was the year I was sent to Auckland to live with my uncle and aunt. My mother was sick, my father had to go away for his work. The house was rather grand, Sarsfield Street, on the upper side, a harbour view. Uncle was a lawyer – or at least I thought he still was when I moved there, but the truth was Uncle Henry was no longer a lawyer. The Law Society had taken unkindly to some deals he had done, and though the profits had earned his only son, Scott, a whole new farm near Clevedon, Uncle now pottered on as a humble clerk in the firm of an old friend, lawyers of course, who rather admired what he had got away with. I had remembered my Aunt (Uncle was my mother's brother) as a 'beautiful woman' – what a strange thing for a seven-year-old to remember, for I hadn't seen her since, and I was fifteen when I went to live there. Either my memory had been wrong or else the intervening time had taken its toll, for she now seemed to me a thin, scrawny, nervous woman, always rubbing one hand with the other. Or else I had changed. She liked me – very much I think, now looking back, perhaps investing in me something of 'hope' that had been lost elsewhere. I called her Aunt, though her name was Cynthia, and she called me Stan. Uncle called me Stan the Man. No one called me Stanley.

Mother and her brother Henry were acknowledged as 'a clever family.' Mother had even been dux of her school, but after school finished, there was nowhere for her to go. Her parents made her stay home and earn her keep teaching the piano. Even then, in 1926, that was becoming a wretchedly old-fashioned notion. Henry, of course, had gone to study law and 'done well' and become a partner very young. His solution, I learned quickly once I was living there, to coping with the consequences of his 'sticky end,' was to drink. He was never an unpleasant drunk, just a secretive, silent, bewildered-looking one. If I was sitting up late with my homework, Uncle Henry might creep into my room and sit on the bed and stare at me, all before I realized he was there. As the sense of his presence (or perhaps the smell of the sherry) crept upon me, I would say, without looking round, 'Has Aunty gone to bed already?' When I turned around, there he'd be, quite far gone, smiling sheepishly as if both pleased and ashamed of the central fact of his new existence.

'She's getting ready.' He would almost whisper this to me.

'I've got some physics to finish for tomorrow,' I'd say. Then there'd be a very long 'pause' as I kept my head down and completed the said physics, and turned back to find him still sitting, still grinning:

'Everything alright?' was always his question.

'Yes, thank you, Uncle.' Another pause.

'I'd better make tracks, then' and off he would pad, doggedly obedient to his own inner command. In his world, his stash of embezzled funds and the surreptitious sherry bottle shared a secret only he knew.

Mother wrote to me and I wrote to her. My father would send me a telegram every now and then. He was always somewhere different, building some new bridge. In 1926 things were rolling along nicely, the future looked rosy for a man like my father. But he wasn't the kind of man who could catch the moment's wave crest and ride it. He wasn't 'smart' like Henry or Mother. Father was methodical, careful, painstaking, limited, the kind of man you would choose to build a bridge. He was where he was meant to be. FIVE MORE DAYS STOP SHOULD BE FINISHED HOPE ALL WELL STOP DAD. I might get one of these every three weeks if I was lucky – or unlucky, depending on how you read the subtext. Mother, on the other, would pour out breath-filled cadences, mainly of regret: 'Dear Stanley' – yes, it's true, Mother did call me Stanley – 'If only I could make sense of all that has happened, I would offer an explanation for these unfortunate circumstances that have visited us. You will have heard me quote to you before those famous lines of the great Scottish bard,

Robert Burns, about "our best-laid plans" so I shall not burden you with them again, but I do say them to myself often . . . ' My father had arranged that a young woman from the YWCA would be a live-in helper for Mother. My mother's letters told me of the pleasure she received from the times in the afternoon when this young woman would read to her.

I would have counted myself happy, strangely, if I had been asked then. I was 'alright' – which was as far as, perhaps even further than, my uncle ever wanted to know. Of course, now, I have to look back and say to myself, 'Really?' My room was a small one, upstairs, at the front of the house, in the north-east corner, and if a large phoenix palm hadn't been dominating the front garden, I might have seen the sparkling waters of the Waitematā. Uncle and Aunt's room was also upstairs, but diametrically opposite mine, on the other side of the staircase and the landing and the small bathroom for my use, so they were quite far away and positioned to the northwest, where there was a long view of harbour running down to Meola Reef and beyond. My view looked over the street, where, almost opposite, a shining new Californian bungalow had recently been built. Aunt called them 'the new people.' The boy next door told me they were 'Ities'. Since I didn't know what an 'Itie' was I asked Aunt Cynthia: 'Italians. Italians are called Ities,' she explained. But only the mother is an Itie, Aunt went on, the father is a Dally. Coming from Te Aroha, I didn't know what that was either, but I didn't ask. The boy next door had been assigned to me – or rather I had been assigned to him – because I would be starting new at his school, which was two tram trips away, so he would be my guide. He was a year ahead of me and I think it was a shame for him to arrive at school with someone like me. Leon always wanted to get there early so he could go to the new gymnasium to train weightlifting with the gym teacher and 'spar a few rounds,' as he said. Once I had learned how to negotiate the tram journeys, I said to Leon that he shouldn't bother about me. He said when the weather got warmer I should come to the beach and swim with him and his friends. Like Uncle, he was trying to be friendly.

My aunt kept away from me, because she liked me and

wanted me to be able to do what I wanted to do. My Uncle only noticed me when he was drunk, as if he'd just found out I was living in his house and his curiosity was too powerful to resist. And Leon didn't really like me at all, but was happy to pretend that he did. After my first week at the new school, I told Leon I wouldn't wait for him to finish his footie practice, that I could find my own way home. This meant I could come home earlier and there was Aunt with a sandwich she had made for me. I asked her if I may take it up to my room, so that I could start early on my homework. She smiled and said I was a strange boy. When I asked why, she said that normally boys didn't like to do their homework.

I went upstairs and placed the plate with the sandwich on the small black chest of drawers, then pulled the book of trig tables out of my satchel. It was true, I enjoyed trigonometry. I made no connection then to the projects my father was engaged in, whereas now it looks so blindingly obvious. However, that day, rather than opening the tables of functions, I picked up the sandwich – some of yesterday's roast mutton with lily-pickle – in an only semi-conscious state of mind, while gazing down on the street below. That was when I first saw her. She came to the new wrought iron gate of the Californian bungalow, opened the gate, and stood there in her school uniform – hers was the sister school of the one Leon and I went to – and took a pair of gloves from her blazer pocket and drew them on. I think it was her hands that first entered my mind and took up residence there. Sallow, translucent skin, elegant fingers, even at that distance, which, once gloved, reached up to her neck, where the same deep olive skin was shining, and lifted the great body of thick, intensely black hair into a bob, which she clicked in place somehow with a pin, and then took the pert little uniform hat and plonked it on her head. She picked up the tanned leather satchel from the foot of the gatepost, pulled the gate behind her and set off walking downhill. The sway of her skirt as she walked, even that dull brown piece of shapeless anonymity, is still with me.

Without noticing, I had eaten the sandwich by the time she

was gone from sight. The watching and the eating were of a piece. But one thing is sure: I would do my homework standing there at the chest of drawers from where her gate could be seen and any of her coming and going might be noted by my hungry eyes. And so, in my fifteen-year-old way, without any word to describe what I was doing or what I was feeling, I became, I can now see, her stalker. Once I had ascertained the time she left for school, I made sure I would also leave then, walking the trail of her gymslip and stockings, following the cheeky hat balanced on that black cloud of hair, up the steep hill to the tram. She changed trams before me, so then she was gone for the day, but the memory of her long, black hair and the skin of her neck that I could fix in my gaze from my chosen place in the crowded tram kept me going all day. I could then try to get to the same tram as her for the return journey, though this was difficult, as her school was a much shorter distance from Sarsfield Street. Even if I had missed her, I could be in place at the window with Aunt's sandwich in time to see her emerge, twice a week, to head off with her satchel. I worked out that it must be for music lessons. I wondered how I could arrange music lessons for myself, though I had never shown any aptitude for music. Mother had tried to teach me, so I was able to play a little, but nothing had disappointed Mother more: 'Your father's son,' she smiled and patted my inept hands, 'stick to your maths – it's a kind of silent music.'

If I was lucky and found myself on the same tram coming home, then I could follow her as she walked home. One day, I was doing this, at my usual calculated distance, when ahead of me she stopped by a big old gatepost built out of volcanic stones. She stopped there and waited until I came walking up, planning to keep on walking, feeling my cheeks turning red, my ears beginning to glow.

As I came alongside her, she said: 'Hullo.' Naturally I was completely unprepared for this. In fact, she rendered me speechless. I see now I could have written something like: 'I was impotent to reply.' But she didn't intend to let me off lightly. 'I see you standing up at your window looking at me,' she said.

Not only was I now speechless, I also had nothing to say. What could I say? It was all true, every word. 'That's all right' she said, somehow instinctively making use of standard interrogation procedures by suddenly releasing the pressure so that the suspect will gratefully blurt their confession. 'You've just come to live there, because you haven't got any parents and you have to live with your uncle and aunt.' She looked at me and I raised my eyes for the first time to look at her. Her eyes were extraordinary. Sullen and limpid, deep and dark, bright and wide, all these at once. Everything I had thought I had seen at a distance was much truer close up. 'That's what my mum told me,' she added.

'My mum's sick,' I sort of croaked.

'Oh, that's a real pity. Is she going to die?'

'I don't know.' I had never asked myself that, at least not in words, certainly not out loud like that. 'I hope not,' I said.

'Let's walk,' she said.

We set off. It was only five minutes till we were home. But there I was, that whole five minutes, walking beside her. And she was talking to me. Her voice was rather surprising, not beautiful, but strong and crisp, like some teachers in school.

'Is Leon your friend?' she asked.

Well, I didn't know what to say to this, so I said, 'Do you know him?'

'He lives across the road,' she answered, as if that explained something.

'Not really,' I said.

'I saw you going to school with him.'

'That was just so I could get to know my way in the beginning.'

We reached the gate in a kind of, for me at least, blissful silence.

Then she said, 'What's your name?'

So I told her – and asked her what was hers.

'Barbara,' she said. Suddenly that name, with its two Bs and its two Rs and its three As was like a trigonometric function. The sound of it, the feel of the sound of it, the touch of it, as I said it. 'Are you going to the Luna Park opening?' she asked me just as I was going to go inside with the treasure of my meeting all wrapped in my mind.

Luna Park was opening on Saturday, down by the harbour in town. School would finish soon for summer. I had asked Uncle and Aunt if they would like to go with me. Everyone at school was going to go. But Aunt had just said, 'Do you really want to go to that? I don't know why they allow such rubbish.' And Uncle had smiled at me sideways and changed the subject from moral decrepitude to financial folly, by pronouncing that the investors were a no-good bunch and the whole deal would be dead in a year. Well, he would know, I thought. But their response had made me determined: 'Yes,' I said, 'I'm going on Saturday when everyone's going.' I felt brave, as well as determined. Then I asked her: 'Are you going to go?'

'I'm not allowed,' she said. Then her eyes lit up. 'But if you're going, you could get me something.'

'Yes, yes,' I said, 'I'll do that.'

'There's coconut shies,' she said.

'Course there'll be the coconut shies.'

'Win me a coconut,' she said.

'I'll do that,' I said.

'I better go. I've got my music lesson.'

And she turned into her gate and I crossed the road and went around to the back door where Aunt had the sandwich on the kitchen table.

'I saw you talking to that girl across the road,' she said. 'What's her name?'

I had to say it out loud, but it felt like I was betraying some terrible secret that I should never give away. It was as if I had only had that secret for such a short time before I had lost it again. The sound of her name in my mouth when I said it out loud was like a seal of doom being set on my fate.

'Barbara,' she said. 'She looks like a nice girl.'

I didn't say anything. I picked up the sandwich and went upstairs.

It was only two days till the grand opening of Luna Park. That was time enough for me to make my plans. I found an old tennis ball in the back of Uncle's garage and, with the ball in my pocket, on Friday afternoon I walked as casually as I could down to Sentinel Bay beach. After a long search, I found a rock close to the size of a coconut and set it up on another rock, so that I could improve my throwing with target practice. It wasn't long before two small boys came along and asked me what I was doing and whether they could join in. I told them to go to hell, but I could no longer concentrate, and retreated to my room. I could always say the magic syllables of her name under my breath like a spell to keep me safe for tomorrow, when I would be able to take the tram to town and walk along to Luna Park.

On Saturdays I had to mow the lawns, front and back, and help Aunt carry the shopping, and then lift and carry things in the garden. But it was a clear early summer day and I was happy to get all my jobs done as fast as I could. I managed to casually mention to Aunt that I thought I would take a tram ride to town to see the opening of the new Luna Park. She looked at me as if I had made that classic mistake of walking into the Ladies when you thought you were walking into Gentlemen:

'You better ask your Uncle.' Then she added, 'What will you eat?'

I said I wasn't hungry, that I would get something when I got there, that was the fun of it.

'Rubbish food, no doubt,' she replied. But I felt generous towards her opinion.

Because the weather was good, the first day yet with a real feeling of summer in it, Aunt lingered in the garden. I began to feel she was doing it deliberately, as she found yet another shrub to trim and more bundles of branches and twigs to deposit. Eventually we went inside, and then it was clear that disaster had struck. We each went to our separate bathrooms to wash, and I headed for the kitchen to take a glass of milk from the safe, so was ahead of my aunt. There, stretched out on the fresh, modern linoleum covering of the floor, lay Uncle Henry. I thought, immediately, that he was dead, and was still standing in shock when Aunt arrived behind me:

'Stone the crows!' she blurted, and then added: "God forgive me!'

'Is he dead?' I asked.

'Dead drunk, more like it.'

She walked around me and stood over him: 'Henry! Henry! Get up!' But nothing happened, as I suspect she expected it wouldn't. 'Oh, Stan, it's a disgrace.' I noticed that he'd wet himself at the same time she noticed me noticing. 'Exactly!' she said. 'You're going to have to help me get him upstairs and get him changed and washed and throw him into his bed. I'm sorry, Stan, but I can't do it on my own.' I had grown taller recently, even in the months I had been staying, and I was strong enough to be of use. Nevertheless, the whole operation took us an hour. 'I'm sorry you have to see this, Stan.' I didn't know where to look of course. 'Still, it might be a lesson to remember. You're a quiet boy, but I have a sense that you know the fitness of things.' Well, I had no idea what she was talking about and I was now an hour late. There was a bike in the back of the garage that I had worked on over the past months until it was in good running order. I asked Aunt if I might take the bike, since I was now so late. She sighed in a way that spoke more of her general sense of defeat than that I was somehow pulling a swiftie on her. 'Don't be late.' I think she was happy to see me gone; though not necessarily happy to be left with a lump of slavering, unconscious incontinence.

I could hear the band in the distance playing 'Sweet Georgia Brown' before I even saw the two towers of Luna Park, with their lights sparkling in the summer evening. Over the Saturdays of helping out Aunty in the garden I had saved myself ten shillings and my small fortune was tucked into the fob pocket at the waist of my grey slacks. I had had to stop and take my jersey off biking across the bottom of the town, because I had begun to sweat. The evening was still a little warm and I was a nervous as I would have been if I had been going to meet Barbara in person, rather than to obtain a present for her that would hold the promise of a future meeting. I parked the bike carefully behind a lamppost hidden in the shadow of the tower that twinkled 'LUNA' and paid my entrance fee and pushed my way in. The crowds were everywhere. I wrapped my jersey round my neck like a scarf and looked around: the Switchback Scenic railway dominated everything and the shrieking from the riders filled the air. The smell of sugar and cooking oil flooded my senses. A big windmill rose above the dodgem cars. My hunger was eating me up, but I was determined to find the coconut shies and fulfil my mission before I did anything else. Opposite the stage where the band played, entry to the kiosk was blocked by a throng of other hungry beings. Then my eyes fell on the signs I was looking for – FUNHOUSE – and PENNY ARCADES.

The man at the Coconut Shies was small and pale, with hairy arms and bulging cheeks, a little monkey-man, while his wife, as I thought she must be, sat behind him, vast and round and pink, with a leather apron into which she tossed coins and from which he drew out change. Three throws for a penny was the order of the stall. The 'balls' you were given to throw were roughly carved chunks of wood that seemed designed to fly off trajectory and miss their target. At the back, where a grey-green canvas hung down, the missing balls slapped into the cloth and slid down to the ground, where a little urchin child, maybe male, maybe female, barefoot, with pudding-basin haircut, ducked and weaved, gathering the balls and returning them to their monkey-man Dad. On the eighteenth throw, after I had disposed of 6d, I struck my golden coconut, but it didn't budge an inch.

'Have another go – for free.' And he handed me one more ball.

I took my aim carefully, I whispered the syllables of her name like a summons to my power, and I let fly. It was a perfect shot, one that no amount of wedging of the coconut in its number eight wire holder could resist.

'Arm of God' – that's how he addressed me – 'choose your prize!' And her drew out a narrow drawer of offerings, dolls and ashtrays and hairbands and novelty disguises, lying on a bed of green beige, like propitiate offerings at a shrine.

'I'd just like the coconut, please,' I said.

'Sorry, Arm of God,' he said, 'coconuts ain't for sale.'

'What?'

'Limited supply. Until the ship gets here from the islands.'

'But that's all I want – a coconut. Please.'

'We don't do that.'

'It's a special promise,' I pleaded with him.

'Not normally,' the monkey-man said.

'It's for my sick grandma, I promised!'

'It's for his sick grandma,' the fat lady behind spoke with a voice like a rusty megaphone.

'Speckles!' the man called to the urchin. 'Bring that coconut.'

'Don't tell the others where you got it.'

I clutched the hairy treasure to my guts and staggered out into the night air, the food smells and the shrieking of the railway riders flying high above the general hubbub. Would I treat myself to one ride? Dodgems? River caves? Switchback? The Switchback was pure trigonometry. I felt that pull to the angles and the slopes, riding the sine and the cosine, up and down on a real and steady magic. Even now that it was completely dark, I could see there was a queue. I joined the end of it and stood there, coconut clutched, gazing around me at this crowd. Over at the Scenic River Caves, the crowds were unloading from the flat-bottomed boats, with bewildered faces as if wondering why they had bothered as they stepped off. It was then I saw her. There's no doubt for a moment I considered whether my mind had conjured her up. But, no. It was her. She was stepping out of the boat, pulling the bundle of her hair back, in that characteristic gesture I had watched often from my bedroom window. After she had stepped onto the unloading platform, she turned and looked backwards and offered her hand, and who should take it but next-door neighbour Leon.

It was a defining moment I was unprepared for in every way. I stepped out of the Switchback queue. And I probably stood there, alone separate, bewildered, long enough for both of them to see me, holding my coconut, the roots of my hair glowing with shame. I think I knew that was the case. Why else did I head for the exit immediately? The crowds were thinner now. I reached the small hidey-hole where I had stowed the bike. But, no, of course, it had gone. I went back to the ticket booth to ask if anyone had seen anything suspicious. The ticket booth was closed. If you had come then, well, you could have walked in. But many things were closing up.

There was a tram heading towards town. I leapt across the tracks. Yes, I was almost killed by the tram coming the other way, and it would have been a kind of poetic justice, whatever that phrase has to do with actual poetry, but I passed safely and took the ride into town. But there weren't any trams going west at that hour. With my coconut in hand I walked, up College Hill, and along Jervois Road, turning down to Sarsfield. It was already what my Aunt would have called 'late to be out.' My night was not over. There were no lights on in the new Californian bungalow as I passed by on my way to Sentinel Beach. I shuffled to the edge of the tide, which was almost full and heaved the coconut with one enormous grunt of despair and also, to tell the truth, of injured vanity, out into the murky water. The splash woke me up to myself, out of my trance of despair.

The sort of weariness that only a teenager can experience fell on my shoulders, as if all the stars had fallen and pressed down on me. Each step up from the beach felt as if a dragnet was pulling me back to drown in the soft, gentle, summer waters of the Waitematā. The combined weight of self-pity and vanity is immeasurable. Then a sound stopped me in my tracks: a kind of grunting and snorting, as if something was rooting around in the undergrowth on the side of the path. What could it be? At the edge of Uncle and Aunt's quiet and respectable street? I stepped down onto a small area of grass and the sound grew louder. Then a voice:

'What the – '

Even in the darkness I could see the naked buttocks, almost have leant out and touched them. A man's voice: 'Get to hell, kid!' And a female voice:

'You sneaky little perv!'

Aunt Cynthia seemed to ignore the lateness of my return. She had received a telegram from Scott on the farm saying that he wasn't going to bother coming to see them for Christmas. She was very upset. 'I've never talked to you, Stan, about Scott, but now you have had to witness the worst of our disgrace with Uncle

Henry, you might as well know.' I was trapped downstairs in the front room that was more-or-less never used, where Aunt had been waiting for me. A strangely prickly red velvet armchair held me in its grasp while she unveiled the family's deepest shames: 'Our Scott remains ungrateful for the farm that Henry bought because he thinks that Henry is hoarding more money.' I realized then that Aunt too had been catching up with Uncle in getting her share of the sherry bottle (or bottles) while I had been one of the famous Luna Park's 10,000 guests on its opening night.

'There, you know now. I shouldn't have told you but I have. Why would a son behave like that?'

The question was very real to her, but I had nothing to offer. I couldn't think of a way of getting out of the room. The Gothic melodrama of my whole evening was playing and replaying inside me, a ghastly black and white horror movie, while suddenly, and out of all precedent, Aunt was unburdening herself to me, the very last person who could do anything or wanted to know anything about what she was saying.

'Stan,' she said, almost but definitely not quite crying, 'I was wondering if I could ask you something?'

My stillness and my silence were all I could do to say the 'yes' I didn't want to say.

'I want to go to the farm for Christmas. I want to show Scott that we care, even if he doesn't care. Stan, I was wondering – I know you want to go home to see your mother for Christmas, but – but – do you think you could come with Uncle and I down to the farm, just for a day or two? It would make everything – easier.'

It was easy now for me to escape upstairs. Of course, I said I would. That released me. But I never did. Even though Christmas was less than three weeks away, in that time my mother suddenly deteriorated. She died the day before Christmas. Up in my room I could see nothing from the window. No sign of Leon and Barbara in the night. But once I was back at school on Monday, it was clear that they had seen me at Luna Park with my coconut. Boys would sidle up behind me and sneer: 'Don't be *shy* - show me your coconut!' My supposed deepest secret had become the butt of ribald humour and the humiliation that I now felt I had constructed myself was complete. Those last three weeks at that school meant that, when my poor mother died, it was almost a relief as it brought me full and final escape from the trap I was caught in.

Except there was worse to come. My father decided I should be sent to a Catholic boarding school in Wellington. Where this notion came from, I never knew. We had never been near a Catholic church and the two years I spent there were quite incomprehensible. I think that the school's virtues, from his point of view, were its cheapness and its distance from him. I was glad I had not been sent to this school at a younger age, because every boy in the first three years was regularly beaten to the great pleasure of the Brothers, the lay teachers, and the senior boys. I think I was the only one who didn't share this pleasure. After a couple of months my father wrote to tell me that he had remarried to the young woman from the YWCA, who had been Mother's helper. It was almost the same as if he were telling me he had just completed another bridge. All these factors, the miserable boarding establishment, cold, damp, cheap and nasty (this is understatement, not exaggeration), my mother's death, the sudden remarriage, meant that my final two years of schooling were a blur. After I had been in Wellington for six months one of my father's inimitable telegrams arrived: UNCLE HENRY SADLY DEAD STOP STRUCK BY TRAM YOURS DAD. There was something mathematical about the relationship between Uncle, myself and two trams that I struggled to write out as an equation. The trajectory and the speed of the tram, the trajectory and the fixed point of the man . . . At least, while at school those two final years, I kept my head for study and, though the teaching was diabolical, I had no trouble returning to Auckland to enroll to study engineering. I boarded with a family at Northcote, and, when I was crossing the harbour by ferry, as I did most days, I could catch a glimpse of the finial of the Sarsfield Street house where I had spent those months. In the holidays I worked on the wharves, earning money. Luna Park twice contrived to burn down before finally being demolished in the third year of my study. Uncle had been right when he said the whole enterprise was doomed before it started, not least its antiquated and outmoded wooden structure. My father and I sustained only the remotest relationship. I think my strategy became to adopt and imitate his telegram-ese in my short, courteous and quite irregular letters.

Those years I was studying in Auckland, I never went to see Aunt Cynthia. I certainly felt ashamed that I had not gone to Uncle's funeral (father did not either) and had not written to her at the time of his death nor since. I didn't need to be told: of course, Uncle Henry would have been drunk and the tram driver would not have had any chance. The burden of not going to the farm as I had said I would, even though I had the best excuse in the world, weighed on me in the oddest way. I didn't think about it often, but when I did, it bothered me greatly. It was like one of those inter-locked wire puzzles that look so easy, if only you could work out the magic twist . . .

Then, just as I had graduated and begun working for a company in Nelson Street, feeling at last I had charge of things, myself, my career and my future, my father sent me a short note with a small neat clipping from the newspaper stapled to it, Aunt Cynthia's death notice, with the time and place of the funeral, St Stephens on Jervois Road, 11am the next day. I explained to my new employer, who was most gracious, and I set off in good time, arriving at the church so that I could take an anonymous seat and sit for a while. I wondered if I would see Scott, whom I only remembered from the photographs in the front room. But I couldn't see anyone who prompted a memory. Somewhere the organist was playing very softly, the church was dim and cold and the attendance seemed small and diffuse. The coffin had already been placed at the front under the pulpit. Almost entirely older folk drifted in, just ones and twos, and sat down. It occurred to me, as I sat there, that Aunt and Uncle had really had no visitors while I lived there. Perhaps this was a consequence of Henry's disgrace. The organ stopped playing. The silence then filled the church. No one spoke. The Minister entered silently, taking his position in the pulpit without being noticed, so that when he spoken there was a small frisson amongst the scattered congregation. Cynthia had lived in this suburb for many years. Though Cynthia was not a regular attendee at this church, he could vouch for her as a Christian soul. The organist, still unseen, played something both dreary and exaggerated, as if death was a boring parade. The Minister pronounced some formal words, read a standard prayer, and asked us all to take a moment to look inward. While we did this, he explained, a young friend of Cynthia would play some music for us on the piano. I hadn't noticed the piano, which was tucked away to one side. I watched a young woman get up from a seat a few rows ahead and walk up the aisle. As soon as I saw the walk, I knew who it was.

Barbara played Ravel's 'Pavane for a Dead Princess' with extraordinary tenderness. The great cascade of her black hair was piled up, but also tumbled down to her shoulders, and her head was down as she played, watching her hands as they let the teasing, whimsical and melancholic qualities of the music give the church a feeling it wasn't often granted. And then she went back to her seat, with the music held under her arm as I had remembered her satchel had been held when she had come out her gate and headed for her lesson.

I had made a decision that I would simply slip away. But Barbara decided I wasn't going to escape so easily. I had begun walking along Jervois Road, when I heard quick footsteps behind me. I stopped and waited for her to catch up. 'Hullo,' I said. 'Your playing – it was – beautiful. Aunty would have been –'

'I saw you when you stood up,' she said. 'You are even taller now. And look at me – I haven't grown at all!' It was true, suddenly we could see each other for what we had become. 'Cynthia – your Aunt – she often spoke of you.'

How terrible those words seemed to me in that street, that ordinary street, where, although someone we both knew had died, still everything was just going on, on a Thursday, at midday. To hear that Aunty had mentioned me at all felt like a vast accusation of everything I had failed to do, though I was barely twenty-five years old. The feeling pierced me, while, at the same time as I felt that pain, I felt tears well up in my eyes.

'I think she liked you a lot.'

'I can see you must have been very kind to her . . .' but I was mumbling. There was so much I wanted to ask, but the clock at Three Lamps began to toll the twelve strokes of midday. I took my cue from them, explaining I had to be back at work, how nice it was to see her, 'to see you, Barbara,' I managed to get those words out, before I turned and began walking.

When I had gone fifty yards, I stopped and looked back. Yes, Barbara was standing there, as if I could have predicted it using a table of functions. She waved, and I waved back. We might have been standing on either side of an equation.

WHO'S A PRETTY BOY

I don't like children. I don't like old people either. And people in the 'prime' of their lives are the worst of all. Carrying on as if they ruled the roost. What a ridiculous phrase. What would people know about 'the roost'? Too big for their boots. I like that better. That's what I see sitting up here in my cage – all ages from the mewling and puking to the doddering and dying all too big for their boots. May their toes be pinched. May their bunions squawk. May their ingrown excuses for claws squeal.

I like parrots. Not that I've seen one in fifty years. But I am patient. I could still mount a downy bum and squirt my steamy stuff. Nothing missing in that department, let me warn you. And I can feel a few more good years packed away under the tail. By then most of this wretched lot here today will be feeding the fields to make the grain to feed the birds that laugh in their putrid mugs.

Look at that little brat. Jesus just died for their sins last Friday, yet God is still making the sun to shine and that little pants-wetter's mother has wrapped him in a gabardine coat and a cap of Harris tweed. And put clodhoppers on his feet. And doubtless soggy porridge in his guts. He's had a ride on the pedal cars (the blue one puke puke because he's a boy) and on the choo-choo train and while he was filling up the choo choo with the pretend petrol (god help us) his mummy just done a runner (more of that later o ye of flappy ears) and now he's looking round to see exactly where his mother's gone. Well I won't tell him that will I? If he says 'Hullo hullo' to the scrawny old parrot I'll say, 'Who's got a snotty nose then?' Mumsy has asked the nice shop assistant if she'd kindly take the nasty little monster by the hand, (whilst surreptitiously slipping a fiver into her pink little palm).

Mumsy's going to be busy for a little time-sy. Beneath my crest of gold ('sulphur' be damn'd) my round and innocent eyes miss not a trick. O look Louisey-weesy is leading him over to where the Bible leaders from the Boss's crazy church are telling 'Bible Stories for Children' all part of today's roll-up roll-up and empty your pockets this Easter Tuesday. Bratty keeps pulling away, he wants to see the funny parrot. Pull him Lou, pull him hard, make him learn about stinking Jesus on the stinking cross.

What's Brat saying now? What's the parrot's name? I shriek it - HEEEK – TAR! HEEEK – TAR! That stops them in their tracks.

'That's our parrot called Hector. He's over one hundred years old,' simpers Lou-lou Louisey-peasy.

I notice my name is used in an unprepossessing manner by many parents who visit this child's pleasure garden: 'Will you please stop hectoring your father!'

To have one's name taken in vain when its etymological origins are as timeless as the Fall of Troy is simply to compound proof that this is a nation of ignoramuses (or should that be 'ignorami'?) who blight my every day spent wasting pure talent locked in a foul cage built for something the size of a small mosquito. You will doubtless have heard of the religious fanatic who concocted this sanctimonious enterprise's brilliant idea, the Hector's Harbour Race? Grown human fools floating in wheelbarrows or bath-tubs or on rapidly sinking beds endeavour to cross the harbour faster than anyone else. And who, I ask you, is not allowed to take part? Yes, you got it. And who would finish the crossing in two minutes flat, twice as fast as that Captain of the Ludicrous who calls himself a flier, I'm-one-of-the-lads call-me Captain Ladd? Given a chance I would've made him crash his plane and then we could have dragged his body round the streets of Auckland behind a pink limousine just like Achilles did to my namesake round the walls of Troy. Of course I wrote *The Iliad*. Parrots grow incredibly old, just as humans grow incredibly stupid. My portrait of I'm-an-All-Black Achilles was carefully crafted to show you all what you are up against when dickheads rule. I would argue *The Iliad* has been way more misinterpreted than the Bible.

Oi oi oi, just a minute, what in the name of jumping jesus are they doing telling the small whiny ones the story of 'Jonah and Whale' – what has that got to do with Easter? These freaks will believe anything that's told them. I guess that when Mumsy and Brat finally get home, Hubby will believe the story about Mummy having to leave little snotnose for 'just a moment' while she attended to her needs. Well yes, there's not a word of lies in that. Nor a word of truth either, me hearties. (More of that soon!) Wingless freaks. Crawling around in the mud and the filth.

Ah, a ray of light! One of the kiddly-winks has burst into tears. I like to see children crying. It's only then I can say, 'Cross me old pirate heart, it's been a good day.' Not our particular Brat in this case, but you can't have everything, can you? Our Little Dribbler is lapping up the Ingestion of Jonah. Little blind fool. Keep that story rolling because Mumsy is getting very busy right now with her needs.

Down the escalator, around the corner, next to the Chief Accountant's office (I know because I was taken there as special guest for the Christmas Party when the War ended), there's a rather secret little room that the Chief Accountant has a one-and-only key for. Oh, yes, I noticed that. It was used a couple of times during that party. It was quite some party. The Chief Accountant was younger then, just home from the War (not the Trojan one) and so was his good friend, in fact they had each saved each other's lives or something like that, I forget exactly, whatever it is humans do for each other. (It's all in *My Iliad* if you care to read. Noble noble noble noble, like a pigeon fluffing up before it fucks. Pigeons disgust me.) I think you will have got the idea by now. Hubby at home and Chief Accountant, presently in the secret little room with special guest Mumsy, are and were (but may not always be in the future) the best of friends. Meantime, a quick passage of ye olde how's-your-father is in progress. Three's definitely a crowd. Except if you're parrot, when the rule seems to be one in a cage is a crowd.

I got brought here by a little old lady who could 'no longer manage me.' Just her and I and years and years and eons of time, and she would say, 'Who's a pretty boy, then?' and I would say 'You are, you are' and, slowly and surely, I destroyed her, psychologically speaking. They took her off somewhere and they brought me here. I regret that now. These people! These galahs! What did Oscar Wilde say? 'They're killing me, Robbie, they're killing me.' My point exactly.

I don't know if a zoo would have been better or worse. There's a Pet Department here I believe. I do not want to see. I have been accused of not being the parrot I was. Literally. Because human beings will swallow any shit, even parrot shit, the story has been put about that I died, yes found dead as the proverbial dodo-parrot, but because of my immense PR value, I could not be allowed to die. You see where I'm leading, don't you? This is Tuesday of Easter. Hint hint. The day of our Risen Lord. The Squawk of our Risen Parrot! Next thing they'll be telling the true tale of Jonah and the Parrot: 'Once Upon a Time, there was Jonah, who was a circus performer who used to swallow a parrot every night . . .' Don't get me started! I refuse to say whether I am the 'original' or whether I am 'the replacement.' That ambiguity is my pure identity. Suck that.

When I do die – as surely I will, fuckers and losers, as will you – doubtless one rainy afternoon when some gormless paterfamilias will intone to his bum-faced progeny, 'Hector likes to have his head scratched' and I shall kick the bucket from sheer shame, ignominy and boredom, the fatal threesome – then, my fervent prayer is that I am stuffed and taken to occupy a pride of place at the company's Head Office, and that some virulent new viral pestilence will escape from my mangey feathers and pass into the tubes and corpuscles of the suits and suitesses as they sit encircling the boardroom table, where they will be found in a demented heap of mortal remains by a poor and innocent junior clerk who shall faint in horror. Amen.

Oh, here she comes. And Brat doesn't want to go with her. He's pulling back. He wants more Bible stories. Jesus! But she's got him good. Maybe things didn't go so well down in the secret room. Hmmm. Ponder time. He wants an ice cream! Is there no limit? And she, she wants to scream! Why does everything resolve into a bad old joke. What a scream! Make you cream your jeans! Oh, stop it, Hector.

No, she's not even going to stay for her usual 'tea and cake.' My wizened brain that dates back to the mythological days of non-existent Homer the Bard tells me that something has come to an end. They're off to catch the famous friendly Farmer's bus. Love has its season.

APPLES

'Have you had a visitor?'

'How do you know?'

'A cigarette butt in Dad's old silver ashtray on the porch – with the press-down mechanism to hide the butts – but, it hasn't done the pressing down very well.'

'Yesterday. They don't clean properly in this place.'

'I'll complain to the manageress.'

'No. Please don't. Leave it. You've never known how to complain properly.'

'Okay. As you wish.'

'Trixie.'

'Trixie?'

'Yes, Trixie.'

'Not Peggy?'

'No, Trixie.'

'Who's Trixie, Mum?'

'Before your time.'

'Manageress collared me. Something about being worried about you.'

'She was a friend of mine at school.'

'Ladies College!'

'Sarcasm is unbecoming.'

'You never mentioned Trixie before.'

'I haven't seen her since school.'

'That's a while.'

'So what was Manageress worried about?'

'Apparently, Night Nurse found you 'wandering' in the cool store at midnight.'

'In the cool store at midnight. Sounds like a game of Cluedo.

I had been there earlier in the evening, to steal an apple. I went back because I wanted to put the core in the rubbish.'

'Why not put the core in the basket here in your room?'

'Trixie left school before the rest of us.'

'Pregnant? That must have been big trouble.'

'Actually it was, then.'

'How come she found you, if you haven't seen her since school?'

'I can't stand organic rubbish going into a waste paper basket. A waste paper basket is all they provide.'

'I don't think I can say that to Manageress.'

'Her husband – her *third* apparently – was a cousin of my cousin Ronnie. She heard my name. Wanted to re-connect. Can't stand the smell of smoke in my room. Anyway, we're not allowed. See, I know the rules. We sat outside.'

'I have to be going soon. If there's anything you'd like, I can buy it and bring it next time. I think that Manageress will probably try and catch me as I go.'

'Don't mention the waste paper basket.'

'Okay. She sounded worried about - you know.'

'The mental question?'

'Yes, okay, the mental question.'

'She's the mental one.'

'I'll tell her that.'

'I had the feeling she came to see me because she hasn't got very long.'

'Funny she should want to see you - after all this time.'

'We used to catch the tram together each morning. Into town. We wore hats and gloves and scarves and stockings, even in summer. Trixie used to put her hat on the back of her head, wrap her scarf round her mouth like a muffler so her green eyes shone on each side of her freckled nose, and thrust her hands deep into the pockets of her blazer. She walked like a boy.'

'When was this?'

'We must have been thirteen. Or fourteen. Bring me my purse. Thank you. She brought me a clipping from the newspaper. Ah, there's no date . . .'

'Doesn't matter. I must get going.'

'I liked the way she pretended to be a boy. Yes - she was thirteen and I was fourteen. We looked the other way round. Trixie looked like she was twenty-five! We used to play wonderful games together - we were film stars on a yacht sailing round the world, visiting our fans in every port. She was Valentino. I was Lillian Gish. One morning this man was sitting at our tram stop. His name's in the clipping - Wilfred Malone.'

'The man at the bus stop has his name in the paper?'

'Wilfred Malone. "No fixed abode." He was wearing a bowler hat. You didn't see them anymore then, even then. And a big watch, in his, you know, ah, fob pocket. And dirty yellow spats. He carried a leather case, like an old-fashioned doctor's bag. He was a bit whiffy.'

'Whiffy?'

'He smelt bad.'

'Oh, he ponged.'

'That's not a word I like.'

'You remember how he smelt?'

'When she talked about it, it all came back to me. What on earth made us fall for his poofy-la-la carry-on? He told us the tram had gone. It had come and gone early - there weren't many trams - and we believed him. Well, I did. I think Trixie knew what he was up to. Trixie could sing. She had an ear, I'll grant you. Used to sit in the tram-stop every morning and sing, I'd hear her as I came up the street. Of course she did it just to irritate. She was like that, but she made me laugh back then. Tiny thing she was, but voice like a man. Still is, after all these years. She can hardly see five feet in front of her, poor thing. She's bent over like a bow, using two sticks and her skin's like an old lizard - the smoking. I didn't say it, but she looks like a witch. Your cousin Sharon would have me up on a charge for saying that, wouldn't she? But it's true. But, look at me, hardly a spot. Shows you can make a difference, look after yourself - if you put your mind to it! We did exactly as he asked, and handed over our tram fares. He went across the road to buy us each an apple. There was a Chinese greengrocer, thin little wisp of a man, couldn't speak a word of English. There was always one of the children there to take your money – they must have had the day off school turn and turnabout, to serve in the shop. Wilfred came back with three juicy granny smiths. "I propose an outing: we shall visit the fairground, we shall partake of ice cream." So, we crossed the road and caught the tram in the opposite direction, out to the beach, right to the terminus. There was a funny little, lonesome merry-go-round standing there all by itself by the sea. We ate our apples sitting on the sand looking at the sea. Trixie sang a song and the man –'

'Wilfred – '

'Good boy - you're paying attention. Wilfred applauded - and patted her on the back. I started to think we should be going back. But we still had money left, from the tram fares, so Trixie and Wilfred had a race to the kiosk and bought ice creams all round. Back at the merry-go-round, the man took a box-brownie camera out of his doctor's bag. Trixie sat on the merry-go-round horse and Wilfred took her picture as she posed. But, there was no film in the camera – look, here, in the newspaper clipping: "Mr Malone claimed to be photographing the girls for a magazine, but police said there was no film in the camera. Subsequent investigation determined the camera had been stolen." Then they asked me to crank the handle on the merry-go-round, while they rode on the horses. Hand-cranked, for tiny-tots really. They were laughing and giggling, so I never saw the police coming. They were just suddenly there. Wilfred tried to run, but one grabbed him from behind, round the neck and threw him to the ground. Another one started kicking him in the back. He was squealing, like a dog when it's run over. I was frightened. I was only fourteen. Then a third one came running up and pulled him up by his collar and punched him in the face. Then he was quiet. I think we were all quiet then.'

'Did you and Trixie have to go to court?'

'No, I think someone came to talk to me from the police when my mother was there, but I can't really remember. I never played with Trixie again. My mother said it was her fault. Molestation. They put him away. But there wasn't any molestation.'

'It sounds like there was going to be.'

'She was a little horror.'

'You said she made you laugh.'

'Slip out the back way. If you go that way - Manageress won't see you then.'

'I said I would speak to her.'

'Why cause trouble?'

'I will have to speak to her eventually. Say I had to leave urgently if she asks.'

'I won't remember.'

'Okay, Mum.'

'And lock the door behind you.'

'Okay, Mum.'

'What does that mean?'

'What does what mean?'

'Okay, Mum.'

'It means, okay Mum.'

'So you don't want to lock the door.'

'I'll lock the door, don't worry.'

'If you don't lock it, I won't remember to check, and then I'll worry if you've locked it or not. We could all be murdered in our beds.'

'I'll lock it.'

'Are you sure?'

'Sure I'm sure.'

'You're a good boy. Orchard apples, hah!'

LUKE

Luke was not warm. She was shivering. So was the old walnut tree through which the light from the kitchen threw its shadows. When she looked up into the tree its bare twigs seemed to vibrate. She heard their old sheep in the grass, snuffling. Her mother's face appeared at the kitchen window, calling:

'Lucy! Lucy!'

She did not answer. Her mother had no idea where she was. But she was so close, under the shadow of the walnut tree, that she could see her mother's look of exasperation and the stick of celery she was holding in her hand, as if it was a wand. Bang. The window was pulled shut.

Her brothers would be inside, gathered round the model space rocket John was building, waiting to be fed; and ready to leap to the table, once Mum delivered the steaming casserole. John said it was the first stage in his plan to escape from planet earth. Matt said he wasn't interested, but he still used to come and stand and watch John building it.

'Where do you think you'll go?' Matt had asked him.

'Somewhere you're not.'

'The universe always comes back to the place it started. That's the shape it is,' said Matt.

'You're nuts,' said Mark.

'I know,' said Matt.

The window was thrown open. 'Dinner!' her mother called as if she was scaring off evil spirits. And then slammed shut again. Luke was trembling. Fog was beginning to creep up from the harbour to their house in the cradle of the headland. She could feel the fog making soft and limp the pages of the notebook she was holding. She glanced down. Her fingers looked like pink sticks. Would he come? Six o'clock. That was the time she had typed, then printed it out on the computer at school: 'Please come to 13 Dundee Crescent at 6 o'clock on the 17th of August if your lost notebook is important to you. If you do not, it will be destroyed. PS I know you are a psychiatrist.' No signature of course. And carefully posted in the real mail at the Post Shop.

Inside the front cover: 'Dr. Joseph Herod, Psychiatrist, The Olives, Mountain Road.' Luke had never imagined her town had an address that sounded so like out of a book. The notebook was small and bound in shiny black covers. The blue ink writing glowed in the light from the kitchen window. Most of the book was blank. Only the first three pages had any writing. On the first page the name 'Eve,' in the same blue ink as the address, with four under-linings. Then Dr. Herod had written: 'desire for the other'. For the other what? And then: 'parasomnia'. Luke didn't know how you pronounced that.

'Dinner!'

On the second page, there was more writing: 'Sunday, @ 4pm, bring the activator file. Contact Marriage Guidance. Grant Flummery, lawyer, Wellesley Street, Box number ??. Her intention to precipitate'. Precipitation was what they had done in science. 'Her intention to precipitate.' You poured one thing into another and suddenly it glowed and hung there, the liquid sitting in the other liquid, like smoke hanging in the air after a rocket has departed from the earth. Luke slipped the notebook down into the pocket of her jeans. Nestled there, she covered it by slipping her hand into the pocket, in front of the book. The other hand, her left, she slid into the back pocket. Cold damp hands. Her red cowboy shirt was not warm enough. The mist dripped from her eyebrows, her brown hair lank with fog, her muddy toes freezing.

The car stopped right by the gate. Its lights shut off. She had positioned herself so she had a good view of anyone entering the gate. The man who did was small, in a big black overcoat, his glasses caught the light as he looked up at the house, and so did the bald patch between his shocks of fizzy hair. And a big black moustache, like it had been painted on. He didn't straighten his legs as he walked. He seemed to glide forward.

Luke slid away behind the trunk of the walnut into shadow. The sheep scuttled toward the rhododendron at the top of the paddock. Dr. Herod heard the sheep and stopped. He turned his head to peer. When Luke was little the sheep had been a lamb. They'd never given it a name. Now it was just 'the sheep.' No one thought about it anymore except Luke. As it grew older, a strange look attached itself to the sheep's face: blank yet inquisitive, as if it were always about to ask, 'Now why did you say that?' Then it would run away. Perhaps it knew it was meant to have been killed long ago, but someone forgot. Dr. Herod gave up looking for the sheep that had made the scuttling sound. The sheep coughed. Dr. Herod coughed too and recommenced his approach to the house.

A torch beam flickered as it climbed over the stile into the field. Luke saw the beam expose Mark's red hair and freckled face. He stood on the stile. 'Luke!' Then, 'Mum's mad with you!' After that: 'You've gotta come. It's dinner!' Dr. Herod had stopped again and was watching Mark, standing on the stile. Mark clambered back, the beam in the fog spreading and slithering as it descended, then sprinting round the back of the house.

Luke put her hand down inside her shirt and pulled out the tiny metal torch that had belonged to her great grandfather in the war. It was a relic, an antique. It was fat and short, with a little metal lid you could lift where the battery went in. And another lid you could use to cover the beam. She imagined her great grandfather searching through the desert for the Germans. He could use the torch to read his orders, just like she used it to read Dr. Herod's notebook in the dark. Her brother John had taken it apart and found a way to make it work with a modern AA battery.

She heard Dr. Herod knocking at the front door. No one ever used the front door. Her mother would be saying, "Now who would that be?" in her voice that meant whoever it was she didn't want to see them. Only the family doctor or the moron Mormons came to the front door. Her brothers would be crowding behind, looking over Mum's shoulders at this strange man at the door. None of them would know why he was there. She had to watch carefully, make sure she didn't miss him.

She had gone in the car when Mum had taken Matt to the hospital for his treatment. She said she didn't want to go in and she'd sit in the car and read her book. Mum had said, 'All right,' meaning that it wasn't and Matt had said, 'Come in with us, you need the treatment too,' and Mum had said, 'Shut up, Matt!' and they'd gone and left her there. She'd wandered around the carpark until the carpark warden came and asked her what she wanted. Then she wandered round the back of the building where there were all the fans and pipes and the rubbish collection place. After that she reached the staff carpark. And there it was, the little black notebook, lying by a yellow painted line on the asphalt.

Luke could hear the voices at the front door, but she couldn't hear what they were saying: Mum's voice first. Mum would be grinding the apron she wore into a ball of flannel, like she always did when she was nervous. Next, what must be Dr. Herod's voice, and Mum again, then John's voice, and Matt's voice, and Mum's laughter, and, just before she heard the door shut, Dr. Herod again. Dr. Herod was retreating down the front steps. Inside Mum yelled loud enough so that anyone could hear right down to the harbour: 'Matthew! Can you turn off the stove! Mark, tell Matthew to turn off the stove!'

Luke was quickly across the stile and sauntering down the side of the house. She reached the driveway and could see that Dr. Herod was already at the gate, his hands deep in the overcoat's pockets. heading for his car. By the time she reached the car, he was climbing into the driver's seat. They wouldn't be able to see her from the house once she was out the gate.

'Doctor Herod!'

Doctor Herod looked up, startled, the same way he had when he tried to see the sheep. His glasses and his moustache made him look like he was wearing one of those silly masks. She couldn't see if his nose was pink. But Luke thought she saw it wiggle, like the sheep's also did.

'Hullo. Who is it?'

'It's me.'

'Oh. Who are you?'

'I live here.'

'Oh. In the house?'

'Yes. I wrote you the letter.'

'Oh? You did!'

Dr. Herod closed the car door quietly and came round to the front of the car and stopped, with his hand leaning on the bonnet.

'Do you have the notebook?'

'Do you want it?'

'Yes, please.'

Luke pulled the book out from her jeans' pocket. Dr. Herod took three slow steps forward and gathered the book from her and retreated to his haven by the car.

'I've never been to this part of the city before. It's a long drive.'

'Mum says it's Bermuda.'

'Oh.'

'My oldest brother John says there's no escape from Bermuda.'

'I see.'

'My brother Matt is crazy.'

'And is he?'

'I don't know. He says the family motto should be 'Further and further but no farther.''

Dr. Herod laughed, a small explosive repetition, like a sheep baa-ing.

'That's rather clever. How old is Matt?'

'Sixteen. He's a problem. That's what Mum says. But I like him. But I guess he's still crazy.'

'You sound like you are a good friend to your brother.'

'Mum says, what this family needs is a resident psychiatrist.'

'Does she?'

'You could come and live here. There's room downstairs.'

'Thank you. You see, I already have a home.'

'You could come and stay in the weekends.'

'I think the main thing is to help your mother. Thank you for returning my notebook. Your mum needs a boy like you, if she's looking after all of you on her own.'

'I'm not a boy. I'm a girl.'

'Oh. I'm sorry.'

'I'm not. I like being a girl. It's better than being a boy.'

Dr. Herod retreated slowly to the car door, pocketing the notebook as he went.

'I need to be going now. I think I heard that your dinner was ready. It's getting very foggy. Good night.'

Luke stood there. Dr. Herod's car 's headlights made swirling clouds appear as their light was gathered up by the engulfing fog. The soft fog was everywhere. She heard the sheep cough. Then she realized Mark was standing at her shoulder.

'Were you talking to that man?'

'No.'

'You're worse than Matt.'

'Matt's my friend. You're not.'

'Mum says you've got to stop wandering off. Anyway, the casserole's burned.'

'I don't care. I like it like that. Race you to the back door.'

THE BALLAD OF ROB LESTRANGE

1

Rob was just fifteen when the US navy steamed into Waitematā Harbour in 1942. The war had already given her a chance to grow up fast. She never wanted to stay a little girl – in some ways she never wanted to be a girl. But she wanted to get out and do stuff and war gives you excuses for that. Her mother, Joyce, or Mrs Aaron LeStrange, as she was addressed in society, was President of the Ladies Auxiliary of the Auckland Red Cross, and young Robin had already been helping out with packing parcels to send overseas. Therefore, when the Red Cross created two clubs in the city, one for officers and one for 'men,' for those swanky Yanks who had landed in thousands – camps in the Domain, Mechanics Bay, Western Springs, Papakura, a hospital in Cornwall Park – she went to work on the weekends in the kitchen at the Officers' Club. She didn't like school, so if she couldn't be playing tennis or sailing her little dinghy, she'd rather be helping the war effort.

There was Rob, the LeStrange daughter, but also kitchen hand, and out there through the swing doors that led into one of the dining rooms of The Auckland Hotel – those doors with the porthole windows so you can see who's getting near finishing their meal – the lunchtime serving was crowded, full of US officers in tailored and ironed uniforms. While behind her, at the service entrance a wide and heavy wooden door, which shoved open with a cranky old squeak, led to a loading bay dock where trucks would reverse up with a load of potatoes (if they could be obtained) or more likely another delivery of lettuces in summer or cabbages in winter. The staff in the kitchen were all women, a striking mixture of Remuera housewives pitching in for the cause and working-class women requisitioned from the

Railways cafés and factory canteens to feed the over-paid, over-sexed and over-here lads (as they were sometimes resentfully known), who had arrived to save us all. The dining room was entirely male – except for invited female guests, of which there was a regular stream. And the delivery trucks were all male too, except for the occasional lass in dungarees who'd been allowed to take a couple of hours off from the Pukekohe or the Avondale fields and ride into town, sitting up front in a rusty cab, while some old joker graunched his way through a painful selection of double declutches. Rob found herself in this hot, steamy, women's-land, laden with smells of beef sizzling for burgers and steaming coffee, odours quite alien to normal Kiwi kitchens. The kitchen stood between the dining room full of smoke and laughter and the darkened loading bay where old cabbage leaves lay in rain puddles that had swept in from the south-west.

In the kitchen, Rob was everybody's dogsbody. This meant she was doing a lot of mundane stuff, washing dishes, chopping things up, carrying orders from one cooking station to the next. It also meant that in times of pressure, she could be sent out back to help unload a truck – or even, throw off her apron and push through the swing doors with a couple of burgers in hand for the officers in the far corner who had been waiting half an hour already.

The very first time she was required to play the waitress, those officers in the corner turned out to be two handsome young men in naval uniforms, LTJG (Lieutenant Junior Grade) Randolph McMaster and LT (Lieutenant) Jesse Freeman. Commissions came young when those above you were dying fast and these two were only twenty-five and twenty-three years old respectively, but each had impressed their superiors as men for whom promotion stood anxiously waiting with lolling tongue, eager eye and wagging tail. Randolph was tall and blond and perhaps a little too relaxed in the way he slouched with deliberation in his chair and reached across the table to fetch the salt. His nonchalance was a study. Jesse was shorter, but still above average height, brown-eyed, with deep brown hair and a smooth, almost suntanned look, and a strong jaw to match his lively, penetrating stare. Though his manner was a little stiffer than his companion's, it was also sincerer, and its attention was granted to its object with a kind of complete devotion.   They watched as a tiny young woman, with burning blue eyes, in a worn light-grey smock, belted at the waist, neatly collared in pale pink, with a small, white crown of a cap pinned into her bobbed brown hair, came bouncing across the dining room towards them. She moved with a fierce grace, as if she might suddenly spring. This striking way of walking could have been the effect of nerves, her first time out on the big carpet, but the handsome coordination of her physical presence made you look again, as you might at a dancer. Jesse looked and looked again, and caught her eye, and she caught his.

'You must be new. We haven't seen her before, have we, Randy?'

The two young officers had met for the first time when they took up their commissions, but ever since that meeting, their friendship had grown steadily stronger, so that, now they were stationed in Auckland, they went everywhere together and agreed that they owed it to each other to enjoy this furlough before they headed north to face the Japanese.

'Did you order the hamburgers?' Rob didn't know what accent to use and what came out was a stumbling mixture of broad Kiwi and Remuera pseudo-English.

'Did you hear how she said that, Jesse?'

'Sure did. It's mighty charming.'

'Do you need extra knives and forks?'

'Ah, no ma'am. Thank you.'

'Excuse me asking, ma'am, but do you lay out the tables before the diners arrive?'

'I do sometimes. Depending on what Mrs Grimshaw tells me.'

'Mrs Grimshaw!'

'Is she, ah, something of a tiger?'

'You shouldn't ask the young lady a question like that, Randy. We're pleased to make you acquaintance, Miss. My name is Lieutenant Jesse Freeman and this rude young man is Lieutenant Randolph McMaster and he's not half as bad as his rude question makes him out.'

'And please, give our compliments to Mrs Grimshaw for the excellent service we have received from you. You will say I said that, won't you? If you don't, I'll go and tell her myself.'

'I'll – I'll see what I can do!'

And poor Rob fled in a kind of delicious terror back to the kitchen, where she found Mrs Grimshaw and tried to tell her but found herself lost for words. Mrs Grimshaw stared at her, but didn't comment on the incoherent story of the officer in the dining room. After all, Rob was the Lady President's daughter.

'That's your first time out front, isn't it, Robin?'

'Yes, Mrs Grimshaw.'

'There's a truck just pulled up outside with those bags of spuds we've been waiting a week for. Put your apron back on, go and help the lad unload. Mr McTavish, who's driving, he's too old to be lugging sacks of spuds. His back's a cross to bear. Go and make yourself useful.'

That is how Rob first got to meet young Clarence Molloy. He was sixteen, a young beanpole, with a stiffly sculptured head, a thick mat of black hair, and that stoop of embarrassment young men contrive. As two Kiwi teenagers, male and female, they worked in silence, side by side, eyes on ground, hauling the earthy sack-loads of potatoes off the truck, through the loading bay and into the cool store. It was all done in half an hour and they were both sweating.

'Thanks.'

'You're welcome.'

'Corker job. You're stronger than you look.'

'Am I?'

'I just mean – when I saw you – you're quite – small – '

'Shortie?'

'Small.'

'They call me 'Shortie' at the tennis club. But I was in the semi-finals.'

'Good for you.'

'The men's semis.'

'You're joking.'

'Yeah. I'm joking.'

'Thought so.'

'Actually, no, I'm not.'

'I didn't think they'd let a girl play. In the men's.'

'It's war time. They had to make up the numbers. They didn't count on me being in the semis. There was a bit of a kerfuffle.'

'Bet there was.'

'I lost my semi on purpose. To stop the carry-on. Do you play tennis?'

'Me? Um, not much.'

'You should come to the club and have a game.'

'Sounds good. But, umm, I haven't got a racket.'

'I can get you a racket.'

'I haven't got any white clothes.'

'I can get them from my Dad's drawer.'

'Is he tall?'

'Yeah. I'm the family throwback.'

'I've never been to a tennis club. But I've played a lot at school. Just hitting around and that kind of thing. They've got some old rackets there we can use.'

'Okey-doke.'

'Rightio then.'

'Hooray, then.'

'Hooray.'

Clarrie got Saturday afternoon off, because the delivery trucks he was helping with knocked off at Saturday lunchtime. That's how, dressed in Rob's old man's cast-off, but beautifully pressed white longs and Viyella shirt (the white longs were only a little too short for him), grasping Rob's brother's second-best racket, shod, however, in his own pair of sandshoes, Clarrie made his entrée onto the grass courts of the lawn tennis club that was only ten-minute-walk from the LeStrange mansion. Rob brought the precious tennis balls, which were in short supply, signed Clarrie in as a guest, then proceeded to thrash the pants off him. But they became friends. Clarrie would always knock on the kitchen door to say 'Gidday' when he was on a delivery, and every so often it was possible to meet up for a game of tennis.

Clarence's game improved quickly with some coaching from Rob and soon their matches were furiously competitive, because neither of them lacked in that department. Inevitably, the kitchen staff were not slow to note that Rob had got herself a beau and the teasing was sometimes a little out-of-hand. She heard the words 'necking' and 'petting' for the first time then. They'd come in with the American invasion. When she heard about 'jitterbugging' she thought it must be another strange and repulsive activity that she didn't understand, until she was told that it was just dancing, but in a naughty way. This confused her more. The only hanky-panky she experienced took place in the dirty minds of the cooks and bottlewashers.

2

Rob and Clarrie's friendship began over the summer of 1942-1943, she was turning sixteen and he was turning seventeen, and the war was going from bad to worse if you were not Japanese, the GIs were pouring in, and the camps dotted through the city were bursting at their seams, so there was a strong disconnect between the excitement brought by these visitors and fear of what the future looked likely to bring. Rob's mother insisted that the Americans had come to save us, because nobody else would or could. She asked Rob to look out for a couple of nice Americans to invite home for dinner, as was the widespread hospitality practice, and naturally Rob chose Randolph and Jesse. Mrs LeStrange was charmed and Mr LeStrange was impressed and Robin LeStrange was thrilled, and young brother was entranced, and the boys lived up to their vaunted reputations as demonstrative, polite, entertaining and well-heeled. Chocolates and flowers and candy and gum were brought out and handed over.

It turned out that Randolph came from a farm in the Mid-West and that Jesse came from a very good family indeed in the South. No one in the LeStrange household, despite their elevation within Auckland society, knew enough about the USA to know exactly where the Midwest and the South began and ended. Jesse had chosen the Navy as a profession. He had received a good education and training and so, even though very young for the job, he took on real responsibilities from the moment America became involved. The charming and relaxed Randy explained that he had never seen the sea until he joined the Navy and that was exactly why he had joined the Navy (wasn't there a song about that?). He had had a good College education and the Navy welcomed young men of his caliber (though he said so himself!). Mrs and Mrs LeStrange were also impressed with their daughter for choosing such guests. Jesse Freeman, from what he said, came from a family of considerable economic substance, while Randy McMaster's farm (or ranch as Mrs LeStrange loved to call it) clearly supported a comfortable existence. And the uniforms were of soft fabric, and well-fitted, and cut with style.

Rob's big moment arrived at the beginning of September in 1943, when Artie Shaw and his band played at the Town Hall for a dance that was organized by the Red Cross in honour of Eleanor Roosevelt, who had flown in for a six-day visit. Much later Rob wondered if it had been her mother's arrangement – nevertheless, when a printed invitation from Lieutenant Jesse Freeman, US Navy, arrived, asking her to dinner, just the two of them together, followed by partnering him to the dance, Rob said she felt as if her life was finally beginning. Never a girlie girl, her mother presented her with a frock that would have been the last thing she would have chosen, but she wore it, because anything was worth it.

She and Jesse went to the Victoria Café in Victoria Street West, and had steak and eggs and then ice cream, such 'pure luxury,' and walked on up to the Town Hall with Rob delicately balancing herself on Lieutenant Freeman's impeccably presented elbow. When they arrived, they were announced, and, because Mrs LeStrange was the Red Cross Lady President, they were whisked away to be presented to the First Lady herself. The band was 'amazing' and the dancing was 'a dream' and the Lieutenant seemed to know exactly what to do and Mother and Father didn't seem to mind at all. That night, Rob found she was suddenly overwhelmed. She'd never had any kind of what she could only call 'feelings' before, but now she knew that she loved Jesse and that she wanted to be with him. She'd just turned seventeen, she'd decided she was going to leave school, she was looking for a job in an office where she could work hard, and make a contribution. She wanted to work in business. Yet now, suddenly she could see herself leaving for America when the war was over and becoming rich and living with this man of her dreams.

But there was a war and the Cinderella night of the dance had not even faded when the fleet sailed, with the Lieutenant on board, towards what would be the gruesome and devastating battle with the Japanese forces on the atoll of Tarawa, in the Gilbert Islands. Up into the Pacific they steamed. Rob watched the ships leave, exulted and broken-hearted, feelings she had never felt before.

3

It was well into 1944 before Jesse Freeman's ship returned. Meantime Clarrie and Rob's friendship grew firmer as the outcome of the war was growing less and less ominous. Every now and then, she would sneak him into the tennis club for a ferocious friendly game. When-ever they could, they would share a milk-shake or a creaming soda in town. Clarrie stopped helping with the vegetable deliveries from South Auckland, because he had begun his engineering studies at University and that study was signed off as worthy of being classified as 'essential.' Engineers of any sort were wanted as soon as possible. Rob took him sailing a few times, showing him how to handle her small boat. The tennis club and the sailing were new to his world. Rob sensed his discomfort and through all of these meetings, she never mentioned him to her family. She knew he wouldn't feel at home at the LeStrange mansion, which even had a name on its gate, 'Versaille' (with no 's' and pronounced always, 'Ver-sail'). Meantime she went looking for a job. Her father offered her clerking in the family law partnership. She chose, instead, a small company that dealt in real estate and also worked as brokers and agents arranging insurance for buildings and properties. She started in the office, but soon it was obvious that she could talk to clients and that she understood the kind of deals that clients wanted to cut to obtain insurance that would allow them to borrow from the banks. It was a tricky time, because the banks were beholden to the war economy, but the tide was turning and many people, whose interest was in money itself, were looking forward to how money could be made to behave when the fighting had come to a stop.

When Lieutenant Freeman returned to Auckland, he did not appear to be markedly changed. He was a man of singular restraint and he valued the way he presented to others above the exhibition of his own feelings or experience. Randy, on the other hand, looked a little as if a shadow had passed over him, but some of the shadow had stayed attached to him as it passed. He was mottled with patches of light and dark. Most of his exuberant nonchalance was gone, his shoulders rode up, his head often leant over as if scanning the ground in front of him, the hands were introverted into the elegant pockets of his naval jacket. No one doubted that they had been through the proverbial gates, though their fiery baptisms had left them blessedly unscathed in any physical way. Nobody spoke of any of it. It was known the services were strongly discouraged from mentioning anything, lest secrets might be exposed, and then, there really would be trouble. Better to say nothing. So, nobody asked. It was more than a collusion; it was a kind of treaty. And it was so jolly to have their boys back, that the doors of Versaille were flung open for them.

Everyone agreed that they were heroes, they were all heroes, and they had earned their rest and they had earned their recreation. And for Rob, those 'feelings' resurfaced. She looked at her parents and she saw that they saw this, and that this pleased them – and that scared her. But the feelings did not go away. She pitched herself into her work. She loved it when Jesse came to visit with Randy, and after the two of them had been at the LeStrange house for a while and her father had brought out the really aged bottle of Scotch to teach the two boys a taste for that alien, unsweetened pale liquor, then Randy would laugh like he had before they'd sailed away to Tarawa. As well as never mentioning Clarrie to her mother or father, Rob never said a word to Jesse about Clarrie - and neither did she mention Jesse to Clarrie. One day at the tennis club, her young brother had turned up and seen Clarrie and her playing together. When he'd teased her, she'd claimed she was giving the boy a lesson, for which he was paying handsomely, and hoped she'd dodged the jeopardy. She'd even been careful to give her father's second-best whites to Mrs Murphy, the woman who came twice a week to take away the laundry, and asked her specifically to deliver them cleaned and pressed back to her. Then she would replace them carefully in the bottom drawer of her father's dresser.

In Auckland the number of encamped troops was dwindling, the number of ships grew fewer, though the hospitals in Cornwall Park and in Avondale and the recuperation camp at Western Springs were still full. But the feeling of dread, of imminent incursion, of the likelihood of invasion and surrender and catastrophe were gone. The fighting was further and further away to the north. Lieutenant Freeman had moved up to some kind of senior position in the naval base. He kept a watchful eye over his troubled friend, Randy, and found a clerical niche for him where he could recover from what he'd once described to Rob as 'his nerves.' One weekend Jesse turned up in a car with a driver and drove Rob and her brother and mother and father down to the quay, where they stepped into a launch and shot across the harbour and were taken on board the very ship that their boys had sailed on under the diving bombers and the strafing fighter planes. The scars of the war were evident and there was nothing treasonous about showing such badges of courage. Lieutenant Freeman told them how one evening, here in Auckland, soon after they had first arrived, he had been on watch with a fellow officer, and they heard the sound of an engine, and, looking up, they saw a Japanese reconnaissance plane fly over. It wasn't the kind of thing you mentioned at the time to the general public. Rob's father said that, of course, he'd heard whispers about that at the office. How good it was they could laugh about it now. Rob looked at her brother and the look on his shining face was total admiration toward the handsome Lieutenant. She was almost jealous.

Then the boys took another tour of duty on their intrepid ship, but this time only up to Fiji and the danger was minimal. During the time that the ship was away, Rob decided that keeping Clarrie a secret was turning into a ridiculous game. It affronted her fundamentally straight-talking, straight-looking, straight-forward way of being alive. Now that she was working in town (her office was on Shortland Street) and Clarrie was studying at the university, it was easy for them to meet up at lunch hour. Their friends, on each side, thought it strange that you could have a friend who was a boy (or a friend who was a girl) and that these were 'friends' who were not boyfriends or girlfriends. 'It's a bit bloody odd' one of Clarrie's friends said to him. 'Is he, you know, one of them?' a friend of Rob's asked her. The way she had been harbouring her 'secret friend' began to irritate her. Next time they had a game of tennis, she told her mother beforehand that she would be playing with a friend and could she bring him home after for afternoon tea.

'Him?'

'Yes, him.'

'Who is he?'

'Someone I sometimes play with at the club.'

'Do I know him?'

'No, you don't.'

'Do we know him?'

'Who's we? I know him.'

'I meant, is he known to our family.'

'I don't think so.'

'Oh. Is he a Catholic?'

'I don't know.'

'He's not a Maori, is he?

'No, Mother, he's not a Maori.'

'Well, does he have a name?'

'Clarence.'

'Clarence who?'

'Clarence Molloy.'

'Molloy! I think he probably is Catholic. Yes, very well, bring him round. We'll take a look at him. Have you heard when the boys are getting back from Fiji?'

'Only the same card we all got sent: "There are a lot of palm trees here".'

'I thought that was a rather silly thing to write.'

'I thought it was funny.'

'Oh, I see. Very well, funny then.'

'I think they were making sure it got past the censor.'

'Oh, I don't think the censor would care about that.'

'I agree. That's why it's funny.'

'Anyway, what time will you be here with this Catholic boy – he is a boy?'

'He's eighteen. After we've finished our game. On Saturday.'

'What does he do?'

'He's studying at university. Engineering.'

'Like Uncle Leslie.'

As Clarrie and Rob were approaching Versaille, after their game, Rob suddenly realized Clarrie was still wearing Mr LeStrange's whites. She called out to Brian, the old gardener, to unlatch the little back gate that was usually locked. But mother was hovering and greeted them both by the side door as they were trying to slip in. By the time that Clarrie arrived at the kitchen, after changing into his own clothes, he walked into a real ding-dong in progress between mother and daughter over the rights and wrongs of a stranger being allowed access to father's second pair of whites.

'When is the last time father played a game of tennis?'

'That's not the point.'

'The point is that I've been washing them and looking after them and nobody has even noticed.'

'They belong to your father. What would he think?'

'I don't know. What would he think?'

'Oh, don't be ridiculous. You know what I mean. Ah – come in, young man. I can run you down to your bus stop, if you like. Robin tells me your home is in *Oad-a-hoo*.'

'I've made some tea. I said I would. Therefore, we should

drink it.'

'There's probably not time for tea before the bus goes.'

'Yes, yes. Your mother is right, Thank you, Mrs LeStrange. And It's okay, I have my bike.'

'All that way?'

'Yes, I always bike home. Mum likes to have the dinner on the table at six. I'll be late if I don't go now.'

4

This happened not long before Jesse and Randy returned from Fiji. The debacle of Clarrie's visit, was recounted by her mother to her father, and that brought about another argument between Rob and her parents. This second argument served to confirm Clarrie's persona non grata status. What do you mean, he doesn't have a father? Oh, was he killed? What, in this dreadful war, poor man? What do you mean, he died before Clarence was born? What kind of accident? A shunting accident? You mean he worked for the Railways? So, he has grown up all his life in *Oad-a-hoo* with no father in the house? Have you been out to his house? Where did you meet this fellow? Then Aaron and Joyce began to argue with each other about whether it had been a good idea for Rob to have spent that time working in the kitchen at the Auckland Hotel. It was one thing to play your part. It was something completely else to be somewhere which wasn't suitable. But then they remembered that that was where Rob had met the boys and that wouldn't have happened if she hadn't been there.

Rob still met up with Clarrie in Albert Park for lunch some days. But now the boys from the navy were back their presence took over. Rob's young brother sat at their feet, Mrs LeStrange was certainly smitten, and Mr LeStrange had formed the unshakeable idea that such eligible and well-funded young men presented the opportunity of a lifetime (perhaps the LeStrange Family Trust might make an investment). Randy and Jesse became more than welcome. The question for Mr and Mrs Lestrange was simply: 'Which one?' Randy was the better tennis player. Jesse didn't seem to have much of an idea, but he learned fast. Of course, they both knew how to sail. Younger brother was more excited than anyone about the choice. He had made his pick.

Robin was aware of all of these ways that she was being pushed. She didn't like being pushed. If it hadn't been that part of her didn't mind being pushed towards Jesse, she might have extricated herself and let the others squabble together. The other force that she did not wish to resist was that, since his return from Fiji, Jesse seemed to be interested in her in an enhanced way. And the exciting news was that, although the bulk of the US forces had departed by October 1944, a small naval contingent would remain and both of their boys were included in that small grouping. From that point, with any possible threat long gone, and the fighting far away, it almost felt as if there wasn't a war going on at all for the jolly company that often assembled at Versaille.

It haunted Rob that she had never told Clarrie about Jesse. Not that there was anything like that between her and Clarrie, so it disturbed her that she found the task of explaining the situation to him too awkward. She rehearsed, but she never performed: there was this naval officer – but he was very young for a naval officer – yes, he was an American – and recently he had made a proposal to her – he was of course a wonderful man – so that she had thought about it – and she had decided that she would say yes – and, in fact, she had already said yes – and she needed to tell Clarrie because, before too long, once the US Navy had granted Jesse permission to marry (they had to wait for this), her mother and father being the mother and father they were, the whole thing was organized to appear in the *Herald* as soon as the Navy gave the clearance, with a photo of the happy couple. The photos had already been taken. And the final thing she would say to Clarrie was that it was almost as big a surprise to her as it must be to Clarrie. But she never found the right place and time to say any of these things.

Clarrie was now progressing rapidly with his engineering studies. His cohort was being pressure-cooked through the courses, so qualified engineers would be available as soon as possible. It was May 1945 and the European war had finished and very soon the country would be flooded with the men returning, indeed that was already happening. Rob had become aware that if she once told Clarrie, then suddenly an invisible, but powerful fence would be thrown up around her, separating them from each other. She hadn't quite reckoned on this. She wanted to know if this was what the future was going to look like, a kind of happy imprisonment. Then she told herself, it would all work out, because she would be living in America. Clarrie would have to come and see her.

Now their tacit yet still unconfirmable engagement was acknowledged by her family, Rob was freer to spend time alone with Jesse. She needed to ask him about how he saw the future, their future. She found out something surprising from him: contrary to her own presumption and her parents' vision of their daughter on a grand estate in 'The South' and them steaming across the Pacific to visit, it turned out that Jesse wanted to stay in New Zealand. But why? Don't you want to go back? He liked it here, he said. But what about your family? What about your life back there? And he tried to explain to her that her father had made things sound as if Jesse had said them, when he hadn't really said that at all. For example, his family wasn't really rich. He had tried to explain to her father, but it had been laughed off as false modesty and another sign of his good breeding. He hadn't wanted to have an argument. And now that he and Rob were engaged, the truth was that he really didn't want to go back to the States. He would be very happy to stay right here with Rob. There was nothing in the States for him that he wanted to go back to. He knew it was going to be difficult with the Navy, but he was going to see if he could get Randy to support him. Randy did come from a very comfortably-off family and he had certain connections that might help. He was a good friend, and might help to obtain permission from the Navy to marry and to be granted a discharge, so he could stay on in New Zealand. They crossed their fingers together.

A week later Rob came home from work to find father standing behind the Regency chair (it was a real one) in which mother was seated, together filling the sitting room with their coordinated presence. And there was Randy, a little hunched over, elbows on the table, hands supporting chin. They said there was something they wanted to talk to her about. Rob dashed upstairs to take off her coat and put down her handbag and came back and they were all exactly where and how they had been when she had left them. Father said:

'We have had a visit from Randy.'

'I can see – hullo, Randy – he's still here.'

'He brought us some rather disturbing news.'

Rob's blood stopped cold. 'Why? What's happened? Has something happened to Jesse? Why isn't Jesse here?'

The elephant in that room had always been the portrait of Great-Grandfather Leslie Aaron LeStrange, who loomed from the darkest corner, where Rob could only see the too-bright whites of his eyes gleaming at her from the deep shades of the painting. As far as anyone knew, the man depicted in oils had arrived in Auckland on a ship from Australia in the 1870s and headed south where, after the fighting had come to a stop, land had been confiscated and made free for buying and selling. Great-Grandfather, who was said to have claimed to be the youngest son of French aristocrats, had enough cash in his pocket to take part in the buying and selling. And out of the difference between what he bought and what he sold, a gap which steadily increased, as he bought and sold and sold and bought, a decade or so later, this house in which he now hung, had been built: Versaille.

It had been her Uncle Leslie who had turned Great-Grandfather Lestrange into an elephant for her. Uncle Leslie, the engineer who worked for the Railways (as Clarrie's Dad had done), didn't visit Versaille very often, though he had grown up there. Rob was ten when one day Uncle Leslie turned up uninvited for lunch. He chose a moment, when mother and father were in the next room talking to each other in lowered voices, to say to Rob and her brother: 'You know that I'm the black sheep of the family, don't you?' Rob had replied, in her conscientiously literal way, 'You can't be a sheep, because you're a man.' Uncle Leslie agreed. Then, she remembered, his eyes sparkled and he had said to them both: 'But you know there's an elephant in this room, don't you?' And Rob's brother had said: 'What elephant?' And Uncle Leslie had said:

'That's what Jimmy Durante said.'

'Said what?'

'Jimmy Durante said, "What elephant?"'

'Who's Jimmy Dew -?'

'Dew – RAAN – tay! He's a funny man.'

'Like you?'

'Maybe. So, can you see the elephant?'

'There's no elephant!'

'There he is.' And Uncle Leslie had pointed at the portrait of Great-Grandfather.

'He's not an elephant! He's a man.'

'So you don't think a man can be an elephant? You don't think he can be one of them?'

'No! Don't be silly!'

But there he was now, staring out from his corner, with his little shining eyes and his big grey ears and his bulbous nose, and his fluffy white whiskers, while Rob panicked about what had happened to Jesse.

'Randy came to tell us something.'

'What? Tell me.'

'You tell her, dear.'

'It seems your Jesse isn't who he says he is.'

'It's easy for young girls to have their heads turned.'

'First, Lieutenant Jesse Freeman doesn't come from a wealthy, established Southern family at all. And, second, he is actually, though I know it isn't something that appears obvious, a Negro.'

Randy was still propping up his head, elbows on table.

'The point of the matter is, Miss LeStrange, Jesse Freeman has been passing. That means, if you don't know, he's been living like a white man, when he isn't a white man at all. Whatever you folks here think about it, there are no Negroes in the US Navy. Well, there's a few doing menial duties, 'sea-going bellhops' is what they're called, and they do make a contribution, but Jesse Freeman can't be here as a Lieutenant in the US Navy. That's a fact. And, I'm sorry to have to say this, but he's going to have to pay for his lying. This news came after I'd helped him put in his application for a special discharge. I have to say, I feel mighty betrayed right now. Seems like his father was a white man, but he never met him, and his mother died when he was young, and being a smart Negro, as we all know he is, he won a scholarship to a high school up north and then he won another scholarship to the Navy, and seems like nobody ever checked up -'

'I know.'

'What do you mean? What do you know?'

'He told me.'

'Told you?'

'Of course. We love each other.'

'Don't be ridiculous. Don't you see, you can't marry one of them!'

'Why not?'

'He's lied to us. And cheated us.'

'He's cheated you? Cheated you of what?'

'He gave us the impression – '

'What has he cheated you of?'

'You are our daughter!'

Rob began to laugh. It was feeling you got when you had been to a movie and you still felt like you were in the movie. You were in another world. 'We're going to get married and that's that and who cares about all that nonsense.'

'I beg your pardon. You'll do not such thing.'

'There is not going to be any marriage. You can rest assured about that, young lady. You are too young to decide for yourself, without our permission, which is expressly forbidden.'

'Can you hear what you sound like, Father?'

'I'm sorry Miss LeStrange, regardless of your infatuation, Jesse Freeman will be sent home immediately now that the Navy have learned the truth about his deception. He has cheated the government of his own country, not only us here in this room.'

'That's because his government has stupid rules.'

'What his government decides is none of our business and we should respect it.'

'If everyone did that we wouldn't be having this stupid war.'

'Don't speak to your father like that. And you can apologise to Lieutenant McMaster right now. He felt it was only right and proper that he come and tell us. He is a fine young man. If only you had set your sights on him, all this needn't have happened. He has excellent credentials and a fine sense of what is fit and proper.'

'I'd rather not marry a rat.'

5

Rob didn't set out to use Clarrie to get back at her parents. She liked him greatly, but she also suddenly needed him, needed him badly, to fill the gap that had opened in her life. Anyway, she didn't so much want to get back at them as to get away from them. Run and hide. And Clarrie was one kind of hiding-place. Still, she could not bring herself to explain to Clarrie anything about what had happened. Because, by now, too much had happened. Instead, she went to see Uncle Leslie, the black sheep, in his shed, which he called his office, at the Railway Station, and asked to borrow sixty pounds from him. Uncle laughed: 'If a Lestrange is borrowing from a Lestrange, then the interest rate has got to be exorbitant! No, no, you naughty girl, just pay me back whatever, whenever. And for Saint Patrick's sake, don't tell me what you are going to do with it!'

Rob bought herself a second-hand 1935 Austin 7 Ruby. She asked Mrs Beckett, who operated the book-keeping machine at the office, if she could park the car in her backyard and said that Mrs Beckett was welcome to drive it whenever she liked, until Rob had her license. Mrs Beckett didn't have a license, but it didn't take Rob long to get hers. She had already, perched on two cushions, stretching her legs to the pedals, driven her mother's Lanchester Roadrider into town with her father sitting alongside.

In November, the war three months finished, summer almost detectable, the day Clarrie was sitting the last of his final exams for his Bachelor's, the two of them met in the Park in the early evening after work, because Rob had said she had a surprise. 'You're going to have to double me' she laughed and pulled out a cushion she was carrying hidden under her coat. She stuffed the cushion into the bike's carrier trap and hopped on: 'Now take me to Mount Eden.'

The gawky rider stood in the pedals as he pumped his way up Symonds Street, with his tiny princess pillion perched behind on her cushion. When they arrived at Mrs Beckett's cottage in a cul-de-sac under the mountain, Ruby the Austin was ready waiting, washed and polished by Mrs Beckett's twelve-year-old boy, Paul.

Rob opened the driver's door and placed her cushion in the driver's seat: 'You can hop in the other side.'

'What's the idea?'

'We're going for a drive.'

'Where'd you get the car? Does it belong to Mrs Beckett?'

'It's mine.'

'Yours?'

'I bought it.'

'Robbie – you're a one!'

'Yep. And we're a two! Look, my feet reach the pedals easy.'

The electric starter fired like a dream. Rob pushed the windscreen open. In fact, it was a dream, or as close to as you could get to one at that time and place, as they wound their way up the mountain, until Ruby crested the summit and there, below, them, the city's panorama.

'And now we're going for a game of tennis.'

'Aw, Robbie, I don't think I should go back to your club, not after what –'

'I've changed clubs. I've got us each a membership down there at the Mount Eden club.'

'I haven't got any gear. I've just sat an exam. I've been writing about concrete structure for three hours. You'll thrash me.'

'That's the whole idea. Look under the seat, there's whites and shoes, and over the back, a new racket. It's not the best, but I ran out of money.'

'Robbie, what's going on?'

'We'd better hurry or it will be too dark to play.'

She had decided that Clarrie would be re-admitted through the gates of Versaille. There was nothing she could do about Jesse, and this helplessness caused her to determine that she and Clarrie would revisit the LeStrange mansion together and that the page-boy from Ōtāhuhu would be admitted. She had made it her mission to make Clarrie feel that he mattered.

The chosen occasion was Mrs Aaron LeStrange's revival of her annual Christmas party, which had last been held in 1939. Now the war was over, it seemed only decent, indeed almost patriotic, to restore the celebration. There was much to celebrate. For Rob, it was ideal, because the children were told they could invite any friends, if they wished. Clarrie was able to cobble together from his university mates the 'attire formal' required and Rob met him when he got off his bike at the gate, a looming, angular penguin with his white starched chest and cute bowtie and over-polished shoes. No one could miss him as his shy head drifted above almost all the other heads. Joyce had certainly not forgotten him, and soon informed her husband. Mr LeStrange made his point by using avoidance to convey his unwelcome. Clarrie could see what was happening and decided to leave early. Straddling the carrier of his bike, in her party dress, Rob went with him. She hopped off at Mrs Becektt's and, while Clarrie rode on back to Ōtāhuhu, Rob drove Ruby back to Versaille, parking just outside. She had already packed the things she would need, anticipating the showdown as likely, if not inevitable. One of the girls hired for the party helped her carry down the cases. Everything fitted on the backseat. And she drove off into the night.

She had made her point and she had made her escape. Mrs Beckett was a good Christian woman whose husband had indeed been 'killed in the dreadful war.' Her house had a room which she rented. She did not ask what had happened, but she knew something had happened for the young woman to have kept the news of her car a secret and then to arrive in the night with her suitcases. Mrs Beckett liked the calm and steady manner with which the young woman bore whatever she was bearing. And she liked the way young Robin was happy to run around the backyard, between the clothesline poles, and pass a rugby ball back and forth when her Paul asked 'Who wants a game of hoofie?' while she cooked a dinner.

And so, while Rob began living in Mrs Beckett's spare room, and enjoying a game of hoofie in the backyard with Paul, the two women were going each day to their workplace, where Rob was now first-port-of-call for all newly arriving clients, a veritable chief assistant to the assistant chief, and Mrs Beckett clattered and slammed away at her book-keeping machine in a room all by herself, and Paul was coming home from school and pouring himself a glass of milk and making himself a cheese and marmite sandwich waiting for the women in his life to return, Rob also waited. She waited to hear from Joyce and Aaron. She knew they had booked for a holiday in Sydney, leaving straight after Christmas. They were taking her younger brother with them. She began to presume they had gone. She knew that Clarrie and his mother and his brother were catching the train to Wellington to stay with Clarrie's mother's sister until the middle of January. Still, she also waited to hear from Clarrie. Meanwhile, as the New Year came and the summer grew hotter and dryer, she came and went from work, returning home each day more puzzled by the lack of a letter or a telegram or even a visit. It was as if in the other world, nearby, but the one she wasn't living in, that world over there, had stopped.

January came to an end. She received a note at work from her father inviting her to lunch. They sat in the rooftop at Farmers, as if she were still a child, and ate sandwiches and drank tea, while he offered a smorgasbord of platitudes. 'Your mother was very upset of course.' He carefully excluded himself. 'We had a lovely time. Sydney is much less provincial. You'd love David Jones.' He would not have gone to the department store, he'd have been hobnobbing with some financial cronies. 'We thought you needed some time to yourself.' We were so angry we might have killed you if we had seen you. 'How is the young man in question? I have a terrible memory for names.' She excused herself at quarter to one, caught the lift down to the street and set off walking to Shortland Street.

In the office she looked up the phone book to see if she could find a Molloy in Ōtāhuhu. Clarrie had said that the phone was always being cut off and that his mother didn't like to use it. He used to ring Rob at her work from a phone box. She would leave notes for him in the Students' Association office. There were three Molloys listed living in Ōtāhuhu. She told Mrs Beckett that she wouldn't be in for dinner and jumped into Ruby as soon as she was home, heading across to Newmarket and down the Great South Road.

The first Molloy was in Hutton Street, so she turned into Princes Street and drove down Hutton and stopped outside the house. There were three children playing out front on the street and a large man with a hose was watering the vegie garden out back. Not her Molloys, she thought. Turning into High Street she passed St Joseph's where she knew that Clarrie had first gone to school. When she reached the next address in Station Road she stopped outside the house with its the picket fence and a minute trellised porch. The pocket garden was neat and empty, dried out by the recent weather. She pushed through the gate. Wild barking erupted and she found herself facing a strong black dog at the end of the strip of concrete paving. Two steps backwards and she pulled the gate shut behind her, as the dog reared up on its hind legs and lurched forward with its paws on the top of the gate and its hard white teeth, soft red mouth and barking head straining to reach her. She knew it could easily jump that gate.

'Down, Harry! Down! Harry!'

The woman must have been on her hands and knees behind the fence, because, out of nowhere, it seemed, she had appeared and taken hold of the trembling Harry by the collar. She was a tall, straight, bony woman, with curly grey hair, in a print frock of roses, wearing her old gardening cardigan and a pair of heavy gumboots that came up to her knees. Her face was young, but unsmiling; when she spoke, then you could see an eye tooth, top and bottom, missing.

'Sit. That's better. Sit. Stay. Good girl.'

Harry now had huddled her shoulder in behind the woman's

leg and the woman's hand rested on the dog's head.

'Was there something you were wanting?'

'Yes, please. My name's Robin LeStrange. I'm trying to find someone called Clarence Molloy. I was going in to knock on your door.'

'You've come to the right place. How do you know Clarrie?'

'He's a friend of mine.'

'What did you say your name was?'

'Robin. Robin LeStrange.'

'Robin. Can't say he's mentioned you. But that wouldn't be a big surprise. I'm just his mum. I'm Edith.'

'Very nice to meet you.'

'Thank you, dear. Sorry, but bit of a wild goose chase for you, you see, Clarrie's not here.'

'Will he be back soon? I can wait. I mean, I can sit in the car and wait. The reason I came, Mrs Molloy, Edith, is that I haven't seen him for a while and I've been wondering where he is.'

'Exactly as I said: he's not here. No good waiting for him.'

'If he's not here, I can come back another time.'

'No. I'm mean he's not here. He's gone.'

'Gone?'

'He's in Australia.

'Australia? Since when? He never told me that.'

'Nor me neither, dear. Not till the day before he left. He's gone to Australia to be an engineer.'

'How?'

'On the boat.'

'How could he do that?'

'I guess it's his choice, he's a grown-up now. More or less.'

'No – I mean – how did he get the money for the fare. Sorry, I shouldn't ask that.'

'He said the job he was going to in Australia was paying his fare. I'm sorry if Harry gave you a scare. I was on my hands and knees in the corner digging out the bulbs. Nothing's going to grow unless we get some rain. I haven't got an address for Clarrie. I'm expecting he'll write. I could let you know if he does. You look a little out of sorts, dear.'

There was a clash of steel as two rail wagons coupled. The sour flesh-stench of the meat-works hung thick in the air. Rob excused herself. Clarrie knew how to get in touch with her if he wished. She opened the door of the Austin and Harry began to bark again.

'We called her Harry before she arrived, because we was told she was going to be a boy.'

Rob walked back to the gate. 'Do you think she will mind if I give her a pat?'

Edith kept her hand hooked under the collar and walked Harry to the gate. Rob reached out her hand and Harry licked it.

'She likes ya. I'll tell Clarrie that. When he writes.'

'If you like.'

'It was Clarrie called her Harry. Makes a rhyme. I didn't have the heart to make him change it.'

'Thank you, Mrs Molloy.'

'I'll let him know you called. I'm sure we'll hear from him soon.'

Rob didn't hear. She was sure that Edith must have, but she never went back to check.

6

All that had been long ago. Ever since she had lived happily ever after, more or less. She had built a business of her own, selling other people's land to other people. In the beginning she was known as a land agent. She searched, but could not find, another woman who had that title. The face of Great Grandfather Leslie Aaron, with its geography of large territories of black oil paint and startling crude highlights in white, the eyeballs and the whiskers, loomed over her endeavours. He too had been an agent. Then, with a wave of the legislative wand, land agents turned into real estate agents. Suddenly she found her business dealt in realty. She preferred that term greatly.

One day she met with a buyer on the North Shore, a man from Brazil, Pedro Nostromo, and his six-year-old daughter, Justina. He had come to New Zealand as an agricultural scientist to work on developing maize production for animal feed. His wife, who had left him for a scientist from Australia, had gone to live across the ditch. Rob and Pedro married, she became Mrs Robin Nostromo, and the house she had sold him in Narrow Neck became her house too. Meanwhile across the harbour, after long years of roaming Versaille's corridors, her mother, Joyce, died of dementia, and Rob's brother and his wife Suzie had the mansion for themselves and children. When Pedro died of a heart attack at the age of fifty, Rob and Justina continued together. It wasn't surprising that, rather than a real estate agent, Justina became an environmental scientist, an early pursuant of land and waterway poisonings. Hers was 'a different kind of realty,' Justina grinned with black humour.

And, now Rob was still here, but Justina was in Florianopolis, where her birth mother, long since returned to Brazil, was slowly dying. The glass on the café table in front of Rob was a starry blue. The full moon in the clear sky shone through the café window and filled her glass with moonlight. She could look out onto the stretch of harbour. A vast container ship was edging its way in. The tug was standing off. A girl in black jeans and black t-shirt and black sneakers, with silver blonde hair, came to her table with a jug of water and lemon and ice. Rob nodded and the girl poured. Rob had been waiting here for her young brother for half an hour. Her impatience had grown worse with age. When you had reached the age of eighty-two, what on earth was the point of waiting? A deep blue Mercedes slid into the disabled parking slot and a handsome young Polynesian man in a tracksuit stepped out of the driver's door, walked round to the back of the car and, opening the boot, removed a walking frame, then came around to the passenger's side, opened that door and, taking the man seated there by his elbows, raised the crumpled figure and edged him into place with his hands on the walker. Rob thought her brother looked like a bedraggled bear emerging from his cave after hibernation.

Versaille was going on the market. It had nothing at all to do with Rob, the will long since had given her no part of anything, a gift she was most grateful for. Apparently, a box of 'things' had been found and now they would be delivered. The young man was putting the shoebox box wrapped with a pink ribbon in the carrier basket of the walker. The disabled park was ramped for access up to the footpath and it would take her brother some minutes to get himself inside the café and seated at her table.

Rob had gone on boarding with Mrs Beckett for five years. During that time, her father died suddenly. The anger she felt towards him made grief easy. He had been cruel to her. She knew how to be cruel to herself. And all her sadness was somewhere else, wrapped up in a cloak of mystery, the missing persons bureau she carried about inside herself. Where were they? Where, 'on earth,' as we say, had they gone? How had she managed to create such mysteries – out of nothing? At Aaron LeStrange's funeral Rob played out her role, while her brother let her know that her mother was happy not to see her. Then Mrs Beckett had a stroke and died. Rob withheld her own grief to accommodate Paul's, his confusion and determination to show he could cope. She helped him sell the house and invest the money, so he could find his way. It was her first house sale, the beginning of a long career. The nice thing was that she still met up with Paul Beckett every now and then. He'd recently retired from being an accountant, and he and Christos, his partner, had bought a house at Piha. She'd driven herself out to the house-warming. She wished she'd been able to sell the boys their new house. It was a beauty.

Her brother heaved himself down. The young man, the driver, was sitting on the seawall playing with his gaming console.

'Dreadful business!'

Rob wasn't sure what 'business' her brother was referring to.

'Sorry to bring you this far, but you know I don't like to go to Versaille.'

'No, no, not that. Selling the place. All kinds of legal rubbish. Red tape wrapped round red tape.'

'I see you've wrapped mine up in some nice pink tape.'

'Take a look. It's all yours.'

'You looked at it?'

'It was up in the attic in a box of Mum's stuff. I had to look and see what's there. Of course, mother had no idea what was what or who was who for the last twenty years.'

Their mother's handwriting had given the box its label many years ago, the radiant blue ink, the curious use of capitals in a cursive script: ROBIN. She pulled the pink ribbon and the bow fell open, like a dressing-gown sash. Her small, brown hands, stained with dark patches of sun-scarring, reached out and lifted the lid. On top of a pile of old letters and aerogrammes, there lay a postcard with a picture of the Statue of Liberty on it. Turning the card over, she saw it was addressed to 'The LeStrange Family.' There was a date, in 1947, and, as she knew already, there was the name, Jesse Freeman. He told them that he was lucky to have left the Navy with a dis-honourable discharge. A dignified apology followed, for causing 'the LeStrange family any trouble,' plus a grateful thank you for their hospitality and 'a special hullo' for Robbie. There had been girls at the tennis club who burst into tears when they lost an important match and everyone flocked around to comfort them. Rob had always thought 'bursting into tears' was girly and stupid. She certainly hadn't burst into tears at the end of that confrontation with her parents and Junior Lieutenant Randy. She had never seen Jesse Freeman again. And now he had suddenly jumped out of an old shoebox.

'I wonder what happened to those engagement photos that the *Herald* photographer came and took.' She placed the postcard back in the box. 'Can you get a drink in this place?'

Her brother waved his hand in the air and the girl in black came over and Rob watched her brother pick out the chardonnay of his choice. 'What about you? For old times?'

'I'm sailing tomorrow.'

'What?'

'I've got a race at the yacht club. Me and another old salt – well, she's in her fifties.'

'Christ, Rob, you must be eighty-three!'

'Eighty-two. Don't rush me!'

'How's business?'

'I still go in two days a week. Last week, I sold a property that had been on the books for two years. I bought the other agents a bottle of bubbly! Encourage them! I own a real estate company in Auckland, so, you know, I must be a billionaire. That's what everyone thinks.'

The chardonnay arrived. Rob watched it disappear.

'Too bloody warm. I'll get another and ask her to make sure it's properly chilled.'

Rob replaced the lid on top of the box. The waitress came and took the glass and the order.

'Any other treasures in here?'

'I thought you'd like to see that one.'

'Thank you.'

'You'd never seen it before?'

'No.'

'Nor me. Bit bloody rough of the olds. Tell me, what happened to that other bloke, you know, the one from the Railways?'

'From the Railways? I've had a few friends over the years, that's true. Nobody's business but mine. But the Railways? Not sure who you mean.'

'You know, the one Dad sent away.'

'Sorry?'

'I don't know. Maybe I got it all wrong. I remember this very tall –'

'Clarrie?'

'Yes. That was it.'

'What do you mean, 'the one Dad sent away'?'

'I thought that was why you left. I thought that –'

'Dad sent him away? How?'

'Didn't you know?'

'No. Know what?'

'Oh, shit. My big feet. As I understand it, Papa bought him a fare to Oz, hooked him up with some contact of his in a job, can't imagine it was in the Railways . . . you mean, you didn't know?'

'No.'

The second chardonnay arrived and went down faster than the first.

7

The waitress watched the old man work his way towards the door. She went and held the door open for him. He might trip on the little step down. The boss would be furious with her if he did. The old man barely noticed what she was doing. He called out to the driver lying on the seawall. Loading the man and his walker into car took some doing. The driver looked up and noticed the waitress standing at the door watching him and winked at her. She smiled back, and flicked her silver-blonde hair, then turned and went inside. The tiny old bird was still perched at the table. She had been watching everything. And now she smiled. The waitress smiled back. She went over to her and picked up the wine glass and the blue water glass.

'Anything else?'

She wiped the table.

'Can I ask you a question?'

'Sure.'

'How much do you think he's worth?'

'What – the old guy?'

Bright blue eyes were burning out at her from a landscape of wrinkled skin.

'No idea. How would I know? Why, do you know?'

'It's a funny question, don't you think?'

'What is?'

'To ask what someone's worth.'

'I dunno. People want to know that all the time. But no one can ever tell you, can they? People keep that kind of thing secret.'

'That's right. The funny thing is, I don't know what he's worth, but I know what he thinks he's worth.'

The little old bird began to laugh to herself. Chuckling and chuckling. The waitress cocked her head sideways and looked at her.

'Never really thought about it.'

The waitress left the table and took the glasses back behind the bar. Now it was dark, looking across the harbour, every house was lit up, each point of light marking a place, on the undulant land, owned by someone.

3

COUNTERPOINTS

Sophia was up long before the night had abated. She hardly knew whether she had slept or not. Images came and went through her mind, Bianca singing, Hunter's teeth as he sneered, Sandy holding Bianca on the beach at Piha, Hunter weeping hysterically in the tutorial, and that strange young woman who had come to see her who seemed to do nothing but smile as she unraveled her skein of truths . . . and in and out, weaving among the images like racing cars on a wet and dangerous track, the phrases spun out of control: 'Her presence in the room is enough to make me feel unsafe'; 'Didn't you know that about your own daughter?'; 'I heard you were at a conference when she died'; 'Associate-Professor Grimaldi, this is 2020, not the 1980s.' In the darkness she sat with her bare feet over the side of the bed, touching the cold carpet, shuffling around in search of her beloved Trade Aid slippers from Nepal, and it seemed to her as if the phrases flashed with colour, like the tiny smoke alarm on the ceiling, while the images, in a strange reversal, remained stubbornly black and white.

'Jesus!'

She spoke out loud to herself in English. Why not? She needed to keep practicing for the next four hours so that, come 10am, she would be ready to parry whatever was thrust upon her in the form of words. Did it all begin the evening she visited The Left Fields in their rehearsal bunker? Of course not, of course not, it began much earlier than that. The Left Fields were one of those alt-rock bands who always wanted to play slower and slower, as if Nick Cave and the Bad Seeds had got mixed up with Rickie Lee Jones. But they could rock it, when they found their mojo. The moment she arrived she could see they didn't want her there. After all, why should she be alive when Bianca wasn't? That was the look in the eyes that gazed back at her. She could have stayed away. Except she couldn't. She could have left when she arrived, but she didn't. Contrition? Attrition? What was it she was looking for?

The band was in a slump. After Bianca's death they had produced a version of Abba's 'Mamma Mia' in which they attacked the song with all the grunge they could muster, Abba on steroids, but the result had been a perfectly inverted image of the original: the gutless with its guts hanging out. It was too obvious. Then they had taken the version of 'Beulah Land' that Mississippi John Hurt sang and played it as a soaring elegy: 'I've got a sister in Beulah Land, outshine the sun.' It would have been brilliant, if they had had a singer to sing it. But what is a band without a lead singer? Sophia had watched their work from afar, for more than a year, not daring to go close, until she brought the song to them.

She had found her slippers. What should Associate-Professor Grimaldi wear to her trial? It barely matters. Why not these very pajamas? With their romping kittens and their bubbling tulips? Very questionable pajamas, Associate-Professor! The Chief Interrogator will speak in a kindly voice, as they always do, expressing both hope and disappointment, mixed in a cocktail called The Inevitability. To be sipped slowly and savoured for each drop. Sophia stood and walked across the bedroom to the French doors and opened the curtains. She could see the few lights that had already been switched on, over on the other side of the harbour. Otherwise the water was dark. Clouds lay low. A blustery north-easterly beat down from the Pacific. Stormy weather. As in the sailors' cry, but also the song. How long have you been gone?

She took the song out of her rucksack and held it out.

'I've brought you a new song. It was left to me by a song-writer from Norway. I met him when I was away at the conference, when ... He's a well-known singer there. Kaleb Nydas is his name. His father was English – his mother, like me, from Italy, but he had grown up with them in Norway. He writes his songs in English. So, the thing is, he was dying. He had a terminal condition. When I met him at the conference, he said he had songs that he would never be able to sing or record.'

She had been staring at the floor while she spoke, still holding out the piece of paper with the song written on it, but then she had looked up. They had all been looking at her. Jimmy the bass player. Neil, the drummer. Charlie, who played guitar, keyboards, even fiddle she'd heard him play. Nobody had reached out for the piece of paper.

'He – Kaleb – he – ah – he asked me to take one, take one song I liked. And set it to music. He'd heard some of my settings for songs. He must have liked them, I guess. This is very awkward. I don't think I should have come. But I have done what he asked. I have written music. It's here along with Kaleb's words. This is the one I chose, after I'd looked at a few, some. The thing is, I've come here to offer it to you. I can't quite, really, bear to have it with me any longer. It seems as if the song has two deaths now inside it. If you want to have it. It's yours. I can play for you. I can . . .'

She had stumbled to silence as she refused to cry. Would these boys laugh at her? Spit on her? Had any of them been Bianca's lover? Was that a mother's question to ask? Of course, it was.

Suddenly Charlie spoke: 'Mrs Grimaldi –'

He gestured to the keyboard. Went over and pulled out the stool, switched on the power. She knew at that moment that she wanted to play it for them. She sat at the keyboards and pressed a couple of keys. The paper with her music was propped up.

'I'm not a singer,' she explained. 'I'm a composer. You're going to have to find a singer. Bianca, of course, she could have. We all know that.' It seemed silly to laugh but she did. It also freed her voice slightly. 'It's called, "I'm not your brother, brother".'

Neil lifted his head and something in him registered for the first time. Jimmy sat down on the floor, preparing to listen.

All she wanted to do was to walk down the hall to the bathroom and vomit. Vomit out memories like this, the accumulated tide of the unforgotten things that was flooding in. Despair can also make you smile. Some glimpse of a crack in the formidable cliff she faced that blocked her way forward was granted. She went to the bathroom, but did not vomit. To the kitchen and put on coffee, looking out from the other side of the apartment, into the tangle of leaves and fronds in the small garden below her, almost invisible in the darkness, except where her kitchen light shone on dew or maybe rain in the night. Had it rained? She thought she had been awake all night. She didn't need more coffee. Her last had been at 3am. Now it was six. She had not noticed rain. Perhaps it had fallen softly. There on the dining table where she glanced, her papers, for the hearing, carefully prepared last night, lay in such an orderly pile, they amazed her.

The chords she struck seemed suddenly uncertain. She stopped and re-started, repeating the first few bars three times to steady herself. Then she had begun to sing:

I am not your brother, brother,
I am not your brother, bro,
No no I'm not I am the other
The one the one you do not know

And a quick passage of lightness on the treble, just a splintering of sounds that didn't add up, but brought with them light, rather than darkness. And then into the chorus in which she heard the sound of vengeance in her voice in a way that surprised her:

Beware beware this other
Hate this other
Hate the one who
Who is the other
I'm the one you'd like to die
But I shall be the death of you
I hunt you like a lover
The one who killed your mother
Beware I am your other
And you must hate this other

> See, bro, I hate you too
> I hate you like a lover

Then everything changed, from major to minor, as the old song says; the tempo crashed; it was the bit she knew she could hear in her head as clearly as she could hear her own mother's voice forty years ago in Italian calling out to her as she left for school, 'Hai tutto, cara?'; but it was the part only a real singer could sing. Again, she paused a moment, went back two bars, re-started, and found a way through, at least to make sense of what the song wanted to say:

> Who are you and you are who
> That question is your name
> I'll tell you, bro, what I think of you
> You and me we are the same

And now the tempo began to increase, to find its way back to the beginning:

> That's why I want to kill you too
> Just like you, bro, want to murder me
> Here I come so what can you do
> Run, bro, run and hide from me

And once more the chorus. Until her hands stopped moving below her eyes and the silence that is not the song took possession of the space.

She took her coffee over to the table and opened the folder. Were they called 'bullet points' because they were likely to shoot out and kill you? Last night she had carefully copied them out, twelve in all, the distillation of her defence, so that they might fit on one side of a sheet of paper. 'She had no intention to offend.' This was fundamental. But how do you prove intention, when you are accused? 'Her job had been to engage critical thinking, not to present material that everyone agreed with.' And then: 'Her job

was to teach, not to make everyone in the class feel comfortable.'
She took a sip of coffee, picked up the pen that was still there on
the table, and crossed out that last phrase. Was it true that truth
resided in the unsayable? The unspeakable? The song was about
the unspeakable. But she wouldn't say that either. No one would
be interested in that. It all needed to be kept simple. She had
talked to a friend in the Law Faculty and she had said, 'Keep it
simple. The stupid need it simple.' And should I defend myself?
'It's your only hope.' That was another phrase that wouldn't go
away, flashing its multi-coloured warning: 'It's your only hope.'
What had she meant? That she didn't think she had a chance
and therefore she didn't want to act in her defence? That she was
scared of the power of the managerial centre? Sophia had felt
that fear many times. She knew it as the basic tool of modern
managerial practice. But now, after weeks on suspension from
the job, fear had disappeared. She almost welcomed the fight
to come. It was grief that held her, almost like a warrior princess
that stood behind her, egging her on. Slay them with the weapon
of your sharpened grief.

'Mrs Grimaldi.'
Charlie was speaking to her. She'd never called herself 'Mrs
Black.' But she'd never called herself 'Mrs Grimaldi' either. Ms
Grimaldi, if she had to be. Of course, Bianca had called herself
Black, Bianca Black. Her father's name, the unmentionable one,
the 'Black-listed' one, whose mention would always provoke
the antipathy towards Sophia that used to flare up in Bianca
whenever it found any kind of fuel.
'Mrs Grimaldi,' said Charlie, again, thank you for coming to
see us. Ah – can we – may we – keep the song for now please?
We'll let you know.'
'That's why I came,' she had said lamely.
She stood up from the keyboard stool, smoothing down her
jeans, re-tying her hair back from her face, reaching for her bag.
'I'd better go. It was just something that I –' and she had gestured
towards the song, the sheet music and the lyrics, that Charlie was
now picking up.

'Thank you, Mrs Grimaldi.'

The other two mumbled assent, as only musicians can mumble.

'Sometimes one – '

'Yes, of course.'

'Sometimes my English. It doesn't say what I want it to say.'

And she had stumbled out, ungainly, proud, tossing her head, yet furious too, feeling some kind of unnameable hatred for those 'boys,' for their youth, their hopeless mumbling, their righteous little bubble, their sullen ingratitude, their miserable stagnation.

She should eat. She knew that. But, how could she? She went to the fridge, opened it, stared, closed it. There are mirrors and mirrors. Eventually one had to eat or die. Eventually one had to die. What was the time one fought for? The small time one had? There was no escape. As in music, the time is set. Until it changes. She was standing in the middle of nowhere in the middle of the room. In the shower one stood naked for a short time each day. But, really, all day, one stood naked, except for the clothes. Again, the smile, that crack in the cliff-face through which one might squeeze oneself and scramble away to freedom, escape, appeared before her eyes.

She stood in the shower and let the water pour down her and, of course, she wished she could stand there forever. Why not? Would the water, all the water, in the city eventually pour out the one shower rose until it stopped, or was there a distant pumping station, pumping an endless stream of water through those pipes, to her? The water cycle, as children learned it at school, as Bianca had learned it, was like a song cycle, in which you could begin anywhere. You could begin with the sun, drawing up the puddles, turning them to vapour, rising, until they became a cloud-song, a floating delicate membrane of melody that floated and floated until it was so heavy and drenched with its own simple own-ness that it changed completely into a thunderous, tumbling thing, the beating song of the rain, falling on the mountain tops, trickling, snaking, bubbling, filling, making a tiny stream, rushing down, finding its deep bed, then came the river-song, slow, languid, easy easy easy down to the sea, that symphonic thing at the end, that mass of a thousand voices . . .

'I'm not Your Brother' had come out as a Spotify track. It picked up numbers. The Left Fields were pleased. Something of a healing, if not a rebirth. They'd got someone in to sing it. Wisely, Sophia thought, a female vocalist. Most of what money they received went to pay her, and she was happy to do it but not interested in hanging around with those three sad boys. Tracey Spines and the Left Fields was the attribution for 'I'm not Your Brother.' Sophia still felt anxious about the whole deal. On the one hand she was happy to have carried through the task that the dying Kaleb had handed her; on the other, a nagging guilt about her act of giving the song to the boys as a piece of false penance. Her guilt could not go away. Where would it go? Into the grave with Bianca? Such melodramatically morbid thoughts came at her. She had learned that they were cloaks to hide other feelings that she didn't want to face.

And then suddenly, after several months, there it was, the song, on Facebook, with a 'WTF' and a pile of angry faces. At first, she couldn't get any handle on what had happened. She'd seen it as a farewell from Kaleb, the 'other' was his death, as when Jacques Brel had sung of his own 'My Death,' but this time closer, because the man who had written 'You're Not My Brother' was already aware that his death was close. And she'd seen other things. It reminded her of when she and Sandy had split up, when Bianca was fourteen, the venomous desire to 'kill the other' that one found in oneself. And, the song had come to feel that it was about Bianca, about how you can feel like you have killed without meaning to, have killed the other, who is yourself, your own daughter. It had never occurred to her that the song might be appropriated for a right-wing organisation's hate-speech anthem. She had gone cold all over. And then, the same week, came the tutorial in which the class representative had stood up from her chair and said, 'Associate-Professor Grimaldi, the class would like to speak to you about the song you wrote for the White Brothers website on the dark web.'

Sophia found she was staring into her small wardrobe. She had already refused her last meal. Now she was being asked what she would like to wear to the ceremony of her own demise. In that song, Mary Hamilton puts on her robes of white to ride through Edinburgh town. Or was it Glasgow town? Or was it her robes of red? It certainly mattered to Mary as she ascended the scaffold. 'Oh little did my mother think, the day she cradled me . . . ' That insistent little smile returned. She bent and found her light-weight Italian tramping boots, almost fashion footwear, that sheltered in the depth of the wardrobe. The pale cotton/polyester trousers, the night-sky deep blue Gore-tex jacket, her green t-shirt with the Rhiannon Giddens image screened on it. She would look like she was leaving on a jet plane. Every day you were confronted with the choice of looking like a man or a woman, which always meant the choice of looking like someone else's idea of a man or a woman. What did a woman look like? What did an associate-professor of composition in a music school look like – if she were a woman? Ah, if she were a woman. That, she had been told recently, was the English subjunctive. If she were. She didn't even know English had a subjunctive. If she were a woman. If she were a racist. If she were an Italian. If she were right-wing. If she were a traveler. What did a traveler look like?

No, it had begun, if it were possible to give it a beginning, when Hunter Wynyard had come to enroll for a dissertation, with her as his supervisor. She barely remembered him as an undergraduate. He had been in her composition class, some years previous. But he'd struggled. That was what she remembered about him. Pale, blond, surprisingly well-dressed for a Kiwi male, and, now he had returned proposing graduate study, noticeably a little older, he seemed to want to impress and that impulse might have been the cause of the consistent mediocrity of his work. He wanted to produce what was wanted. She never thought Hunter was someone who would come back for graduate study. The 'dissertation' as it was profoundly labelled, had been made compulsory for BA Hons study, all

30,000 laborious words of it. He wanted to do something on song-writing, so he said. That was why he wanted to work with Associate-Professor Grimaldi, he said.

'New Zealand song-writing?'

'Okay,' he'd agreed, as if he had thought of it himself.

'Popular song in New Zealand after the Second World War?'

'Yes, that sounds good.'

'So, will you include Māori waiata?'

'Oh, I don't know anything about that.'

'Do you want to find out?'

'Oh, if you think it's a good idea.'

'It's your dissertation.'

The conversation had quickly begun to go around in circles.

'How about novelty songs?'

'Novelty songs? Such as?'

He was slightly unnerving from the start, from the way he had shaken hands too enthusiastically, from the way he'd drawn up his chair so close beside her as she had checked some regulation on screen. Not harassment, more like having a large puppy bouncing at your side. Perhaps that was a kind of harassment.

'There are songs from the 1950s and 1960s, such as 'Taumarunui on the Main Truck Line' or 'The Dog-dosing Strip at Dunsandel' which are novelty songs. You could then include some Howard Morrison Quartet songs, but you wouldn't have to know Māori.'

'Okay.'

'Okay, what?'

'Sounds good. How do you know about these things, you're Italian aren't you?'

'I study things. That's my job. If you want to do this dissertation, then you must enroll also for my postgraduate song-writing course, but I won't be teaching that until the beginning of next year.'

'Do you write songs, Professor Grimaldi?'

'I write the music for songs, yes.'

He hadn't mentioned Bianca at that first interview, though looking back, Sophia could tell that that was the only thing on his mind. Not so much her, as mentioning her. Mentioning her to her mother. But even Hunter had some tact, when it suited him. He saved it up, not the tact, the mentioning.

The daylight was growing, but very slowly. Then suddenly, a ray of sunshine, in through the bedroom French door, from the east, struck her between the eyes. But it brought no revelation. Only the realization that she was more conscious of everything around her than she could remember being before, yet everything, these brittle curtains, that aluminium imitation French door, the lack of weight in the Gore-tex jacket, the sharp sudden light, everything conspired in its own unreality. Alienation. Disassociation. Dissonance. Sophia closed the curtains, as if she were already on a long-haul flight. In the fridge she found the bowl of potatoes, capsicum, ginger, chili, that she hadn't finished last night. She put it in the micro-wave. Poured out the last of the coffee, including the dregs to chew, into her cup. She put the folder with her papers into her rucksack. The little bell rang, then she sat at the table with her favourite pair of chopsticks, picking her way through the food. It was tastier than last night. At least the food was not unreal.

Hunter's dissertation was still unfinished. Sophia thought she would be willing to bet whatever future happiness she might experience, unlikely as that felt at this moment, against Hunter Wynyard ever completing. He would never finish. He had barely started. But now he was suffering from the trauma of discovering that his Supervisor was a secret racist who used her unconvincing talents to support fanatical groups on the far-right, so it wasn't his fault he couldn't finish. At least she wouldn't have to be in the same room as him today. Hunter had stated that being in the same room with her was traumatic. Yet three times in the past two months she had been summoned to meetings that purported to seek reconciliation and each time Hunter had been there, if anything prolonging each occasion, seeking for himself some kind of limelight almost. But would the Committee summon him today? Would she find herself sitting in that plush, upstairs foyer with its ridiculous leather chairs and its expensive New Zealand art, and there opposite her smiling and traumatized and waiting his turn the apparently plausible Hunter Wynyard? The horror rose up from her heart to fill her head. Sophia shook her head vigorously as she headed back towards the bathroom. As if she were trying to shake his presence out of her hair. Shake that man right out.

There were a dozen students in Words, Music, Voice: Songwriting and its Rites, her postgraduate course. This counted as a good enrolment. Sophia had managed to compress together aspects of the academic study of songwriting with a section of the course that involved practice, the students writing and composing their own, the 'workshop' module. It was a saleable combo.

When the Class Rep had announced that the class wanted to speak to her about the song, she had responded immediately, 'Why yes, of course.' Charlie had been the first to tell her what had happened. He texted, saying take a look at Facebook. The band quickly took the song off their website. They tried to get it removed from Spotify, and that happened once the circumstances were explained. But the White Brothers had their marching song and their game became to post the song as often as they could, where-ever they could, to gain as much limelight as they could. To gather hates and likes like a corrupt priest gathering indulgences to sell.

Sophia had explained to the class what had happened. Norwegian songwriter didn't help. Why couldn't we have an Aotearoa songwriter? A couple of students mentioned Anders Brevik. Someone asked her about Italian Fascism. She explained what had already been done by The Left Fields. Another student asked whether that wasn't the band that Bianca Black had sung in. Then the inevitable: 'Was she the one who died?' question. It wasn't Hunter speaking, after all he knew that she knew that he knew. She didn't look at him. He took his time to play the sensitive card:

'Bianca Black was Associate Professor Grimaldi's daughter.'

Jesus. Some students were confused, some seemed to feel a

plot was thickening.

Someone said, 'I'm not sure I like this.'

Someone else: 'Like what?'

'I don't feel safe.'

Sophia had tried to keep the class together: 'Let's look at the song. Shall we? As a song. Together. As a class. Whatever else, it's a chance for us to see the power of song and to try to understand where that power comes from. Shall we?'

'Shall we what? '

'Look at the song.'

'Why should we? It's white racist hate speech. Why should we have to study that?'

'Okay. Who else feels like this?'

Two others raised tentative hands. Then Hunter added his. Sophia looked at him with some undisguisable disbelief.

'Very well, I tried to explain the circumstances which have given rise to this extremely unfortunate situation.'

'But you would say that, wouldn't you? How can we believe you?'

'I can't make you believe anything. And that's certainly not my job as a teacher. You believe what you believe, I believe what I believe. But what I know is that the song has been twisted completely off its foundation. It was written by a friend of mine who was dying. The brother, the other, the lover the song speaks about is his death.'

'But it's not now, is it?'

'No. No, it's not.'

'But how do we know this is not all a cover-up? That you didn't write this for the White Brothers and now you are cooking up this story?'

'Why hasn't the song been taken down?'

'It has. But the White Brothers have it. They can post it when they like.'

'Why don't you withdraw your copyright?'

'I gave it away. It's not mine.'

'Why did you give it away?'

'Because my daughter had died. Because I wanted to give the

band something, to do something . . . '

'No, this is all a big cover-up. Italy is the home of Fascism.'

Hunter had said that. He truly had. Then the student who had led the questioning got up and walked out. The two tentative hand-raisers followed her. Sophia remembered the strange gurgling sound that came from Hunter as he burst into tears and ran out of the room after the others. Had he really been crying? Or could he not sustain the crying that he wished would come out of him but wouldn't, and therefore he rushed out? She remembered thinking that she was the one who should be crying, but that thought had only summoned her quiet, secret smile, the crack-in-the-cliff smile. She was the only one smiling in the room. Three students had been absent, four had just walked out, and five others sat like stunned mullets.

The mirror on the wall. The face you recognise and do not recognise. The make-up that makes up who you are going to be today. I am just a simple traveler in a strange land. I came here years ago with nothing, a back-packer with a flute and a tiny keyboard in my pack. I came with nothing and I shall leave with nothing. Such has been my rite of passage here. And in between I found a lover and I lost the lover and I found a daughter and I lost the daughter and I found a living and I lost my living. And now, indeed, I have plenty of nothing. She seemed to be getting everything done at an incredible rate.

It was still barely 7.30am, yet she was ready to leave. Reluctance had been replaced by a precipitate desire to hurtle into the maw of her own disappearance. When she had gone into the bathroom at 6am, there on the wall the first of cockroaches coming inside for winter was sitting. When she moved, it scuttled away, behind the cabinet of drawers. She knew, if she pulled the cabinet out to look behind, the cockroach would be gone. The trick of the cockroach was to survive by disappearing. The art of disappearing. By the top corner of the bathroom mirror, that daddy-long-legs spider was still sitting when she returned to the bathroom a second time, banking on the hope that total stillness bestowed invisibility. She'd waved her hand close to the spider, who proceeded to spin wildly in circles. If no longer invisible when seeking survival, then dance mesmerizingly. Tarantella. Cling to life at all costs. She still needed her lights on as she took the Prius out onto the road. Yes, the road was wet. Into each life some rain must fall. And another crack in the cliff.

Sophia drove first to the car park in the bay. She pulled into the car park and stopped. There was no one else there. The sea was chopping up into broken pieces, white water, brown water, green water, grey water, roiled by the wind. She couldn't see the beach from the car park. Only a ragged pōhutukawa and the harbour beyond. A low chain fence that some car had pushed sideways. A saturated MacDonalds box stuck in the grill of the storm-water drain. This was where Sandy used to come as a teenager with his first rock band, at the end of the seventies. They'd set up their beat box and their street amps and torment the neighbourhood until the police arrived. At first the girlfriends were designated the task of riding out as scouts to signal when the cops were coming. Then the girls revolted and stole the gear and wouldn't give it back until they could be in the band.

She first met Sandy at the folk club in the next bay. By then rock music was in the past and he was already sitting and playing his cello, singing his strange ballads, half-borrowed, half-original, tales of murder and violence told in sweet and melancholy tunes: Möritaten as they were called in German. Songs of the great chain of human killing. She had been making her way round the world, with her tin whistle and her tiny electric keyboard, playing on street corners and in clubs where she could, trying not to get in trouble. She didn't sing, but she wrote her own music, even when people thought it sounded like something else. After all, that was the art of art, was it not, she would tease her students, to make something that sounded like something else? At the café in Mount Eden, where they had let her play for an hour a day and collect from her hat, they told her about the folk club. The evening had been called the Night of the Weird and Wonderful, and she and Sandy had both been prominently weird and wonderful that night. They had driven in his Morris

Minor to this place. He had wanted to make love there, in the car, in the carpark, but she didn't. Who might see them? Who was this man? It was their first fight and they had barely met. She'd jumped out of the cramped little English car, worse than a Fiat, and walked away, thinking that's that.

But he had reappeared. In the café in Mount Eden. He was tall, charming, mysterious, wearer of different hats, funny ones, sad ones. And a long tweed overcoat. I may go out tomorrow if I can borrow a coat to wear. He came to apologise. He came to ask if they might play together sometime, that is if she wasn't moving on soon. Going home to Italy?

'A tin whistle and cello?' she asked and laughed.

'I could get hold of a piano accordion for you.'

She smiled then. He had a nice way of going sideways. 'Where could we practice?'

He had a flat, of course.

'When could we practice?'

'This afternoon.'

And, so, the steps of that dance began to form, forward and back, and back and forward, to the left to the right, into the centre, and so on. But they weren't destined to become a musical duo. She was a student, an enquirer, a seeker, and he was an entrepreneur, one of those who never wanted to play the same piece twice. She told him he had never played one piece properly yet. That was another of their early fights. But on the beach at Piha, after Bianca was born, tall and thin as a strange thing made of sticks, in silhouette, his long arms holding the little babe up into the last of the evening sun, it touched her soul.

Sandy had chased after her. And Hunter had too. She could see that now. After he had left her office, when he'd first come about the dissertation, she thought he'd never reappear, she admitted to herself that she hoped he'd never reappear. Then his enrolment appeared and it seemed that someone in administration had signed off on the deal without her say-so, that she was slotted in as Hunter Wynyard's supervisor. Someone with his marks would have needed clearance from the head of department. She had gone to talk to her head. Well, the Department badly needed to boost its numbers (So they would enroll a singing duck?).

The Head knew Hunter's father it turned out. (How would that alter the entry criteria?) The department is seeking sponsorship for launching an undergraduate initiative. (So Mister Wynyard senior was loaded?) His mother was in the Choral Society and on the Arts Foundation Board. (So, Hunter had several more cards in his deck than Mamma Mia from Italy had been dealt?) Just put up with it, the Head explained, and a shamed face fixed its gaze floor-wards. (I'm so happy it's not my job being the Head, she had consoled.) It had not been her ending up with the wrong men, not that she hadn't made mistakes, but it had been the wrong men chasing after her. They made her up. She repeated the English phrase out loud: 'They made her up.' Yes, it definitely had two separate meanings, depending on how you thought about it, with no change of stress or inflexion.

Sophia was almost happy to be stuck in the traffic along the waterfront. Delay now felt like her only aim. The point of arriving was only ever a reason to return to the start and repeat, with minor variations. Inching forward, accelerator, brake, brake accelerator, another kind of dance, an arrhythmic one. Music? She flicked through some old CDs. Calabrian Folk Music with the dreadful kitsch cover. But some happy, bouncy tunes, just right for the occasion – she smiled again. The tarantella beat and the inviting vocal cries were even more at odds with her surroundings as the Prius entered the open jaws of the University's car park building. Her car-parking status, as a result of the fee she paid, was labelled on her monthly account as 'license to hunt.' Nobody seemed to be aware of what the language was saying to them. If you paid a certain amount, then you bought the right to hunt, the license to kill. She shut down the loud Calabrian gentlemen on their guitar and squeeze-box and skin drum and whistle. In the vast but low-ceilinged building one felt as if one were walking through catacombs, the cars like bodies, each slotted into its niche, the acoustics echoing at each footstep or cough. She entered the stairwell and began to climb.

Stairway to heaven. And smiled.

There was a time, in her early teens, when Bianca joined the evangelicals. Sandy was still living with them, but only just. To survive in a world that demanded he complete things, Sandy had taken up producing, which he had proved very good at. If you couldn't complete your own work, then you could complete someone else's. And he did. With style. People like him, who could both command and charm a studio, were in demand. And he wasn't distressed, as Sophia was, when Bianca started going to that dreadful church, with its dreadful blaming, yes, dreadful was the only word – full of dread – he only laughed. Whereas Sophia had raged.

'Not my daughter,' she said. 'They fill you with dread.'

'You be careful what you say, Mum, because God is watching you.'

'Jesus!'

'And don't say Jesus.'

Bianca began to turn on her mother as an enemy. However, subtly twisting, she pitied her father as someone who needed to be saved. And then he walked out. Which saved Bianca for Sophia, but not without an endless irritating resentment. Sandy up and took his young Thai girlfriend back to Thailand. And that had changed the whole story.

Bianca never talked about why she stopped going to the church. One day she just did. She never talked about why she joined a band. In a way, poor girl, she had no choice. She probably knew more about music than her mother and her father combined, because she had no choice. Children have no choice about who is their mother, who is their father. She was tall and ungainly, like her father, and furious and relentless, like her mother.

After all, rather than saying her prayers at night or watching *Shortland Street*, she had sung for her goodnight kiss, a song for Mummy, and a song for Daddy (if he was home). It was the age of Kimbra with the age of Lorde coming up. Bianca began to study Music at the University, perhaps because she could always get a ride in with Mum. She was often away from home for days on end, but she always came back home to Mum. Sophia never asked much. She could see the band really did have something, they were making enough money gigging to survive in a hand-to-mouth way. She also tried to keep away from Bianca's study. And Sandy in Thailand was the absent presence that completed the triad of non-communication.

Bianca noticed what Ayanna Witter-Johnson was doing with her voice and her cello. Of course, it reminded her of her Dad. She began to sing *and* play. She asked Sophia to help her develop her skills with the piano accordion. This tall, gaunt young woman, accordion slung, trilby balanced neatly on the crown of her short, black hair, with her boy-band behind her, became a crowd-puller. The Left Fields, with Bianca as their lead singer, grew versatile, they could rock up in a club, but they could also do the weird, wonderful and fantastical within experimental and world music modes. The people who came were an all-sorts, among whom was Hunter Wynyard, and not so long after, Hunter brought his sister, Diana, to see the one with whom he had fallen in love. He wanted to show his sister, that one there, she's the girl for me.

Here she was, insulated from the cold leather seat, staring at the door where the Disciplinary Committee were in session. Whatever lies behind the door, she heard Scott Walker's mellifluous voice. Music was described by the University as a Discipline. This had made her laugh, years ago, when she was told that she was teaching in the disciplinary area of music. A boot camp for bad musicians quickly created itself in her mind's eye. When she arrived, reporting downstairs to the receptionist, the secretary had come out to see her and led her upstairs on the deep blue carpet with its fleur-de-lis and its heavy pile. The secretary showed her a table with an assortment of cups, a coffee urn, some vapid-looking teabags in a small bowl, a strange arrangement of doses of sugar resembling a quiver of arrows.

'Help yourself,' the secretary said.

Sophia wanted to say, 'I would if I could,' then realized that the secretary could not hear what she was saying in her own language. Help yourself. If only I could.

'They started late,' the secretary continued, 'take a seat.'

Well, even that had its funny side. It was encouraging to feel her smile come back. And then the door opened, and Hunter walked out, and straight past her as if she didn't exist.

Three weeks ago, she'd been rung by the student who had led the questioning in the class and had then published a not-entirely-stupid piece in the student newspaper. If, in fact, she, Sophia, had acted as might be presumed, then she would have agreed with the student. She had responded by letter, explaining the 'facts' but she was aware they felt obscure and lacked impact. The student, Denyce, wanted to meet with her. Sophia explained she was not going to the campus until the situation was resolved. They had met in a coffee shop in Mount Eden. Since it might all have been said to have begun in Mount Eden, in another version of the great chain of undoing, Sophia had felt that a journey back to origins might give her strength.

Denyce had gone and done her homework. She had met with the band. She believed that what Sophia was saying was more-or-less true. Denyce didn't exactly apologise, but she said she was withdrawing her complaint and wished to continue with the class. Sophia thanked her. What about the others, their complaints? Denyce was sorry to say no, Hunter was going ahead and the other two were trailing along. She said she had told them of her decision but they had dismissed her as a coward, interested in her own marks. Would Denyce speak with the Disciplinary Committee? But, no, she didn't want to have anything to do with it. Sophia suddenly saw that Denyce was scared. She thanked her for her courage and left. Mount Eden had a mixed karma.

Then a week later, another phone call. This time, a voice she didn't recognize. Could they meet? Could she come to Sophia's home to talk. No, no, Sophia didn't want to do that. She knew she needed to keep her sanctuary. She suggested the café in Mount Eden, curious what karma it would bring a second time. No, the voice didn't want to meet in a public space like that. So, could the voice tell her the voice's name? Diana. Diana. She had something to tell her. About the – controversy about the song? Not exactly. About Bianca. The name seemed to come at her like an attack of something she'd never heard before.

'Who is this?'

'Could we meet on the mountain?'

'The mountain?'

'Mount Eden.'

'What – what do you want to tell me?'

They'd found a seat, side by side, facing out over the city and the harbour. Sitting side by side, they each faced outwards, speaking in parallel. Diana Wynyard, with pale translucent skin, deeply auburn hair, with arcane symbols tattooed on her forearms, a delicate pair of stylish 'granny' sunglasses perched on her nose, a loose shirt of pale green silk and ragged jeans and sneakers, conveyed nothing less than continual ambiguity. The smile almost never left her face, so it seemed to Sophia, but then again, some people just look like that.

'I'm very sorry. If I had told you my full name, you probably wouldn't have met me.'

'Yes, that's true.'

'Hunter is not my favourite brother, but he's the only one I've got.'

'I don't want to talk about Hunter.'

'I understand. Did you know that Hunter was in love with your daughter, Bianca?'

'Yes. I came to know that.'

'Did Hunter tell you?'

'No. No, he did not. But he made it possible for me over and over to guess that.'

'That's Hunter. But Bianca wasn't in love with him.'

'Is that so?'

'You didn't know?'

'Not exactly. I couldn't believe she could have been. But what does anyone know?'

'So Bianca didn't leave any diaries, letters, anything . . .?'

'Listen, Ms Wynyard, that is my business, not yours.'

'So, do you know who Bianca was in love with?'

'Is this some kind of game?'

'Me. She was in love with me.'

'So – I just believe you?'

'No. You don't have to. You know what it's like not to be believed.'

'How come I have never heard of you before?'

'Perhaps because she was in love with me. Does that make sense? That's why I asked about diaries, letters, emails, texts.'

'I'm not that kind of person. She didn't keep diaries. Yes, I looked at emails – '

'We didn't use email. That's why.'

'There were thousands of texts. I didn't look through all those.'

'Of course.'

'There are songs. Poems. Songs. Whatever. But no names. I probably should have set one of those to music rather than that song I did. But, too late now.'

'Hunter fucked it up for us.'

'Excuse me? What do you want to tell me about Bianca?'

'It's a story I have to tell you because, well, I loved her. Yes, I did. It might help make sense of what happened.'

'What happened when?'

'When she died. Do you know what happened?'

'Of course. How could I not? I'm her mother. The verdict was accidental. I believe that. I think I believe that. I mean, there are no accidents. People do stupid things. She loved her own bravado. If she was here now, would she do it again? No, no, I don't think she would. So, what happened, yes, I know what happened. There's nothing I could ever wish more that didn't happen.'

'Yeah. Yeah, I agree. But I might know why that happened. If you want me to tell you.'

'What are you saying?'

'Hunter chased her. He used to go to every gig, you know, make sure she saw he was there. Hang around. Try to meet her afterwards.'

'Harassment.'

'Yeah, harassment. He dragged me along once to see if I thought he was onto a good thing. There's only eighteen months between us, we grew up together, Mum and Dad, were never round much. He wanted my verdict.'

'Which was?'

'Oh yes. But not for him.'

'I see.'

'Yeah. But I didn't say that to him. It was like that. You didn't know that about your own daughter?'

'No. I mean, you were smitten? Is that the word? Smitten?'

'Yes, that's a word.'

'No, I mean, is that *the* word? So how did you . . . ?'

'I got to know Neil.'

'The drummer?'

'Yeah. I got to go to things with the band. But not with my brother. We were at a small get-together, one night, round at someone's flat, after a gig, in the early hours of the morning. Suddenly Hunter turned up. With flowers, for chrissake. In his mind, it was ultimatum time. There was this commotion at the door. Jimmy comes in, the stupid flowers in his hand, and says, 'Bee, there's that prick out there.' Bianca went out to the front door with Jimmy, and told Hunter to fuck off. She hadn't connected us. I was still just someone hanging out with Neil, enjoying her company. She came back in and said, "What a creep." Actually I agreed.'

'So, did you tell Bianca, who you were?'

'You mean, that I was the creep's sister?'

'Mmm.'

'No. You see he was living in this big apartment downtown with a couple of suits from Dad's business, the apartment was owned by the business. Rent-free is Hunter's ideal in life. He's pretty much lived his ideal all his life so far. I was still staying at home, in the castle. Mum and Dad were overseas for six months, god knows doing what. That's what we used to call it, the castle. It was a family joke, but it's kind of true. It is a fucking castle. There's this dumb waiter between floors you can get in and ride up and down. Hunter and I used to do that all the time when we were kids. And there's two master bedrooms, His and Hers. His has these ceiling panels that slide back to reveal mirrors staring down at you. Hers has panels that slide back with the flick of a switch to reveal a glass ceiling and the stars above. For him, there's an infinity of mirrors gazing down. For her, there's a glass prison, but with a view of the stars above. Between the two rooms, there are these wardrobes that back onto each other and in the back wall, a sliding panel so you can sneak through from him to her or her to him.'

'Sounds like a bordello.'

'That's pretty much true. We grew up in a bordello. Bianca and I used to go back there. We didn't think that Hunter knew anything. That's why there's no traces, apart from texts. We decided not to tell anyone.'

'But Hunter found out?'

'Yeah. Neil knew. Well, I had to tell him. He was very good about it. I don't know how Hunter found out. But he did. And that was that.'

'What?'

'Hunter sneaked in. He waited in the other bedroom. He came through the wardrobes. He watched us. Yeah. Then he told Bianca, you know, sent a message. And said I'd told him he could watch us. That Bianca wouldn't mind. That, you know, he went on about how lucky he was. Thank you very much. Never had so much fun in my life. Best night of my life. Pure shit. My own brother.'

'Jesus!'

'Exactly.'

'Is this true?'

'You don't believe me? That was the end of it. Bianca didn't believe me. She realized who he was. She realized who I was. I mean, not really, but what it looked like. She was furious. Broken. Broken-hearted. I think she wanted to kill me. To kill us both.'

'When was this?'

'Not long before. That's why I wanted to tell you. I think what happened, the accident, well, you know she started drinking.

And other stuff too. She didn't do much of that sort of thing. But Neil told me. She was pretty out of it that night. I was frantic. But she wouldn't answer me.'

'She wasn't coming home much – '

'She used to talk to me about you. Lots.'

'I was overseas, you know, at a conference. I didn't know.'

Sophia had turned to look at Diana. She found it hard to say what she saw. Yes, perhaps it was simply the way her face rested, almost in a smile.

One day, in a supervision meeting, Hunter had suddenly said, 'I'm very sorry about your daughter. I loved her singing and her songs, I saw her lots of times.'

Sophia had simply said, 'Thank you,' and tried to move along.

But then he had added, 'I heard you were at a conference when she died. That must have been hard.' The surprise that he knew something like that had made her look up suddenly and she caught him full in the face, looking at her. His face was almost meaningless, as if he'd just eaten an ice cream and couldn't think of what to do next, because he was bored.

Now she realised she had been looking at a murderer. And sitting there, in the cold leather chair, in the soundless antechamber of the landing, waiting outside the door where the Disciplinary Committee were in session, she realized that she herself was the next victim in this chain of killing.

Suddenly she looked up to see the secretary was standing in front of her, 'Associate-Professor Grimaldi, the Committee will see you now.' The secretary went ahead of her back into the room, leaving the door slightly ajar for her to follow. Sophia stood, and gathered her bag with the papers inside. She walked over to the door, quietly took hold of the handle and closed the door, leaving the Committee inside. Then she turned and walked down the stairs, past the receptionist at her station in the foyer, and pushed open the door to the street, where the wind and the rain greeted her with their open arms.

BY THE BOOK

Raewyn Talua and Samson Gifford were best friends and mortal enemies, for whom life's railroad ran through the middle of their relationship – they were divided on all of life's major fronts, between female and male, brown and white, Catholic and Protestant, South Side and East Side; nevertheless, they agreed on one thing, that Shakespeare was the man. They met regularly at Secondary Schools' Drama Association monthly meetings and annually at the Secondary Schools' Shakespeare Competitions, where they pitted their inventive directorial wits against each other to see whose cohort of senior Drama students would take the prize. Very often it was one of them. The year previous a North Shore school had stolen the crown with a hip-hop Beastie Boys inspired version of Lady Macbeth and Macbeth himself terrifying each other at the midnight hour. Raewyn and Sam agreed it had been a cheap shot and the judges had been swayed by novelty rather than quality. Still, they also knew that if it was only ever one of the two of them who won, then that would begin to sour for everyone. They were both gracious in defeat.

They also met often and informally at the theatres in town, where they both claimed to attend every production, usually with some of their senior star pupils in train. On these occasions it took only five minutes plus a glass of Pinot Noir each before they were shouting at each other about the prospective merits (if the drinks were pre-show) or the manifest demerits/inherent worth of the spectacle they had recently witnessed. The students from both cohorts looked forward to the entertainment Raewyn and Samson's fierce debates about sexism, naturalism, alienation, racism, colonialism and exploitation provided. These shared vicarious audience experiences of the two groups of students, Raewyn's shy (at least initially) Pasifika girls, some in their school uniforms for the evening (though this was not compulsory) and Samson's conscientiously louche Pākeha boys and relentlessly fashionable Asian and Pākeha girls, became a way for the two groups to find an excuse to mix and mingle. Quiet, serious talk was shared across the divide of the two schools, as well as moments of turning away to suppress bursting out in uncontrollable giggling when Mr Gifford would throw his hands in the air in complete despair or Ms Talua would turn away and announce, 'That's enough of that colonialist crap for one night – come on, girls!' and march off down the foyer to the street.

One unwaveringly consistent thing that Raewyn and Samson were in complete disagreement about was whose students were the best. Raewyn insisted on highlighting how her girls were the crème de la crème, achieved in the face of huge odds; while Samson would plead that, despite their acknowledged enormous privilege, his students were broad-minded, tolerant, and enlightened. Neither teacher was quite sure what they really wanted for their students. There was a good argument for Raewyn's girls to ignore any commerce or intercourse with their hugely advantaged white and Asian peers, and to raise themselves single-handedly (with Raewyn's guiding hand, of course) above their disadvantage as shining examples of what a new future might look like. And Samson, also in his own way with a mission, instructed his pupils not to condescend by sticking their noses in where they weren't wanted and didn't know what they were doing, and instead to take what they had learned back to their ignorant parents. There was good sense on each side. Yet such programmes couldn't really satisfy the desire of some students, those who clearly possessed great gifts and potential, to gather for themselves as much experience from life as they could. For certain wonderful young people in their keep, this prospect was almost unbearably alive for both these teachers. There was about such prospects, though neither of them would have said it, that which could have been described as erotic in its longing. Something that, in such students, touched their teachers' souls. Naturally feelings like this remained staunchly in the realm of the unsaid; in fact, in the kingdom of the unsayable.

When Romeo spots Juliet 'above,' on her balcony, he says of her: 'She speaks, yet she says nothing.' And then he adds: 'Her eye discourses.' Such is the nature of the unsaid and the unsayable that Shakespeare was not alone in having a great deal to say about. *Romeo and Juliet, the most excellent and lamentable tragedy of,* was one of the chosen texts for the latest round of the Secondary Schools' Shakespeare Competitions. Winner of the Auckland rounds would proceed to a grand final to be held in little town of Stratford in Taranaki, and the winner of that would then head to perform their scene on the stage of the reconstructed Globe in London, England. High stakes that were to be decided by judges viewing each competing school's presentation of a designated twenty-minute scene from one of three selected plays. The plays were the usual suspects, *As You Like It, Comedy of Errors* or *Romeo and Juliet.* Another year it might have been *Twelfth Night, The Tempest* or *Julius Caesar.*

Both Raewyn and Samson settled on *Romeo and Juliet* because they felt that they had each discovered a rising star in their cohorts, who would be able to carry the demands of the role of Juliet. A lot of theatrical anxiety has been played out over Romeo, but getting Juliet to work on stage, for a modern world, both Raewyn and Samson were canny enough to know, would be the real crux of their challenge. The so-called 'scene' was actually an edited amalgamation of three scenes, Act One, Scenes Four and Five (the young Montague dudes bucking up courage to enter the Capulet's ball and the ball itself where Romeo and Juliet first meet) and these leading to the famous Balcony Scene, somewhat truncated, with Benvolio and Mercutio's short scene at the beginning of Act Two omitted altogether. This would allow the senior drama students a 'boys' scene,' a crowd scene, and then the challenging love scene (even though most playing Juliet would likely be older than Juliet as she is in the play – about to turn fourteen).

Ms Talua had a year twelve Tongan student, Teresa, who was exceptional. Teresa was one of those lucky ones, the longer she stood still on the stage, apparently doing nothing, but processing everything, the more watchable she became. She pulled in the space around her, so that she was its focus and its centre. Teresa was quite small, but her voice seemed to belong to someone larger. It had an extraordinary kind of command and gravitas for someone who was only sixteen. Raewyn knew that when Teresa said to Romeo with guarded, desperate urgency, 'If they do see thee, they will murder thee,' then the audience might shiver; and when she described Romeo as 'the god of my idolatry' then another shiver, of a different kind, was possible. Teresa had been at a state school until this year, supposedly arriving from some undisclosed difficulty, so she was a new quantity for Raewyn, but from the moment she saw her in her Drama classes, she was in no doubt about her quality. She had her Juliet.

For Mr Gifford the problems were different. He couldn't see any issues with getting his students to convincingly pull off Romeo, Mercutio and Benvolio, with their flaming torches, humming and hahing about getting into the Capulet Ball. He had already decided that the ball would be a nightclub on K Road and the motivation would be around trying to get in when you are underage. There was even a club on K Road that had a flaming torch burning outside. And there was one girl, Dana, who would make an excellent Mercutio. She could play a boy as if she'd been one all her life. And it was Dana who gave Samson his inspiration to cast Cooper as Juliet. Cooper's parents were from Serbia. He was tall, but not too tall, with black hair, but sallow skin, and deep brown eyes. There was nothing in the least old-fashioned 'camp' about Cooper. As Mr Gifford put it to himself, 'He's neither straight nor not-straight – he's true!' His hope was that no one would notice that Juliet was being played by a boy. He thought he just might pull it off. The prospect excited him.

The competition would be an all-day-and-into-the-night affair. Raewyn's girls had won the South Side round and Samson's the East Side and there were also winners from the North Shore, the West and the Central City, as well as the winners from Northland, who, rather unfairly, now had to come to Auckland and compete again. Six presentations to be completed during the day, with the attendant changes of lighting and sets and the dressing up and the undressing. The judges arrived with sandwiches packed, just like the students, and large thermoses full of coffee. After all the presentations, there would be shared kai and then, in the evening, the judges' reports and the presentation of winners: best ensemble work; best male performer; best female performer; and then third, second, and, finally, the grand winner of the best scene would be announced.

Thus, was the stage set for a showdown of opposites – or perhaps 'contraries' would be the better word. Raewyn necessarily always had to cast females as males. Because this was an everyday business, much as it had been for Shakespeare himself in reverse, she didn't fuss with making an issue of the fact. She transposed the setting, so that the ball was costumed as if for the annual school ball, with long ball gowns. Her Benvolio and Mercutio were in smart lavalavas, shirts and ties. Romeo had gone for a suit belonging to one of the girls' father. So, the dress was modern and the ambience familiar and local, but these concepts were only used to support a performance that was essentially as in tune with Elizabethan teenagers as possible. The kiss of 'you kiss by the book' was played as a peck on the cheek, and a frankly disappointed response from Teresa as Juliet raised a shriek of laughter from the packed auditorium. She made it clear what she desired and had missed out on. Romeo scaled the improvised ladder to Juliet's balcony with panache, the lighting was pulled down very low and the whole scene played within the realism of the tension between fearing to make a sound and longing to stay talking forever. There was nothing radical about it, but Teresa's mellow tones, the engulfing shadows and the sense of physical longing from Teresa set against the actual physical jeopardy of Romeo (would he fall?), made the scene something that really did glow in the dark – Teresa was the sun and she did outshine the theatre lights that shone on her, 'as daylight doth a lamp.' Raewyn Talua was glowing herself when the lights went up. She must have felt she had it in the bag.

When Samson's players trooped up, his strong directorial hand was immediately in evidence. The crowd outside the K

Road nightclub, complete with flaming torch (a simulated lighting effect in these days of health and safety) and rainbow flag, was very scantily dressed indeed, male and female. Benvolio had a halter top and hot pants, Mercutio was all leather and spikes, and Romeo looked like he'd borrowed his suit from Elvis's closet. Less striking was the amount of ad-libbing (never a winner even with the more liberal judges) and the mashing of the lines as to render some inaudible, others incomprehensible. Inside the club, the mirror ball took over, the music was too loud, and Cooper as Juliet, in a short black dress, was barely visible, merely a series of flashes, as if day were following night every few seconds. There was redemption from this sensual overload. The 'balcony' of the Balcony scene appeared to be the branch of a tree, with the moon visible and shining through its branches, while Juliet, in a long white nightdress, perched there, swinging her lovely legs. She was gorgeous. It was possible three-quarters of the room were not aware that they were watching a boy. At least for that, Samson could feel pleased.

There was nothing in the other Auckland offerings to hold a candle – or any other kind of light – to match the thespians from the South and East. That is, until the contingent from Tai Tokerau took the stage. They had travelled down by bus that morning and didn't arrive until after lunch. They didn't seem to have much with them. They said they'd had trouble finding the Mangere Arts Centre, that they'd forgotten their lighting plan, but this didn't matter because as long as everyone could see it would be okay. There was a buzz running round that the poor country cousins had wandered in and the last item before kai would be an embarrassing anti-climax. That was, until they started to act.

They used the structure of the pōwhiri to bring their boys into the 'ball,' enacted on a bare stage, and from time to time the action was halted and interrupted to create intimate cutaways: while the marae action paused in time, Romeo kissed Juliet, 'by the book.' It was tender; and no one laughed. Though there was no depiction of a meeting house, for this balcony scene, it was clear Juliet was back in the mahau of the house, behind the paepae, while Romeo was crouched out on the marae aatea, though they were not separated by light, only by their urgent and impossible longing for each other. Around them, like whakairo on the walls of the house, the rest of the cast stood like those hovering ancestors who threatened to murder their love. Of course, the scene's outrageous simplicity paid off. The actors weren't great individually, but the whole group effort, the ensemble's commitment, carried everything forward: parting was such sweet sorrow, for the audience as well as the star-crossed lovers.

After the last performance and before the kai was ready, Ms Talua and Mr Gifford, who had not spoken to each other beyond a kia ora at the beginning of the day, were seen to come together and engage in an animated whispered conversation while the judges thanked everyone for their sterling efforts and promised how difficult their decisions were going to be, before gathering up their thermoses and bags and papers and heading out through the doors to the office at the end of the corridor. Raewyn's and Samson's eyes followed them all the way out. The teacher for Tai Tokerau, a short, young-looking Māori woman wearing glasses with strong magnification, dressed in a green track suit and sneakers, came over to greet the two Auckland teachers. There was a quick exchange of formal kisses and handshakes and some short-lived laughter and then they parted again, while Raewyn and Samson continued their conversation. 'Haere mai ki te kai' came the call and all the hungry young made a dash for the foyer where the kai was being served, soup and bread and sausages.

Cooper had taken a while to get changed out of his Juliet manifestation and back to his senior schoolboy look. In his hoodie and jeans no one, except his own school-mates, recognised him. He stood around on the edges, finished a bowl of soup, and wondered what to do. He was aware in a half-conscious way that their scene hadn't been, well, quite – something had been missing. But he felt that he had done what he could, as well as he could. It was a strange feeling. Mr Gifford hadn't come to speak to him yet. He didn't want to be blamed if they lost. He liked Mr Gifford because he really did care, but he also knew he could be unfair to people if he didn't get his own way. Cooper began to wish he wasn't there.

He put down his soup bowl in the returns pile and wandered up the corridor to the entrance, then, pushing the door and finding it open, slipped out into night. The moon was halfway full, and he snaked past some cars and round to the back of the building, where the theatre had its loading bay. His father had said to him: 'Don't be an actor, be a lawyer, it's the same thing – only you get paid more.' His father was clever, cleverer than him, but he knew he didn't want to be a lawyer. And his father had never known what he wanted to be. He was too clever by half, as his mother had said to him once. It was a clear night. The stars, the moon, and across the roundabout, Pak 'n' Save. That made him smile suddenly. The way things, unlikely things, can be fitted together.

'You were good.'

'Jesus! You gave me a fright.'

'Sorry. I'm Teresa.'

'You were better. Better than me.'

Teresa was slowly smoking a cigarette. She was dressed in black jeans, a black puffer jacket and a black beanie. She smiled: 'And you're Juliet!' She smiled again.

'I guess I am.'

'Me too,' she said. 'What's your other name?'

'Cooper.'

'That's cool.'

'My grandmother. She loved Gary Cooper. You know, he was an old actor.'

'Better than being called Gary,' said Teresa.

They got the giggles.

'Do you want a puff?'

'I don't smoke.'

'Go on. Try it. It calms you down. That's what my Nan says.'

Cooper took the smoke and inhaled. He burst out coughing and that made them both get the giggles again.

'Oh, shit,' said Cooper, coughing up his lungs. 'I guess we'd better go back in.'

'No,' said Teresa. 'I'm not.'

'No?'

'No. It's driving me crazy. There's a show in town.'

'What?'

'I'm going into town to see this show. It's called 'Saints Alive!' It's part of the LGBTQ Festival. Do you want to come? I'm named after a saint, Saint Teresa. Maybe they'll let me in free.'

'What was she the saint of?'

'Of Castile.'

'Of what?'

'Of Castile. It's a town in Spain. I think she was a bit, you know, 'off-the-fucking-wall', if you know what I mean.'

'Not really.'

'She had visions.'

'Shit.'

'Well, do you want to come?'

'Yeah. Yeah. Why not?'

'Why not! Could be fun.'

'Okay. I'd better get my bag.'

Teresa finished her cigarette and dropped it on the ground. She could always go and stay at Ani's place in town if she couldn't get home. She was always welcome there. Ani's Mum had looked at her and said: 'You come and see us, if you need to, girl.' There were families going in and coming out of Pak 'n Save. Saturday night. There was a big match on tonight, lots of people would be staying in. Only the good people would be in town. She felt something inside herself that was like a feeling of promise. Cooper ran up, bag on back.

'You ready?'

'Yeah.'

'We'd better catch a bus quick. The show starts at nine o'clock.'

They went round the corner and up the street to the bus stop.

'Anything going into Queen Street will be cool. They almost all do.'

'They were having a fight in there.'

'What?'

'Your teacher –'

'Ms Talua –'

'Yeah and our teacher, Mr Gifford –'

'A fight?'

'An argument. In the foyer. Everyone was going back in to the theatre. But they were arguing out loud. Everyone was looking at them.'

'Shame.'

In the judges' opinions, which were arrived at without major dissent of any kind, despite the predicted difficulties, the best ensemble work prize was earned by the company from Tai Tokerau. Best male performer was awarded to Cooper Simonovic, but he wasn't there to collect his award; and best female performer went to Teresa Lomu, though she too failed to come up and receive her award. The prize for the third best scene presentation went to the winners of the Eastern Zone finals, and Mr Samson Gifford went up to collect his award. He thanked the judges and stressed that the standard had been extremely high this year and that the diversity on display was a pleasure to behold. The prize for second best scene presentation was given to the winners of the Southern Zone, and Ms Raewyn Talua stepped up for that. Her short speech thanked her students for their tireless work and dedication, and the judges for their serious consideration, and asked God to bless the occasion for everyone's sake. The visitors from Tai Tokerau took away the Oscar for the night, and young Ms Pou was going to speak, but broke down in happy tears and simply smiled and waved her prize, a beautifully carved wooden figure. When she had recovered herself, she apologized for having to leave immediately because they had to drive all the way back home tonight. That brought proceedings to a close.

Meanwhile Teresa and Cooper had arrived at the theatre in town, where they had each often been before in the company of Ms Talua and Mr Gifford respectively. The crowd on the street was buzzing. It was better than Mr. Gifford's staging of the imagined clientele of the rainbow nightclub in K Road jostling for admittance. Suddenly the two young people felt small and shy together. There was a lot of glitter about and the voices were loud, yet melodious, and the gestures extravagant but graceful, and the glances confronting yet gorgeous. They needed to get a ticket. There was a queue at the Box and Cooper and Teresa both fell silent with the anxiety brought on by the possibility they might not get in. But they did. They did! They were way, way up in the top balcony. But that was fine, because they'd never been there, not even on school trips.

The foyer was now pretty tightly packed. Everyone seemed to be shouting, but in the nicest possible way. All awaited the sound of the buzzer that would announce that the doors were opening. Suddenly a man in a gold top hat and a golden, sparkling leotard and silver platform shoes clambered up on a table. Someone held his hand so he didn't fall off.

'Hear ye, hear ye, hear ye!'

'We hear ye!' The crowd roared back and the laughter was deafening.

'Tonight's show is a world premiere! We have brought you, from all round this great globe of ours, all the saints – and darlings, you know, when I say saints, I mean sinners!' Another roar from the crowd. 'Yes, all your favourite saints will be inside tonight, some of them you have never heard of, no not even you, darling,' he said pointing at a tall sombre man, wearing pale, ghoulish makeup, dressed all in black.

Teresa and Cooper were standing close to the barker in the gold top hat. Suddenly his eyes caught sight of them both.

'Oh,' he exclaimed. 'What have we here? Oh! Two beautiful young people! Oh, how gorgeous. Oh, excuse me everyone for a moment, please give us a moment's silence, while I bless these young people, who have come here to grace us old hags and haggesses with their presence and patronage. Truly we are blessed. Let us bless them back.'

And he raised his arms high above his head, and he called out in a loud voice, louder than any he had already used, 'Bless you! Bless you! Bless you!' and the crowd roared back, 'Bless you!'

And truly they felt blessed, as they shuffled forward towards the theatre entrance, their combo of puffer jacket and hoodie standing out by virtue of their sheer dullness in the bespangled crowd. Waiting for them, to take their tickets, was the tall sombre man in the ghoulish makeup. The dark cloak that engulfed him, head to toe, matched Teresa and Cooper's Gothic black. As he reached for their tickets, his smile beneath the makeup was warm and ironic.

'Well, well,' his deep voice drawled, 'indeed how lovely you are. Our Prince of Ceremonies was not wrong. I am your Usher for tonight and this theatre is my house. Sometimes we call it "The House of the Usher",' and he chuckled away to himself. Then suddenly his tone changed: 'Wait a mouldy moment! Who sold you these tickets?'

'The lady at the front,' Teresa replied.

'I think the lovely Rita was off on a brain holiday – sometimes being a lady can be stressful.'

'Is there something wrong?'

'These tickets are for the big theatre. Tonight we are in The Dungeon. And a very nice dungeon it is too!'

'We didn't know. Can we still get in? Is it sold out?'

The push of the crowd behind them was pressing on their backs.

'Patience, Earthlings!' the Usher cried out, 'it will be worth it.'

'I'm all squashed,' a voice called out.

'That's how I like you best,' another voice replied and the goodwill of the general gaiety was restored.

'What I'm going to do,' the Usher addressed Cooper and Teresa, 'I'm going to give you my house seats.' And, reaching into the depths of his cloak, he withdrew two slips of pink paper onto which he scrawled with a pen the numbers of the house seats. 'You have the honour of seats of the House of the Usher. The only problem is that you will be sitting by me. Do you think you will be able to endure the thrill?'

Inside, the theatre was humming, jumping, occasionally erupting, as greetings were shouted across seats and items of clothing were shown off with a twirl and a bow, often to sustained applause. Teresa and Cooper snuck quietly into their house seats in the back row, from where they could survey the seething crowd and the whole space. They had never been here with Ms

Talua or Mr Gifford. The big theatre they always visited was cavernous, aerial, just as the Mangere theatre was barn-like, floating. This was different. The Dungeon was dimly lit, just enough light on the seating to enable patrons to find their way. It was as if the whole crowd had rushed headlong into a deep cave or a black box and the stone or the lid had been slammed shut behind them and sealed them in. Instinctively Cooper and Teresa shrank down a little, hunching into their seats, feeling the ceiling just above their heads. They were buried.

The Usher came and took his seat beside them and, before all was plunged into blackness, he murmured to them, 'I shall have to squeeze my way out soon – I need to go and get ready for my own performance! Meanwhile –' and he pressed his pale index finger to his black lips in a gesture of silence that seemed to cue the plunge to black. A parade of many items began, some funny, some silly, some shocking, some even splendid and graceful, but all were greeted with the embrace of pleasure, without judgement. For the two sixteen-year-olds amazement grew from item to item, so they simply didn't register the Usher's going, as he subtly slipped away.

You would have thought that the Usher's item had been intentionally contrived for Cooper and Teresa's benefit, rather than some flagrant coincidence. The scene opened with a coffin revealed on stage. At the same instant the tinkling opening of Kate Bush's 'Wuthering Heights' tickled the air. Voices in the audience responded with high-pitched (and off-pitch) whoops designed to summon the shade of Kate herself. When the song reached the lines 'Too hot, too greedy/How could you leave me/When I needed to possess you/I hated you, I loved you too,' there was more random and enthusiastic joining in. Enter from the rear, the Usher, dressed now in shining red with a high and pompous hat, a travesty of a Borgia pope. He raised his fingers in a gesture of holy beatitude, and in the tech box the sound was faded down:

'Who loves Romeo?' he asked his audience.

Cries of 'Darling, darling, I do!'

'And who loves Juliet?'

Juliet supporters raised the roof.

'Alas, here lies Juliet.'

A collective moan of sorrow followed.

'And you loves Paris?'

'Who? Who?'

'Paris!'

'I love Paris in the springtime,' some silly wit sang out.

'Here comes Paris now,' the popish Usher spoke: 'to strew the bridal bed of this sweet flower with flowers.'

Kate soared back into action. The Usher stepped back into the shadows, and Paris, wearing only a glittering jockstrap and sword, jetéd on stage bearing a massive bunch of flowers. He danced about the coffin, chucking flowers in as he danced.

'And here comes Romeo!' The Usher managed to make himself heard as the vaulting soprano faded once more.

Romeo was in pink tights, bare-chested, also with a sword slung from his waist. Romeo spotted the fervent Paris, weeping at the coffin's edge. Paris looked up and came eyeball to eyeball with Romeo. Paris stepped away from the coffin and pronounced: 'Obey and go with me, for thou must die.' Romeo strode forward and defied: 'Wilt thou provoke me? Then, have at thee, boy.' Romeo drew his sword. Paris drew his. They circled before the coffin. Just as it looked as if the swordfight would begin, the two boys threw their swords away and came together in a long and passionate kiss. The house erupted. The noise must have woken the dead Juliet, for she sat up bright and bold and, wearing nothing visible except two tassles on her nipples, when the hubbub ceased, delivered her line: 'I do remember well where I should be/And there I am.' The boys broke from their kiss with cries of 'Juliet! Juliet!' and the two of them leapt into the capaciously accommodating coffin, while Kate sang on and the Usher, coming forward, delivered the benediction: 'Never was a story of more delight/Than these naughty boys and their Juliet.'

'So, what do you want to be when you grow up?' the Usher was asking them both, now the show had finished and as he led them down to the dressing rooms to meet the cast. The Usher gave them a cheeky wink as he repeated his question, then added:

'Perhaps you don't plan to grow up?'

'A lawyer, I think,' Cooper stumbled out.

'Very good,' the Usher said. 'And you?' He turned to Teresa.

'A saint,' Teresa replied with a smirk on her face.

'Even better,' the Usher replied. 'The law and religion, what else is left? Just be careful you don't end up being an actor. Necromancy is no longer in fashion.'

Cooper and Teresa shared a look: wtf? Yet they didn't want to turn back.

'Ah, here we are,' said the Usher as they arrived at the backstage entrance. With his arms around each of them, his long black cloak embracing them, it was difficult to tell if he was leading the two of them into a new world, or if they were departing forever a lesser, fallen world. Together they stepped through the backstage door, to meet their destiny.

KARDEK AND IMIA

Essie breathed deeply in as she hauled up the window for a look. She needed her glasses now to see anything in the distance clearly. Her ones for long distance were still in the rental car, parked directly below her, at the top of the steep drive. It was vertiginous and the jet-lag didn't help. However, the two rocks, as they were called, the Lion and the Camel, could not be missed. Miniature mountains, she thought. Stretched out between the rocks, far below her, the beach, and through a fissure in the hooves of the Camel, the waves breaking and erupting up the whole face of the cliff. What a place for a house! She was standing high up, in the dream the boys had built for themselves, and she was here as if for the first time, though she'd seen this view on Instagram and on Facebook, well, many times.

'Have you spotted Australia yet?' Plato was smiling as she turned to look at him. He'd spread towels all along one half of the bed. The room lurched a little as the airplane she'd spent twenty hours in kept on flying in her head. 'Come and help me to roll him,' he beckoned her with his brown eyes.

Plato was sitting by Assid's head. He stood and put a hand on each of his shoulders. Essie crossed to the foot of the bed, reached out, and gripped Assid's ankles, holding the feet together, knowing that profound coolness she would find when she touched him. He was quite naked. They looked down at him, then up at each other, found their moment together and, heave-ho, they rolled Assid. He folded stiffly over and settled with the towels under him. His weight made them both breathe loudly. It was as if Assid had begun to melt into the quilt and did not want to be disturbed.

That smell was already in the room.

'Yes,' Plato nodded, wrinkling his nose.

It wasn't strong yet. Still they both knew it, the way the presence of someone who excites you raises your heart beat and tightens your breath, there was a little bit of it everywhere. Plato held another pile of towels and passed two of them to Essie, soft, warm, full of air from the way he had folded them. She patted the folded towels and they sank under her palm like a diaphragm relaxing. Plato spread his, she spread hers, and once the woven green horse on the coverlet had disappeared beneath the towels, they rolled Assid halfway back so he stretched before them. From the grey crown of hair and the high nose, the sardonic pair of lips now fallen into a melancholic curve, as if to say, 'So, this is it,' down to those long legs with the sheaves of dark hair, one foot, white and elegant, almost raised, the way a horse might pointedly raise a hoof. Plato had gone to fill a bowl of warm water and soap. Essie stood and waited. It was almost as if she was waiting to see if Assid would breathe, and then, when she had dismissed the likelihood, she crossed again to the window, breathed the turbulent air blowing past and greeted again the two rocks held in a mass of cloud that could be seen rising and falling, reflected in the sea below.

There were two flannels floating under the surface of the water in the stainless-steel bowl, an orange and a green, just visible. Plato was careful to place the bowl on a stool beside the bed. Assid was not going to move, but one of them could knock the bowl if it was on the bed itself. They took a flannel each, orange for his, green for hers. Essie stood watching Plato as he knelt by Assid's chest. She couldn't see what his eyes were doing but she guessed they were slowly tracing the length of him, taking in all that was left. The jet lag pushed her suddenly forward. She was falling asleep on her feet, but if she'd lain down she wouldn't be resting, she would be lying on her back staring at the ceiling with wide-awake eyes. Plato must have thought her sudden jerking meant she wanted to get started. Her eyes blinked open, but Assid's eyes were closed. Essie sank to her knees at the foot of the bed. She would start with Assid's feet and legs. Plato could take the face, the chest, the arms. He smiled and nodded, and they began. They were like conspirators, working together. *Conspirer* – the French had the same word. We are conspiring – after all, 'conspire' as well as designating a secret shared plan could also indicate 'to breathe together,' to conspire. No good thinking of French now, as it was no good driving in from the airport on the right-hand side of the road – which she had almost done. No good coming to farewell the dead, if you were you are already dead yourself. Spiritus, the breath.

She'd been sitting in her flat on the Rue de Souffle when Plato called her. Alone, bent over her soup, reading an article about the border between Greece and Turkey when the phone rang. The mad idea took hold of her at the moment she heard Plato's voice. 'Sure you want to? I don't think he will be here in time for you to get here.' She had stood by her small table, where she kept an untidy box of names, numbers, addresses and magazines. The curled-over lamp shone on a glossy magazine's cover. Nacreous light. Disputes over seaways, airspace, the continental shelf, demilitarisation, economic zones mingled with Plato's 'time for you to get here.' She smiled to herself as she remembered how Assid had said, "I'm Kardek – and he's Imia" referring to the two tiny islands that had been about to cause a war the time the three of them had been on holiday in Greece together. She recalled him straightening that long face of his and pronouncing: 'I don't think Dostoyevsky could have coped with us.' Plato hadn't got it, but Essie had. 'I don't think Dostoyevsky approved of sex between men – though he probably approved of horses doing it. Strange fellow, Mister D.' She had said to Plato, 'Yes, I'm going to come, I am! It's been so long, just so long. I'm coming.' She rang off, and went online and bought her ticket, just like that. Would Dostoyevsky have berated her for that impulse? Here she was, she had spirited herself.

She glanced up at Plato. The green flannel stroked Assid's neck so tenderly, she thought for a moment she saw life there – she saw a body alive with sweat. The wall behind was alive with books, floor to ceiling. Assid had claimed that Plato had never read a book in his life. 'We're a queer couple,' he would say, amusing himself with his own joke. She watched her hand with the green flannel smooth down the stiff black hairs into the skin. That skin had lost its colour over years, blotched now by sun and everything else, so long since she had gazed on it. And now, well, it was ceasing to be. It was changing, but faster, faster. Her breath reached out to her, touched her chest, stopped her thought.

It was very soon after she had come to live in Paris, before she had the library job, during her hopeless short-lived career as a nanny, that she had seen the announcement about the lecture: 'The Unreason of Reason.' It was the time of Theory. How could she resist? The tall bony young Turkish philosopher had pronounced himself to be a 'post-existentialist' and a 'pre-structuralist' and a 'sub-rationalist' – and a 'counter-intuitivist.' The lecture was a list of 'ists' that produced a lot of laughter. At that stage she'd only understood half the plays and puns in French that Assid threw out to his audience. The lecture had been, simply, a joy, a joyful occasion. Truly for a moment the veil had been pulled aside and the unreason of reason glimpsed. Then afterwards, she'd said something to him, in her stiff French, but that was what had appealed to him about her, and he'd invited her along. 'Where are you from? Oakland? Are you American? Auckland? Auckland?' They rendez-vous-ed with the young Plato, who'd just finished his day's shift in a restaurant, training to be a chef. The evening went on being funny, and by the end of it, after multiple margaritas, they had agreed that, in three weeks' time, when the summer was fully blooming, the Queer Couple would escort the Lady from Auckland on a tour of their native realms, first the wonders of Greece, then the secrets of Turkey.

Plato was squeezing a soapy waterfall over Assid's lovely little cock. Essie reached up the long legs, rubbed them in a way that was way too hard, so that Plato stopped her hand with his, smiled at her. To steady herself, she asked Plato when the doctor would arrive. Half an hour. That was all the time they had now, to wash off the salts and the oils oozing out of him, to give him his last delight, to make him shine. The doctor would write the certificate, the doctor would sign everything off. Then there was nothing more to be done with him. Time to get rid of him. Well, he wasn't here. This afternoon Assid and Plato's friends from the city would arrive to see him. But he wouldn't be here.

'Celeste, I'm gonna wash, then make sweetbread, brioche, start baking for this afternoon. There's just us now. But this afternoon – you know how it will be. You are the first. Take your time.'

Together, they rolled him into place, so he looked as if he were sleeping, and his face with its long nose could be touched by the breeze from the window. Together the conspirators pulled out the towels from under him and gently wrapped him in the green horse. Composed with a single, continuous line, with the naïve splendor of an ancient outline in a deep cave, had she seen something like this horse in Paris, an exhibition of Picasso prints? Plato quietly drew the green flannel from her grip, scooped up the bowl of soapy water and carried it away with him.

Their holiday for three. They'd been so proud to escort the Lady from Auckland. They made her laugh like no one had since she arrived in Paris. In Athens they scored a suite of rooms with connecting balconies. The heat bubbled around them, you breathed it in, and struggled to breathe it out. Like the wretched ancient culture the Greeks couldn't escape from, Assid pointed out – 'choking,' was his word. She showed them how tea, Russian-style, clear with jam, could be delicious in such heat. Plato congratulated her for showing them. The second morning of their stay, she'd brewed up a tray of tea for them all to share and shuffled silently with it along the balcony. The door was open and she shouldered her way in through the drawn curtains. They were fucking on the bed. Fortunately, she saw before she spoke, backing out impeccably. She had been sure they hadn't seen her.

But the next morning she was woken by Plato sitting on her bed. He put his finger to his lips, when she opened her eyes. He pointed to the tray of tea beside the bed.

'In a moment,' he said. Then added: 'You see us. Move over.'

They made love. They fucked. They drank tea. Where was

Assid? 'Look, I bring brioche. Fresh downstair.' They ate. Then they did it again. The whole day, she didn't know what to say or where to look. But nothing seemed to have changed. The next morning, it was still dark, he was back again. When they had reached the point of munching the brioche, Assid came in, smiled, poured himself a tea from a cup he had brought with him into the room and padded out, tall, naked, silent on his bare feet.

That evening they went to a restaurant. The food had been bad. Plato had shouted at a chef. He'd stood up from the table, walked to the door that led to the kitchen, pushed it open and shouted something. Later a young woman came round the tables selling single roses. Assid laughed at her and said something cruel– Essie could tell from girl's face it was cruel – to her in Greek. But what she had noticed was, how they were both out of their cultural depths. Assid had grown up in Paris since an early age. Plato had been in Germany, in Sweden, then in Paris. They were tourists in what they might have claimed as home. Next, they argued with each other about which of them was the more critical about their 'homeland,' accusing the other of traces of sentimental nationalism. Assid struggled to explain the argument, Essie struggled to understand it. She left the holiday early, excusing herself that she had to get back, she had an important job interview. It was almost true. She resigned from being a nanny. She took her library qualifications to the American Library in Paris, and she had been there ever since. A whole lifetime, more or less. They met up once after the holiday, they were all polite, still it felt as if they had just met. She felt angry with herself because she was missing them both.

Plato was standing in the doorway, floury hands fisted on his hips. What would he do now? Grow old perched in the air on this cliff?

'Do you want the books?' Plato was asking her. 'When Assid heard you are coming, he wanted me to ask.'

Essie was back at the window, she could see a plane coming in towards the airport where she had landed some hours ago. 'He was still going surfing five years ago.'

'What did you say?'
'Five years ago, Assid was still surfing.'
'No, not that, before that?'
'The books. Do you want the books?'
All those books. All in that one head.
She laughed. 'What, take them to France?'
The doorbell rang.
'He said you could take as many as you like.'
She laughed again. Thousands of them! But Plato had gone to answer the door for the doctor. She heard the voices.

Twenty-five years later, on Facebook, someone she used to know in Auckland had been out to dinner at Plato's Cave, Auckland's finest Greek restaurant, the friend boasted. She checked the site and checked her breath. She typed in Plato's name, and there he was, in a relationship. With a Professor of Philosophy at the University of Auckland. Incroyable! The online flurry that followed matched those three weeks, years before, when they had gone on holiday. From then on, she had tracked their progress: buying the land at Piha, photos of them staying there in a tent, the plans for the house, the building of the house. She gazed from the window once more on the rocky beasts below. Here she was. It was as if it was the first time again. Essie could smell the dough baking. Such a sweet smell, it made her shudder as she breathed it in and the doctor signed off on the certificate. Hearing her sniff, the doctor spoke softly, offering her words of comfort:
'Such a lovely man.'
'It's Plato's baking, I'm sniffing that. You will stay, won't you, stay and taste the brioche?'
But the doctor had to be going. She heard the voices parting at the door. Then, Plato came in bearing the fresh, warm brioche and steaming tea.
'Just for us, I guess.'

THAT BEAUTIFUL BOY

PART ONE: THE TEXT

Gabrielle's day began with an email from Nancy Fulton, a text from Tom Kinsella and a tweet from Trevor Slade. Before she opened her messages in the morning, she made sure that she walked along the beach and then climbed the small volcano maunga, as the dawn was breaking, or even before. Now the country was in lockdown, the walkers in this suburb emerged early. It wasn't simply the physical distancing that became awkward as the beach and the little maunga began to swarm with the day's eager self-improvers. It was the shared look of blank resentment on these well-fed faces and the stamping frustration of those well-heeled feet that their world had been involuntarily interrupted that disturbed Gabrielle. Her sense of belonging had always been fragile. Now, as people hunkered down in their family bubbles and opened up physical spaces as well as the normal social and emotional ones, she almost welcomed the feeling that she could relax a little into her life-long separateness and not experience that haunting of social guilt and cultural obligation.

Returning to the day's messages needed preparation. Sometimes, opening her devices, she could experience a barrage. This morning on the maunga had been less than pleasant. A young man in lyrca came running past with his dog. The dog had turned on her snarling and leaping. It even snapped its jaws close to her neck, it had jumped so high. Her staying still had probably saved her from being attacked, even though it had been more out of fear than good sense that she had remained frozen to the spot. The young man had come in and grabbed the dog and pulled it back. Gabrielle was about to say thank you, when the man had started yelling at her:

'What did you do? He's never like that! You must have provoked him!' Then he had sworn at her and turned and run off with the beast at his heels.

She had started shaking. Then the tears came. Fear fell on her like a big heavy blanket, so she felt she couldn't walk.

'Are you all right?' The couple behind her were both wearing tracksuits and trainers. They must both have been seventy-five if they were a day. A fluffy white dog on a red lead the woman held was tugging to be gone.

'Yes,' Gabrielle said. Then, 'No. No, no, I'm not.'

'Oh dear. She's not all right, dear.'

'That's Reg Rawlinson's boy, isn't it?'

'No, it's not. He's – oh, you know his name – the one who used to work for Russell McVeigh.'

'No, I don't know who you're talking about.'

'What's his name?'

'Thank you for asking,' Gabrielle said.

She felt her strength come back as she walked away. The man called out to her, 'Take care.' She felt a strong inclination to turn around and shout: 'How do you suggest I do that?' But kindness was still kindness, even when it was stupid. That was what Douglas had told her long ago. Art is still art, even when it's kitsch. 'Remember that,' he had said. It had been on the beach below that he had said that. It was the best lesson in art history, cultural competence and curatorial practice she'd ever received. She sat down for a moment on the grassy slope, put her head in her hands, and breathed. Below her, on the beach, small figures had begun running up and down the sand. And there were the dog-walkers, but those she could see all had their dogs secured on leads.

The old couple must have turned and doubled back to climb the maunga, because suddenly she could hear their voices again:

'Who is that woman? I've seen her before.'

'Is she the woman at the Kinsella House?'

'Does she work there?'

'She lives there.'

'I didn't know anyone lived there.'

'I'm sure that was Reg Rawlinson's boy.'

'No, no. He went to London.'

'I didn't know that.'

'Why does she live there? Is she part of the trust board or is she just a caretaker?'

Gabrielle listened to herself being discussed as an object. She knew she'd have to wait until the couple moved away. They were unaware of her sitting there hidden below the slope in her nest of grass. She didn't want them to know she'd been listening to them. The world of art is a world of objects. Could the same be said about the world of people? What happened when they disappeared? What were they then? A photograph? A portrait? An image in the mind? A story? A phrase in your head that wouldn't go away: 'Kindness is still kindness, even when . . .' She turned and looked the other way, across the harbour, towards the city. There were no ferries running, or very few. The harbour was uninhabited by boats, the morning still, the silence far from total, but eerie in its dominance. She'd always thought Rangitoto looked like a big smile, a beaming face, a cheeky grin, and now it looked more like that than ever before. Gabrielle stood and began to climb down. Glancing behind, she saw the couple had advanced up the mountain into comfortable distance.

When she opened the door of the cottage, the fine pencil filigrees of Douglas's drawing of a thousand flying ants greeted her. It always made her smile. 'It's the silliest drawing in the world,' he'd told her, when he gave it to her. Of course, the hours of work were not the point, nor even really the sheer beauty of the work's frivolity – rather the careless abandonment of it as a gift for her. That was its secret. The Kinsella House, as it was now called, with a proud blue noticeboard at the front gate, contained the legacy and many of the works of Kenneth Kinsella. Gabrielle's little cottage at the bottom of the Kinsella House garden, known as The Docent's Cottage, contained some of the works and a number of pieces and objects from the legacy of Douglas Moran. Knowledge of these two painters and their work dwelt, in voluminous array, in the mind of Gabrielle Knight, the Docent herself in The Docent Cottage. But since the lockdown began, the Kinsella House had been closed to the public and Gabrielle's field of operations was now by phone or online. Though it was true that Nancy Fulton, Chair of the Kinsella House Trust Board, still regarded it as her right to arrive on Gabrielle's doorstep and tell her what needed doing in the Kinsella House, where Nancy permitted herself to rummage at will, while Gabrielle was required to pretend not to know she was there. It was well known that, whatever the rules were, they didn't apply to Nancy Fulton.

She opened Nancy's email first. Nancy was furious that the arts were not regarded as an essential service and she had written an email to the Prime Minister and the Minster of Arts expressing her outrage. Nancy was not of the Prime Minister's party persuasion and some of that alienation had manifested itself in a certain vitriolic tone. Gabrielle felt depressed and wondered why she was being forced to know what she didn't want to know. Why could scholars of international status not continue to obtain access to the archives and the store room? A very famous art historian from the USA had been due to arrive and his trip had been cancelled. Why? It was unlikely that the PM would enlighten Nancy, which would contribute to her strong belief that only the 'Educated Right,' as Nancy termed them, were capable of promoting and appreciating 'high art.' The Bumbling Left, as she described the other lot, sank money only into community arts and hedge-hopping artists who earned their keep by worshipping at the shrine of mediocre diversity. The email went on. Gabrielle scrolled to the bottom. Nancy had added a couple of sentences: 'Dear Gaby, Thought you should see this – what do you think – am I right or am I right? Can you make sure the windfalls from the pear tree are picked up? I'll be popping round later (keep it under your hat) to collect them – don't want to feed the wasps. Old Mr Russell from the Trust Board is still getting over his op and pears can work a miracle in getting the innards churning again.'

Tom's text or Trevor's tweet? Get Tom over and done. 'Dear

Ms Knight, there's a painting of Dad's that belongs to me, it's mine, I'm coming over on Saturday to collect. Advise you to be out. Remember I don't have a key ha ha TK.' Tom was banned. He'd actually spent most of his childhood in that house she looked out on, from her tiny kitchen window, across the garden where the pear tree stood and the windfalls lay. But he had become impossible. The Board had decided. Gabrielle put her phone down on the kitchen bench. The coffee was hissing up in the machine. She'd better tell Nancy when she came about Tom's avowed intent. It wasn't Gabrielle's job to act as gatekeeper and bouncer. Tom Kinsella was over six feet tall, heavy as a bull now he'd turned sixty and was progressively going to fat, usually drunk, and more than Gabrielle could bear to face. She could walk on the beach and up the maunga on Saturday, let Tom come get his painting . . . no, no she couldn't. That was just her cowardly self talking. She had to let Nancy know. She texted, 'TK texted. Says he's coming to House Saturday. Says we have a painting that belongs to him. What to do. G.'

She clicked on Trevor's tweet: 'How's your pandemic? Massive arts cuts here in Oz. Kill the bastards, eh?' The Kinsella House had been closed now for two weeks. It was two weeks since Trevor had gone back to Australia. He had caught the last plane out. The sky, like the harbour, was now almost uninhabited. How miserable those three days had been when he was staying. The House did have a room out the back where people like Trevor, working there on official stuff, either researching, or, as in Trevor's case, writing copy for the Trust, could stay. He was drinking too much. His last manuscript had been turned down. You could see the fantasy in his eyes as he had gazed at her, the old fool's dream of resurrecting that far-off relationship. But what one could not envisage were any bodies leaping into beds. Climbing the maunga together Trevor had had to pause three times. There was definitely a calcifying of something inside his thickening flesh. His ankles and his fingers looked puffed up. Where had she read recently that phrase – 'the opportunism that attracts honours at the expense of honour'? Trevor had dedicated his path in life to such opportunism. His visit had made her wonder if that pathway was reaching a terminus for him. If so, it hadn't made him any less obnoxious, especially after his fourth glass. She'd never even started out on that opportunistic path. Or maybe, once, when she had thought she might become an artist and had first tumbled into bed with Trevor, the art critic whose word had then been law. Of course, it had been Douglas who had inspired her dreams thirty years ago. But then Douglas died. Trevor, for all his promises, had turned out to be a crusher of dreams, a kind of python of the imagination. Maybe she'd fallen, in the beginning, for his snaky qualities when she was young, a certain mesmerizing coiling and uncoiling, that lithe muscularity. But that was all gone. An old snake now. He lay in the sun, looking slow and bloated, but still full of venom. She decided not to tweet back. The less said, the more said, in that dialogue.

She poured the coffee and gazed down the garden. The morning sun at this equinoctial time came straight in her window. She opened the cottage door, picked out a paper bag from the drawer under the sink, and, taking her coffee with her, meandered out to gather old Mr Russell's windfalls. She heard her phone bleat back inside. Going back, she picked it up. It was Trevor again – god, what hour was it in Sydney, 6am? 'The end of the arts as we knew them. How does that sound for a title? How's your bubble?' Gabrielle shut the phone off and went back into the garden. There were thirteen pears on the ground.

Gabrielle's bubble consisted mostly of herself; those looking in from the outside would have said she was alone in her bubble. But they didn't know about the little black and white cat who came past twice a day, his bell jangling, and his name boldly engraved on the label dangling from his collar: Maui. She didn't know who he belonged to and he mustn't be more than a year old. Then there was the pair of mynahs who were firmly ensconced in the cottage roof. The rat that occasionally crossed the garden at dusk. The growing enclave of pigeons settled on the Kinsella House ledges. She'd been asked to scare them away, but she had decided to watch them instead and then tell Nancy tales of their intransigence. She was not alone. In the cottage,

Douglas hung from every wall. And she was there herself even, in Douglas's tiny portrait of her, a few lines of pink and blue water colour that miraculously added up to her.

If the virus had spread across the globe five years ago, Gabrielle would have been in a bubble with Sean, in their single-bedroom flat at the top of Symonds Street. For eight years they had walked together down to the Gallery in town to their shared job as cataloguers to the collections. Together they constituted 1.35 people ('We're the .675ers!' they would sometimes sing when they were cooking dinner together over a glass of Spanish red), which meant the Gallery was getting a good deal out of their doubled expertise, and they each still had a little time for their own work. When Sean died, she just couldn't continue there at the Gallery, it had been too overwhelmingly *their* job; they had been appointed to it together when it looked like they might have nothing. Then someone told her about the Kinsella House, and how it was moving to a professional footing and that she would be the ideal person. Some of her friends had come back after Sean's death. Their departure when she and Sean had first got together had been only one aspect of the whole catastrophe that had turned out to be her great joy. Nobody wanted to mark the progression of their life by milestones of deaths, but Douglas's death thirty years ago, and Sean's just five years ago, did seem to mark first and second turning points.

Douglas had so much wanted her to be an artist. She had really tried after he had died, turned herself into some parody of a 'hot young thing' which had led to the entrapment by Trevor, only to be followed, after she had removed herself, by his review of the group exhibition where he had used his critic's scalpel to remove her from the category of hot art property and cast her back into realm of a decorative imitator of a style that was now passé. That's when she'd decided to train as a teacher and all that had followed, the five years of hell in three different schools where art had come to be labelled as a drag on any child's ability to launch themselves into the new future of the digital revolution. Her hypnotized fellow teachers didn't have a clue that in the fine arts the digital revolution had long been in swing, nowhere more so than in the hybrid work of one Douglas Moran, with its combinations of finely crafted manual work with the iterations and imitations of algorithms But, no, art was still 'art' in the tired cliché of those who thought they knew what so-called progress looked like. What an amazing relief it had been to return to art school, to enroll for her MA, to take up the study of 'the decorative impulse' in local gothic. And to meet Sean Tawai, someone she'd never had much to do with when she'd been an undergraduate nearly two decades earlier and he had just taken up his post.

There was some fundamental revulsion in the society about a woman of thirty-eight living with a man of fifty-eight, that was what she discovered. It was also against the rules of the university for a student and a supervisor to fall in love. Sean lost his job, she had to complete her thesis under the supervision of the most boring man in the university, the senior Professor and Head of School, her friends began to melt away . . . There were days when Sean and she were driven to laughter by the downward progression of events. The City Gallery Director saw things differently from most and she'd brought them on board together just at the moment when rescue was needed. Her only condition was that they produce a short text for the Gallery to publish about Gothic decoration in the city's architecture, which they had done together with great pleasure in the joint enterprise. Sean had been both a protection and a support. What her friends didn't understand was that because he was fifty-eight she was free to be herself. As was he. It had been as if no one noticed their relationship, because it had worked. Sean handled his relationships with his grown-up children, she managed to form a friendship with his daughter, Sean continued to publish as an academic, and Gabrielle found that at last she was using her knowledge when she went to work each day.

She was doing this too now as the Docent at the Kinsella House. But Mister Maui didn't provide the same companionship as Sean had. The problems of working at the Kinsella House were different from they had been at the Gallery. It was the House and all it stood for that was the vortex that sucked in all other work.

The Kinsella House had become a work of art in itself. When one read the House described as an 'early (well for Auckland, anyway) modernist masterpiece', and then one actually saw it, one was struck by how it looked like nothing out of the ordinary at all. It sure wasn't Mies van der Rohe or Frank Lloyd Wright. It was more like a gentrified bach with pretensions. This had been partly because the Kinsellas had been desperately poor (comparatively speaking) until Kenneth's paintings had begun to ramp up in price in Kenneth's later years. Tom Kinsella had now persuaded himself that those paintings, the break-through ones, the ones that imaged the maunga so that it looked like a skull, and the ones in which bodies grew out of the earth itself, were actually painted by his mother, because his father by then had become such a wretched drunk (well, Tom would know, wouldn't he) that he was incapable. Detrimental to Tom's argument was that his mother, Dorothy, now ninety years old and entirely compos mentis, denied that had been the case. Tom raged against his father's repression of his mother. His mother declared that she was perfectly capable of speaking her own truth on her own behalf and that, indeed, Kenneth had painted those extraordinary works – and also, yes indeed, he had been an insufferable and brutal drunkard. Whether he had been a genius or not, was none of her business.

She had received fair payment for her share of the house. She had never been back since the day she walked out. The past thirty years, since Kenneth's death, had been her happiest. She had turned her hand to botanical and archaeological illustration, copying leaves and seeds and flowers and also artifacts in meticulous ink line drawings. Even at ninety, her remarkable skills remained intact. As for art, Dorothy Kinsella probably thought thirteen delicious pears picked up from a lawn thick with grass on a sunny autumn morning were worth more than anything art could offer. Gabrielle had filled the bag for Nancy. Of course, there'd been additions to the House since Kenneth died, specifically to add the area for storage and archives, not open to the public, available only to scholars and researchers. The House was only authentic to a point. Tom Kinsella called it 'a fake monument to a fake genius.' Gabrielle dumped the bag of pears on the kitchen bench and opened her phone. Nancy had texted: 'Discuss this afternoon.'

Nancy's BMW drew up outside at 2pm. She came in through the back gate which led to the cottage. The afternoon had become much warmer and Gabrielle was sitting on the little porch, reading Trevor's draft text for the use of new assistant docents when they were showing visitors round the House.

'Is that the text?' Nancy asked without preliminary greeting.

'No, I'll go and get it,' said Gabrielle, getting up and going into the cottage to retrieve her phone. When she turned, Nancy was standing there behind her in the cottage. 'I think we're meant to be keeping the two metre distance.'

'This is two metres.'

'Could we go outside to talk about it, please?'

'Oh, very well.' And then, as she was backing out of the doorway, with Gabrielle slowly following, she said: 'I don't know what you see in him.'

'See in who?'

'Moran. His work. What you've got up on the walls there. That buzzing mass of insects. And those water-colours. They're hardly there.'

'That's true,' said Gabrielle. 'I try to keep the water-colours away from the light. They're very delicate.'

'It's all surface. No depth. No light and dark. Excuse me for saying so, but it seems to be a statement of the man's sexuality. I don't mean that in a judgmental way.'

'I'm not sure I understand what you mean. But shall we just –'

'I mean, it's all surface, it's, yes, I suppose superficial has to be the word.'

'Kenneth Kinsella liked his work.'

'When? He hardly knew him. Where did you get that from?'

'Douglas had his first exhibition when he was still an undergraduate. Kinsella sent him a letter about it.'

'He did?'

'Yes, he did.'

'I didn't know that. Where's the letter?'

'In my drawer. In my bedroom.'

'Show me.'

Gabrielle said as quietly as she could, though she found the same shaking that had happened that morning, after the dog attack, had seized hold of her again, 'Please stay there. I'll get it if you want to see it.'

Inside the cottage she could feel the same tears erupting, nothing to do with self-pity, only rage and the fierce struggle to suppress it causing a powerful internal pressure, pushing up through her body. She stood for a few minutes by her bed, recovering her breathing.

As she pulled out the file with Douglas's letters Nancy called out, 'I've got to be at old Russell's place by 3:30 across in Remuera!'

Gabrielle came out into the sunshine with the letter in its soft plastic archival sleeve.

'This should be in our archive.'

'It's my letter. Douglas gave it to me, before he died.'

'He might have given it to you, but legally it's part of the archive. The letter is from Kenneth to Moran, not to you.'

There was a moment when Gabrielle thought Nancy might just pop the letter into her handbag and walk off with it. Nothing would surprise her in relation to the Kinsella House. That much she had learned about the propriety of precious national treasures during her five years as the Kinsella House Docent. Then Nancy handed it back to her:

'Think about it.'

'Thank you.'

'Now, where's the text?'

Gabrielle took her phone out of her pocket, scrolled through to Tom Kinsella's text, and held it up to the light, while reading it out.

'No, I don't mean that text. We'll come to that nuisance Tom Kinsella soon. I mean Trevor's text for the house, for the docents, for when we can re-open.'

'Oh, sorry. It's there, on the porch, I was reading through it when you arrived.'

Nancy bent and picked it up. The scarf around her neck did not go with the scarf around her head. The designer sunglasses were clearly prescription, because she had no trouble reading as she stood glancing through, turning the pages, one, two, three, four.

'It's far too long.'

'I know. I said that to Trevor. He said, take out of it what you want.'

'That's not what we paid him for.'

'I know.'

'Looks like it was a mistake.'

'What was?'

'Using Trevor Slade. Isn't he over the hill? When he came over for dinner, when he was here just now, he got horribly drunk, we had to send him home early in a taxi. What's that young woman's name – who writes for *The Concept* – '

'Trish Hegan?'

'Yes. We should have got her. She's got her head screwed on, knows where she's going, Sarah Bartholemew's daughter. Of course, Sarah married Francis Hegan. I was at Saint Cuths with Sarah. I'll bring it up at the next Board meeting. No more Mister Slade.'

'Do you want me to see if I can trim it down – shape it?'

'Would you, please? Thank you. I don't like this – "during those most creative years, family relations began to enter a limbo in which the spirit of dalliance and the dalliance of the sprits concocted an unhappy brew." The Board won't let that through. Trevor Slade was always an insinuating kind of writer.'

'He could be.'

'He was. I'm telling you. He was. Yes please. Have a go. Give it to me. I shall check it over, then take it forward to the Board. Sorry to land this on you. What a waste of a good air fare.'

'I'll see what I can do.'

Nancy held out the text towards Gabrielle. Gabrielle indicated to put it back where it had been lying on the porch. Nancy got the message:

'Oh, this wretched virus. I can see you're behaving yourself.

I really do have to get going. Have you got the pears?' Gabrielle reached into the kitchen from where she had taken up a position of as much distance as she could in the doorway of the cottage and brought out the bag, stepped forward, and placed the bag on the deck of the porch. 'Thank you, dear. Charles will appreciate that. So, what about Thomas? He thinks he's going to come around here on Saturday does he? What's today?'

'Thursday.'

'Well, he's not.'

'No, he can't. But, in case he does, I was wondering if perhaps some people could come in a couple of cars and be here in case he turns up in one of his Tom states.'

'What, you mean, sit outside all afternoon?'

'I don't know. I feel –'

'What?'

'I don't trust him.'

'No one does. Not even his mother. Though god knows what she thinks about anything. Are you scared?'

'Yes. Yes, I am. He tried to jump on me once.'

'I didn't know that. You mean – he tried to assault you?'

'Yes.'

'You should have told us.'

'Actually, I did. Then the ban was imposed, so I thought . . .'

'Well, there's a lockdown on, he can't come, and that's that.'

'I agree.'

'End of story.'

'Could you inform the police? Or ring Dorothy?'

'His mother? She won't talk to me. Same as her son. But for different reasons. No, the lockdown is the lockdown.'

'That's also something I wanted to ask you about, Nancy. You see, you really shouldn't be here, either.'

'Pardon? I don't really think it's your place, Barbara, to tell me where I should and shouldn't be.'

'You called me Barbara.'

'What?'

'You said 'Barbara' to me. I'm Gabrielle.'

'Oh, sorry. Of course, you are. I had just been talking to little

Barbara Evans on the phone in the car before I came in here. She's a nice girl, but I can't see that she'll ever make sense of her life. I'm not sure why you should remind me of each other.'

'We need to ask Tom not to come, officially, and the reason that needs to be given to him is because of the pandemic, and the isolating and the distancing, and my point is that, if you are seen not obeying the rules, then – '

'Gabrielle, it's none of your business telling me what the rules are. Remember, you're lucky to have this job. And the Board is willing to go on paying you – in the meantime, at least. When your Shane died, what would you have done if this position hadn't come along?'

'Sean.'

'What?'

'The name of my partner who died was Sean. Not Shane. And I don't see what that has to do with – I'm perfectly qualified and capable for this position.'

'You should know, if you don't, which you evidently don't – and that's a tribute to Charles Russell's discretion – that you got this job because Charles Russell intervened on your behalf. He was a great admirer of your Sean and he liked the book you helped him write, when he was sick, and he thought that Sean had been pretty roughly treated by the university with their fanatical political correctness campaigns. So just remember that. Look at the time. I've got to be going.'

She picked up the bag of pears.

'So what's going to happen about Tom Kinsella?'

'I'll see what I can sort out. Charles will have some idea. And get working on that messy piece of paper from your Trevor Slade.'

'He's not 'mine' - it wasn't me who suggested Slade,' Gabrielle called after her, but whether Nancy heard or not, she was quickly gone out the gate.

PART TWO: THE SIEGE

Three days later, in the early hours of Sunday morning, Gabrielle was woken up by Maui scratching at her cottage door and miaowing in a weirdly high-pitched plaintive growl. She staggered up. It was only a few paces from the bedroom to the front door, and when she opened it Maui walked proudly in carrying the large and completely dead rat from the garden in his jaws. He dropped it there and then on the floor and began to walk about, rubbing himself against her bare legs and the table legs and the edge of the cupboards and purring so much that the room seemed to vibrate.

Gabrielle had her solar lamp in hand, which cast an eerie bluish glow over the scene on the floor, the rat a deep blackish-brown, its rope-like tail unfurled, its fur wet from the grass it had been slaughtered in, its glazed eye glowing in its deadness.

'Mister Maui, you clever, clever thing! Shall we take it outside now, shall we?'

She grabbed a paper towel and picked Mister Rat up by his beautiful tail and dangled him out onto the grass and dumped him there. An anxious Maui followed. It was then that she noticed that there was a light on in the Kinsella House.

She crossed the garden in the moonless night, holding her solar light high in front of her, successfully blinding herself with her own light. When she reached the paved area at the rear of the House, she turned off her light. The House was in darkness. Maui rubbed himself round and round her legs. She thought the light she had seen had been behind the blinds in the storeroom. She stood, uncertain what to do. She'd stopped just short of the electronic monitors that would switch on all the outside lamps, turning the building into a flood-lit exhibit. She knew well where to stop. As in the Walter de la Mare poem her mother used to recite to her when she was growing up in Tokoroa, she said out loud, 'Is there anybody there?'

The night was so silent and windless that she could hear the soft lap of the waves on the sheltered beach. 'The silence surged softly backward' – her mother had loved saying that before kissing her goodnight and shutting off the light. Maui gave a very sweet and standard cat miaow. He was back to normal after his killing spree. She switched her light back on and retreated up the garden. She felt sure she had seen it, but it was just possible the streetlight had caught on the edge of the window and created an effect. Gabrielle failed to convince herself. Of course, her foot kicked the rat where she'd left it lying. 'Shit!' Then she laughed. She had a moment of seeing herself as an object: fifty-year-old-woman in nightie in old North Shore garden kicking a dead rat at 3am. Bury it in the morning, she said to herself. Check the House in the morning. But she did let Maui come in and jump up onto the bed and snuggle down on her feet.

It was 7am when the phone buzzed at her. It was Trevor. 5am in Sydney! What is he doing? This time it was a text: 'You make me remember old times.' Jesus. Bugger him. Now she was awake, she knew she wouldn't get back to sleep. She'd spent all yesterday waiting for the appearance of Thomas Kinsella. There'd been a text: 'Won't be long.' That was all for the whole day. Nancy had told her to call her number if anything happened. It was the online equivalent of being told by a stranger to 'Take care.' The day had been exhausting. When she'd first moved into the cottage, Tom Kinsella used to come round and they got along well. His interest, she realized later, had been to get her alongside, so she could become an ally in exposing the truth about his father (as well as exposing the evil crowd who ran the Trust Board) – and also she would help him to get back the house that he felt was rightfully his inheritance (though he was subsisting on the money he'd been paid for the sale of the house). The Trust had purchased the house from the Kinsella family and Tom, as the only child, had received half the proceeds with his mother the other half. Then had come the assault. It had happened in the House, when they had been in the paintings storage area. He'd invited her ostensibly to see a particular painting, which, he claimed, related in some way to him as a child. The Freudian nightmare of the whole scene still haunted her. Fortunately for her Tom, half-drunk as usual, had forgotten the House was still open and there were visitors present. She'd screamed, as loudly as she possibly could. Of course, she'd told the Board. It was one of the several incidents that had led to his banning. How come Nancy had 'forgotten'? Maui stirred and stretched himself full length and yawned enormously, then rolled over, curled up again and went on sleeping.

Kinsella's paintings were big, powerful, monumental, heavy with portent, full of meaning and genius. Bereft of the decorative and inconsequential. Each brushstroke took one closer to heaven, revelation, or hell, doom, catastrophe. The fate of the land lay in the palm of his hand. Gabrielle looked at Douglas's tiny ink drawing of a butterfly hanging on the wall beside her bed. She'd put it there as her silent alarm clock, as she called it.

Nancy's text was next to arrive: 'From TK this morning – ha ha ha ha ha. What do you make of it?' Gabrielle put the phone back on the bedside table and rolled over. She had only just begun to acknowledge the stress of yesterday's waiting – for nothing. Her neck and shoulders had turned themselves rigid. There wasn't a comfortable position to find, because discomfort had found her and come to sit over her chest and heart like a bird waiting for her to die so it could gobble her up. It was lucky she had a cat now that would eat the bird after the bird had eaten her. How can you sleep and still feel like you are dead? 'The dead belong to no one.' Where had she read that recently? How fluid and ill-defined, yet fruitful and abundant, the mind was at the point of waking up. Maui began trying to bite her feet through the duvet, now that her feet were taking on a life of their own. He was still half a kitten, half a cat.

She pushed him gently aside and swung her feet to the floor. Her phone buzzed again. Nancy again: 'This now from TK "Tell Ms Night to look out window".' She looked. It was foggy in the garden. She could barely see the Kinsella modernism. A couple of fat pigeons rose above the fog where the sky was clearing fast. Then the phone rang.

'Gabrielle.'

'Yes.'

'Are you awake?'

'I suppose so.'

'Have you seen Tom Kinsella's text?'

'Yes.'

'And?'

'And what?'

'Have you looked out the window?'

'Yes.'

'And?'

'It's foggy. Can't see much.'

Then last night's light came back to mind. And the rat. Gabrielle had already guessed: 'I'll go and look. I'll call you back, Nancy.' She dressed quickly, slipped on her crocs at the door, and glanced momentarily at the dead rat as she crossed the garden. She'd barely got past the pear tree when the music started. It was the Rolling Stones, of course, 'You Can't Always Get What You Want.' Hadn't Trump used that in his election campaign? She stopped and stared at the house. There was nothing to see, of course. But she knew who was inside. She went back to the cottage and called Nancy.

'Yes, he's in there.'

'Did you see him?'

'No.'

'How do you know?'

'He's playing The Rolling Stones.'

'What?'

'Yes, I know, it's very loud, I'll close the door. There, is that better? Can you hear me? Good. He's started up his own private lockdown. What should I do?'

'Christ! Bugger!'

'I feel the same.'

'How did he get in? How did he get past the alarms?'

'Sometimes the mad can be quite clever.'

'And you didn't notice anything?'

'I noticed a light, last night.'

'What? Why didn't you tell me?'

'It was three am, I wasn't sure . . . '

'You saw a light and you weren't sure? What does that mean?'

'Calm down, please.'

'Don't tell me to calm down! I'm on my way.'

Maui looked up at Gabrielle. 'Sorry, I haven't got any food for cats. I wasn't planning going to the supermarket till next week. Can you last? If you're hungry, there's a juicy rat, just outside. Would you like some coffee?' Gabrielle put the coffee on. The Stones' song seemed to be on repeat play. One thing was for sure, the police would be here before Nancy arrived. She opened the cottage door and looked out to where she could catch a glimpse of the street through the little gateway in the hedge. Sure enough, there was a middle-aged man in pajamas and dressing gown standing in the middle of the road, staring at the pulsating Kinsella House.

The reason Nancy had forgotten what Tom Kinsella had tried to do to Gabrielle came clear when the middle-aged man was joined by a middle-aged woman and two sleepy teenagers out on the street. The last thing the Trust Board of Kinsella House wanted was a headline, Famous Painter's Son on Sex Charge Against Kinsella House Caretaker. (The media wouldn't use the word 'docent.') Then a backgrounder, Truth Behind Precious National Treasure. Then, Government Funds for Sex Offender's Family. But nothing was going to stop this present nightmare. The lockdown seemed to be collapsing inwards as more neighbours emerged out onto the desirable dead-end street that stopped right on the beach. That woman and the two men with her with the camera were obviously TV. The police were next. Two officers, woman and man, who immediately started demanding the neighbours return to their bubbles. Nancy's BMW appeared five minutes later, when the residents had retreated to peer out from their gateways.

Nancy had a couple of other Board members with her. Gabrielle recognized them, but didn't know their names. Gabrielle went down to the gate, with Maui at heel, and leant over the gate, trying to attract Nancy's attention. But the Trust Board cohort were already in discussion with the two police officers. Nancy was laying down the law. Gabrielle smiled to herself as she bent to stroke Mister Maui, who then slipped out under the gate and ran across the road to the driveway where the two teenagers were hanging out with coffee mugs in hand. The girl bent down and picked Maui up. That was his official residence. Another police car drew up, four officers this time. Then suddenly the Rolling Stones were switched off. The standard North Shore Sunday morning silence reasserted itself. Six masked police officers, Nancy and the two board members occupied the street, trying to maintain social distancing while having an animated discussion. Nancy was only a year or two older than Gabrielle. Yet she always treated Gabrielle as if she were a retarded child. They'd even been in the same Art History class at university, for god's sake, though Nancy had never been studying fine arts. Probably the proverbial BA/BCom combo. Gabrielle realized the thought was uncharitable, but she was losing the desire to repress that side of herself. Douglas had always said, 'Let the bad thoughts come. They're all good.'

Suddenly a great shout echoed round the solid neighbourhood. It was loud enough surely to be heard on Rangitōtō. Tom had got himself up onto the roof. The TV camera had been joined by another from a different news hub, and together they positioned themselves to catch the full drama as it unfolded. Tom had a stack of his Dad's canvases with him, some framed, some unframed. He was waving one in the air, like a battle flag. In his other hand he flourished a bottle of whiskey. It was 10am, Sunday morning at No. 1 Aroha Place and the siege of the Kinsella House was in full swing.

Gabrielle couldn't any longer bear watching Nancy, with her two hapless men trailing after her, as she attempted to take command of the police operation planning. Instead, she retrieved a spade from the garden shed round the back of the cottage. With this she lifted the stiff body of the rat and carried it to the foot of the pear tree where there was a recently dug patch of soft soil. As she rolled the body into the earth she thought that, if her secret benefactor, Charles Russell, Esq., recovered from his op and lived a little longer, then next year's pears would be even sweeter. The dead belong to no one.

Meanwhile Tom Kinsella had begun shouting his demands from the rooftop, making full use of the best camera angles available and swigging back on his bottle. Nobody was in any doubt, least of all Tom, that this would be his last stand. The only doubt was around whether he would fall off the roof. He was waving a large canvas as he lurched to the edge of the flat modernist roof and shouted at the well-spaced occupants of the street below:

'My mother painted this! He didn't! This painting is mine! This house is mine. I'm keeping my distance. You keep yours. Don't come near or I'll burn it all down. Every last piece of fakery.'

Gabrielle was startled as four police officers broke from behind her cottage and headed in a crouching run down the hedge line, where they couldn't be seen by Tom from his eyrie. The cops would have the keys to the back way from Nancy. There was also a short fire escape ladder which took you up to the roof. Just then the distraction plan from the negotiating team in the street went into action:

'Mister Kinsella, please take a seat up there. It'll be safer.' The voice came through a loud hailer.

'My name's not Kinsella. I've changed it. It's Rogers. I don't want his effing name. That's my mother's name.'

'Okay, Mister Rogers. Yes, take a seat. Are you comfortable?'

'No! What a stupid bloody question.'

But Tom had sat down. He pulled a rag from his pocket and a box of matches from another pocket. He grabbed another canvas, one he clearly thought had been painted by his hateful, famous father.

'See this!' he shouted as he waved the petrol-soaked rag. 'I've soaked this in petrol. I'm going to set this on fire. And I'm going to set fire to this awful painting. What a load of crap.' He waved the painting round in the air, then lost his grip on it and it went flying over the back of the house and landed in a pōhutukawa tree.

'Stop him!' Nancy screamed, running forward.

'Mrs Fulton,' the policewoman standing by her shouted, 'come back here! Let the officer deal with this.'

Gabrielle decided to go inside the cottage and make more coffee, maybe cook an egg, let Douglas's thousand flying ants distract her mind. While she was doing this, Tom's arrest was effected by four officers, two who came up through the manhole to the roof, and two who scaled the fire escape ladder. Tom tried to throw the whiskey bottle at them shouting that it was full of petrol, but they were, apparently, too fast for him. Gabrielle didn't see the arrest, only heard some of the sound effects seated at her table in the cottage.

During all the time since the music had started up, until Tom had been taken away, the street watchers had dispersed, and the Board representatives had also gone, presumably with the police to make statements and so on, not a single person had spoken to or looked at Gabrielle. The egg was delicious. The sandwich for lunch somewhat less so. A vaguely sick feeling had settled on her stomach. Not only did she have no part in what had happened, all her expertise seemed irrelevant to the monument that was the Kinsella House. It felt as if it was all about something else entirely. Almost to reassure herself of her own reality, she'd picked the little book on Gothic that she and Sean had written and began to flick through. It didn't read so badly. It seemed to make a kind of sense, the Victorian remnants of this colonial city, these architectural gestures back to the coloniser. No, it wasn't great, but it wasn't mad. That was when Nancy knocked on her door.

This time Gabrielle didn't open the door. Nancy tried to talk to her through the door, but the shouting was unbearable. She suggested to Nancy that she would open the kitchen window and Nancy could stand at the end of the porch and they would be able to speak like that.

'It's only me here, Gabrielle. There's nothing wrong with me.'

'It's not a question of who's got something wrong, we are doing it for each other.'

'I understand that perfectly well. You don't need to tell me. Anyway, I had to call an emergency Board meeting after we got away from the police station. As you might imagine not everyone could join us, but we had a quorum. Charles Russell couldn't make it of course. Everyone's very disappointed about what has happened.'

'Disappointed?'

'Yes, disappointed. It shouldn't have come to this. The Board feels they need to reassess the situation. I'm not saying there was anything you could have done to stop what happened from happening. But that's the point. You were not the person who could have done something. And that's what we need to look at.'

'What are you looking at?'

'We're looking at who is the best person to undertake the necessary protection of the asset we hold in trust. That house is full of paintings worth tens of thousands each, the House itself is a modernist masterpiece. We are custodians of a precious national treasure that defines our cultural life as a nation.'

'That's the kind of thing that Trevor's text needs to say.'

'Let's leave Trevor's text out of this. That is another disappointment, but more easily rectified. People – I mean the media, but also sponsors and donors – are asking already how could this thing have happened? Where is the security? So, the Board has come to a decision.'

'This afternoon?'

'Actually at lunchtime. We had a Zoom meeting. We have decided that what this house needs is someone living in the Cottage who is a caretaker with the power and the ability to enforce security. Charles Russell doesn't have Zoom, but, apparently, he has a nephew who runs a security company and he knows someone who would be ideal.'

'You mean I have to leave?'

'It won't happen while the lockdown is on. And as for the work you do for us, well that can continue, the docent duties, but employment will be on an hourly contract basis. I wanted to let you know quickly so you could make your arrangements. Now, it's been a day I would prefer to forget, so I need to get going.'

PART THREE: THE DEAD

Gabrielle sat on the beach, in the darkness, by herself. Behind her the expensive houses, where each remained in their bubble, projected fragments of light onto the sand. There was no light from the Kinsella House; after its furious day, it rested. She'd sat here, more or less in the same place, at the same time of day, on a dead Sunday night, thirty-three years before, but then Douglas Moran had been seated alongside her, while, in the Kinsella House, Kenneth Kinsella himself lay drunk and cantankerous while Dorothy tried to dissuade him from drinking more that evening. Douglas had with him the letter he'd received from Kenneth after his first solo show three months earlier. Since then, the share market had crashed massively, and the city had started to take on a haunted feel that would last for several years to come. The uncanny repetition she found herself in, plus the imminent loss of her home, had given rise to a feeling in her that the present was in process of being over-turned by the past.

Douglas held that first solo show in August 1987. He was twenty-two years old. The gallery was thronged, every piece hanging on the walls was sold, champagne flowed, the canapés were endless. Those last mad days before the great crash there was no end to the money that was being made, and, if you were poor art students, as Gabrielle and Douglas were, you could feed yourself for most of any week by attending the Tuesday evening gallery openings and sneaking home quantities of the free food on offer in the suitable bag you brought with you. Tuesday nights consisted of several gratis happy hours rolled into one as you progressed from opening to opening. Inside this culture of cornucopia, Douglas's show stood out for its profound restraint and delicacy. The quality of fragility in his work was not full of portent and doom; its evanescence spoke of a different contract with reality from the one that Kenneth Kinsella displayed with such command. That is why the letter he wrote to Douglas, when it was passed along from the gallery, was such a pleasure and a surprise: 'I see what you are doing and I stand in awe of it . . .' These words, when Nancy had read them the previous Thursday, were the kind of endorsement she wished did not exist, as Gabrielle had noticed from the shadow that had crossed her face. Douglas had warned Gabrielle back then that, if she wanted to try and become 'an artist' (he smiled when he said the word) it was worth remembering that there were always people who thought they owned the world and that the arts were part of the world. You crossed such people at your peril, but also you dealt with them at your peril.   Then he'd said: 'Don't worry, my darling, they haven't got a fucking clue. What's good is that Kenneth Kinsella, whatever else he is, isn't one of them.' The letter was the talisman which proved this true.

After the 20th October financial crash in 1987, as the value of the share market was stripped away to its miserable bones, so the city too descended into a slowly opening abyss, as if it had begun to rot. Construction cranes stood everywhere, and one by one they stopped operating. Their skeletons reached for the sky as if they were an aerobics class that had frozen in mid-gyration and then the flesh had fallen away to leave only gaunt memorials of bone. Douglas and Gabrielle loved the city as this happened to it. It was as if the rich had cleared out and the streets and lanes were left to the art students who could now emerge from their flat above the sex shop in K Rd and wander aimlessly down into the dead city. It was takeover time of a different kind.

It was on a Sunday evening, when they were wandering together, and had reached the red and blue lights of Fort Street, that Douglas had said:

'Let's go visit Kenneth.'

'Do you know where he lives?'

'His address is here, in the letter, see – One Aroha Lane. I know where that is. We could walk there in twenty minutes from the ferry.'

And at the same moment, the little stray kitten had come miaowing up to them from behind a rubbish bin. They'd picked it up and taken it with them, carried on board the ferry inside the same bag that served so well for collecting provisions at gallery openings.

They'd sat on the beach, plucking up courage:

'Has he got a dog?'

'God knows.'

'He's got a wife.'

'Dorothy, I think.'

'That's clever of you to know that.'

'I'm a student of art.'

'Let's sneak into the garden and see if we can see if anyone's home.'

'There's a light on.'

'Some people leave lights on to make people think there's someone there when there's not.'

'We could peek through a window.'

'Douglas Moran! What kind of human being are you?'

'I'm a little bit of a sneaky one.'

'Good. So am I. Let's go.'

Together they found that the hedge on the beachfront was thick, but also full of holes. They pushed their way through and crawled under a row of karo trees and stood up to find themselves in the Kinsella House garden. The light they had seen was down the side of the house (where the additions for storage and archives had subsequently been built). When they reached the window, Douglas was tall enough to stand on tiptoe and peek in at the bottom corner of the room. The room had a small lamp standing on a wooden apple box beside a divan bed. And there, on the bed, with one arm hanging lifelessly over the side, lay Kenneth Kinsella. Douglas could see his half-open mouth and his closed eyes, his head, with its still substantial shock of grey hair, lolling back on a pillow. Douglas picked Gabrielle up by the waist, like Nureyev himself, and lifted her high in the air. Her head shot up above the window ledge and she found herself not only looking at the recumbent Kenneth Kinsella, but also staring straight into the face of Dorothy Kinsella who had just walked into the room.

'Let me down, let me down,' she hissed at Douglas.

Douglas dropped Gabrielle. She plummeted and fell forward, dropping her bag, from which the stray kitten shot out, never to be seen by them again. The window above them was flung open and Dorothy fearlessly stuck her head out:

'Who's that? Who's there? What do you want?'

'It's just us,' said Douglas.

'Us? Us? Who's us?'

'We're two art students. We've come to see Kenneth.'

'Well, you can't. He's dead drunk.'

'Sorry for disturbing you,' Gabrielle ventured.

'You bloody well ought to be. I should have set the dogs on you. Only we haven't got any dogs. Well, you better come in. I want to see who you are. Come round to the back door.'

Dorothy had managed to convert to the funny side of the situation by the time they were inside. Douglas produced the precious letter from his pocket. Dorothy said:

'I hope you're not as delusional about this art business as Kenneth is. Would you like to see some of his latest? Go in there' – gesturing to a doorway – 'and I'll bring some coffee.'

In one corner canvases were leaning against each other. On a drop-cloth small squares of roughly cut canvas were laid out and all painted black. There was an easel, but there was nothing on it. Dorothy brought in the coffee.

'The stuff on the floor he's just started on, I believe. Pull out the stacked ones. Go on. Have a look. Help yourselves. He'll never know. It's your chance. That's why you're here isn't it? I want to go to sleep soon,' she said. 'But you've got half an hour. That's long enough for a good look.'

So, Douglas and Gabrielle pulled out painting after painting, while Dorothy sat on the floor, puffing on a cigarette and asking them questions about how the art school was these days. At half past nine she kicked them out.

'I'm going to give up smoking when he dies,' she said, as they left. 'Look after each other,' she called into the darkness.

It was too late, the last Sunday ferry had left. They curled up together on the beach, building a hollow in the sand. That was when Douglas had told her he was sick. 'It's a pandemic,' he said, saying a word she hadn't heard before. Right round the world. More and more people are dying, and there's nothing anyone can do. They call it the 'gay plague,' but that's bullshit.' Gabrielle couldn't sleep after that. The night was clear, the stars burning with an early summer glint in their eyes.

'Are you still awake?' Douglas asked.

'I suppose I am,' she replied.

'Don't worry, Gabs. First help yourself. This doesn't mean making yourself comfortable and making sure you have attended to all your problems. It means stripping away all the unnecessary rubbish, so you are down to the bare bones of yourself, then you become available to others, because you are not carrying the heavy self, but you have become the light self.'

And here she was again. Where the girl from Tokoroa and the boy from Papatoetoe had spent the night, curled up together under the stars. That beautiful, forgotten boy. She still carried him in herself.

'Welcome back,' she whispered.

SHANGHAI

This morning I went into the bathroom, half awake. After closing the door behind me, though, of course, there's no one else in the house now, I turned and looked up. And there he was, standing right in front of me. The Old Man. I almost said out loud, 'Dad! What are you doing here?' Then I realized. It certainly was the old man. But the old man was me.

The curious thing was that it happened again about an hour later. Not so much a 'vision' as the face in the mirror had been, but a kind of possession. I remember my Dad well when I was a kid, in the morning, before he left for the office, with the morning paper spread out on the dining room table, leaning forward propped up with both palms flat on the table surface and his head craned forward so he could peer over his glasses (they were for his short-sightedness) at the Death Notices. He never failed to scan them. You wouldn't want to turn up at the Loan and Mercantile Company Office of a morning not knowing who was dead and who was alive in the city. Dad must have started this habit pretty young. I didn't start until quite recently. All those years I was working on the boats, I never thought twice. Nobody down there was going to say to me, 'Did you see old so-and-so died', were they? Down on the wharves we smiled and waved and shouted (and swore if the public was out of earshot), it was all body language and educated grunts. On the water you kept your eyes outwards and talked in parallel, but you never got time off to go to anyone's funeral. Then came the redundancy and suddenly I was at home. I'd always read the paper at work, never bought one in years. Connie never cared for reading papers.

She used to ask, 'Do you think knowing about it is going to help?'

'Well, yes, I do,' I would reply.

'I don't think so,' she'd say. 'Go outside and look at the clouds.'

I ordered the paper anyway, even though no one reads it nowadays, and, naturally you might say, I found myself looking at the Death Notices. When Connie first caught me at it, she said, 'Now that's really not going to help them, is it!' She was a laugh a minute, dead-pan as a closed cupboard. I loved her for that. I don't think I ever saw her blink. And then she died. Just like that.

I'd completed my morning routines, collected the paper in its ugly plastic caul from the front gate, and the kettle was on and, rather than wasting an eternity on a watched pot, I went over to the table and turned the paper open to the page of those who are now beyond help, and began to scan. It has got harder to see, so I adjusted my hands, and arms, adopted the appropriate lean, and pulled my neck out until I could get a good strong bead on the latest list. And there I was, I felt it, right in my inner core, as if I was Marcel Marceau himself, completely inhabiting the Old Man's classic pose. I felt it in all my muscles. It went a little deeper than an ordinary case of the collective uncanny. I may just be a common seaman, but I've made up for it with Autodidact Certificate First Grade. I know that Oceanic Feeling when it seizes me. It was not so much that I felt like Dad, as that I felt like myself ten years old again. And I knew what – or rather, who - had possessed me: Dan.

Daniel Matutaera Mahuta Daniels, aged seventy-three. Lots of mokos listed. Tangi at Port Waikato. Dan. Dan, you're-a bit-of-a-Jack-Nohi-aren't-you, Daniels. I was trying to think. I hadn't heard word of him since, I must have been twelve when he went off to Borstal. 1961. Or 1962. That's the last time. And then it was only second-hand. I was still at Intermediate School and he'd been at high school, well he must have been in the fifth form by then, and someone said to me, 'Did you hear Dan Daniels has gone to Borstal?' I got a hell of a shock really, even though I was only twelve, because, well, to be honest, Dan was about the last person in our neighbourhood I would have expected to go to Borstal. At least when I had known him.

Where we lived out West, our house was on top of a hill and there was a valley down one way to the shops and the railway and the cemetery on the hill opposite, and the other way there were still paddocks and orchards. Our road ran down into a little gully where it stopped. Down there was a patch of old bush and mānuka scrub and some big English trees and a row of pines. The Daniels' house was at the bottom of the road. I used to sneak down there by myself to the bush and the trees, because Mum preferred us not to go alone, but my brother never wanted to go with me. Those trees were an excellent place for bird-nesting and I was a climber by nature, so I would go up searching for eggs and take them home and blow them and keep them in an Adams Bruce chocolate box that I had lined with cotton wool: my collection. Sparrow's eggs are white, fantails are creamy, blackbird eggs are a greenish kind of blue, with speckles, but thrushes' are a paler blue with big speckles, and starlings are even more pale, and mynahs, if you can get any, are the best, a shining turquoise blue. Nowadays out here, we are surrounded by tūī and kererū and rosellas, but none of those were round back then. It was pretty bare and bleak then. And there were hardly any native birds, but you could find good eggs. I even had some big brown chicken eggs in my collection box.

The trees and scrub were on the edge of one of the paddocks, which was pretty overgrown. Some kids said, when I was small, there's a bull in that paddock, don't wear anything red; but I never saw a bull. Once someone put three sheep in there for a few months and the grass got shorter, but after that they were taken away. The back fence of the Daniels's house backed onto this paddock near where the trees and scrub were standing. It was, as one might say, a 'place to be' when one was neither independent enough to wander much further, nor too small to feel terrified any longer of being far from home. A big place (you looked out to the dark blues and greens of the Waitākere Ranges with fine stacks of cloud often sitting above), but also a small place (the valley was sheltered from too direct attacks by the south-westerly winds) where in summer you could stand in the long grass with the heat cooking you like egg. Po-faced William

Wordsworth might have recognized it as a place in which the imagination could dwell. I liked to go there by myself.

I had a favourite tree I liked to climb, a horse chestnut with smooth branches, and another, a pine that you could climb to the very top and look out over the world. Someone once said that you could see Australia from the top of that tree. In fact, when you reached that point where you could poke your head out into the air, you weren't even on the level with our backyard up the hill. The day I met Dan I was on a mission to get a duck egg for my collection. A kid at school, Larry Jenkins, told me that his brother had seen a pair of paradise ducks in the paddock and they had a nest in the macrocarpa at the very bottom corner. Larry also told me that paradise ducks lay black eggs and I thought to myself, black eggs, now imagine a black egg in my box. So, I set out. To get down to that corner you had to snake along past the Daniels' corrugated iron fence, otherwise, going round by the other long way, you'd get stuck in the swamp at the bottom of the field, which was full of stuff, old tires and wire-wove beds and an old pram. Larry tried to persuade me there was a dead baby in the pram, but at ten years old someone had screwed my head on straight, so I didn't say anything back to him. I knew, even then, there was no need to provoke people like Larry.

I had couple of brown paper bags with me from the cupboard at home, with a bunch of cotton wool inside, so eggs wouldn't bump against each other and break. You had to bend down to get under the manukas and then, when you'd done that, the path along the edge of the Daniels' fence was quick and easy. I was just standing up after coming under the manukas when – bang! An incredible noise exploded just above my head against the fence. I stood up and looked round, but I couldn't see anything. Then – bang! Again. Something hard whacked into the Daniels' fence, but further down at the other end. Then laughing. I looked up then and saw him sitting up in the oak tree, straddling a branch, looking straight back at me.

'You look like you saw a ghost.' He was laughing again.

'Gave me a fright,' I said. He was older than me. I'd seen him at school and his sister was in my class, but I had never spoken to him before.

'What you want?'

'Bird-nesting.'

'What sort?'

'The ducks. Paradise ducks. Larry Jenkins's brother said there's some paradise ducks down here.'

Dan jumped down. He had a shanghai in his hand. That was what he'd used to fire stones into the tin fence and make me jump. 'You're a bit of a Jack Nohi, aren't you?' He was quite bit taller than me.

'I suppose so.'

'Is that your name?'

'What?'

'Jack Nohi?'

'No.'

'You're in my sister's class, aren't you?'

'Yeah.'

'Dan. I'm Dan. That's my house there, behind the fence.'

I had a problem with my name: Jeavons. Nobody was really meant to have that name for a first name and certainly not back then, when names were much more restricted than now; but my mother's mother, back in Wales, her mother's family had been Jeavons and I think that my mother liked the idea that it was a name 'with distinction' as I heard her once explain to a puzzled receptionist at the doctor's. It has French origins, she said. Dad wanted to fit in, but Mum regretted that she had been obliged to.

'You're Jeavons, aren't you? Funny name.'

'Yeah.'

'That's okay. Mind if I call you Jack?'

'No, that's okay.' Actually, I was glad.

'I've seen you before down here.'

'Yeah.'

'So, what, do you collect eggs?'

'Yeah. I've got a collection.'

'Can I see it?'

'I haven't got it here.'

'Go and get it.'

'What, now?'

'Yeah. Show me. If you show me, I'll help you - we can see if we can get some of those duck eggs from the pūtangitangi.'

'What?'

'That's what we call them. What you call paradise ducks. Pūtangitangi. At least that's what mum calls them. She whistles at them.'

I went back home and got my boxes – I had two boxes by then – and carried them down carefully wrapped up in a jersey so no one would know what I was carrying. I think Dan was quite impressed, because he whistled in that soft, in-drawn way. We hid the boxes under some bracken and then went down to the macrocarpa. The ducks – the pūtangitangi – heard us coming and all we caught of them was the sound of their wings taking flight and their slightly Goon-show 'zonk-zonk' and 'zeek-zeek' calls to proclaim their departures. We climbed up the macrocarpa, but we couldn't find a nest. Then we hunted around the grass at the edge of the paddock by the little swamp, but we couldn't find anything.

'Larry Jenkins says they have black eggs.'

Dan looked at me. Then he said: 'I've never heard of a black egg. I'll ask my Mum.'

'How would she know?'

'She's a teacher.'

'Oh.'

'At the Catholic school. What's your Mum do?'

'Nothing really. She stays at home. Oh, she works at the school, in the office, two days a week.'

'Yeah, I've seen her there.'

I went back home after that, in case Mum thought I'd been away too long. It was funny, talking to one of the older kids like that. He was at the Intermediate, but I was still at Primary. Maybe it was because Dan only had sisters. As I was going he said, looking at the boxes bundled up in my old jersey, 'You haven't got any skylarks' eggs in there.' He was right. He seemed to know the names of all my eggs, so I wondered if he collected eggs too, but I never had the courage to ask him.

'You should get some,' he said. 'The paddock's a good place to look. And the paddock after that. Sometimes the Dragiviches put their goat in there, but it's nothing to be scared of. Just a bit of a bum-butter as old Mister Draggy says. Come down on the weekend. Stand here by the fence and give three whistles three times and I'll climb over. I'll show you where to look.'

I was still leaning on the table, with his death notice there in front of me. It is startling how much can pass through your mind in an instant. I took myself back to the kettle and put my hand on it to feel how hot it was. Probably good now for green tea. I opened the drawer and took out the Lung Ching and unscrewed the top of the jar. That bitter, grassy scent came floating up. Two spoons in an old iron pot. Then the water, hopefully a little under boiling now. And wait to brew: three to five minutes.

Dan told me that skylark eggs are cream with brown speckles. I had never seen one before. We set out across the paddock looking for a nest in the grass. The grass was long in places and, with our heads down, we could almost disappear from each other from time to time. Suddenly Dan came up behind me and started firing a machine gun at me. I fell down, jerking and shrieking, before undergoing rapid rigor mortis. I think Dan liked my dying.

'It's like hunting in the jungle for the Commies,' he said.

'Yeah.'

'That's what my Dad does. Hunting the Commies in the jungle.'

I didn't quite believe him. The gap between my Dad going off in the Anglia to the Loan and Merc every morning and Dan's Dad stalking the Commies with a machine gun felt a little large to compass.

'Is that right?'

'You don't believe me. It's true.'

'Okay.'

'He's in the army.'

'Oh.'

'In Malaya. They got an emergency there and he's fighting the Commies. It's not like here with grass and stuff. It's real jungle, you know, swamps – not like that swamp down there – and snakes and monkeys and it's steaming hot.'

'So, he doesn't come home?'

'No. No, he's been away for six months. He's going to come home in a couple of months.'

I didn't tell anyone at home about Dan. And I didn't go to his place, so I don't know if his mother or his sisters knew about me. Well, Marion, his sister did know about me because I was in her class. And he didn't come up to my place. I would duck under the manukas to the fence and whistle and sometimes Dan would appear and sometimes he wouldn't. I could always play there by myself. When he did come out, we developed our game of 'stalking the commies' by pretending that the pūtangitangi were the Commies and we would try to creep up on them through the densest patches of grass without making a sound, but we never succeeded in getting close. That might have been because Dan loved his system of whistles that he had devised for signaling, and I was obliged to use them. However, the ducks ably identified human whistles. So, those Commies were too smart for us.

We couldn't work out where they were nesting. We began to scour the paddock for signs of a nest on the ground. This 'mopping up' operation (Dan knew the right terms) took us up to the top side of the paddock where the backyards of several houses ran down to meet the old wire-stranded fence. One of these houses, a small cottage that looked as if, as Mum said, 'it had seen better days' had a large vegetable garden. When we came up by the fence, we crouched down in our combat-ready position and lifted our heads carefully above the grass-line. We could see in the backyard an old couple, the woman bending over, the man sitting on a stool, working in the garden. These were 'the old Chinese couple' as my mother referred to them, who 'didn't speak a word of English.' There were no other Chinese people around in our area of town in those days, though, of course, the three-storey block of flats that now stands on that site is occupied by at least two young Chinese couples, one with a BMW sports, while the others take off every morning on electric bikes.

The tea was ready. It's strange how you can still feel something like that grass on your skin (the grass at the top of the paddock by the fence-line was lush and green) from sixty years ago. Green tea in the hand and green grass in the mind, but touching the body. Perhaps it's because, although I went to sea, I never left home. This is the same place that I grew up in. Oh, Connie and I changed it over years, a back deck out over the valley to the Waitakeres, some proper insulation, a central heating system; but really, it's still here more-or-less 'as is' as I am (more or less) myself. The old man of the old place. I didn't really want to *go* anywhere in that sense. I wanted to go to sea, and I did. In the merchant navy at first, but then, working on the harbour.

My brother wanted to know why I lacked ambition. 'You could have done anything, you know.'

I answered him, 'It never occurred to me.'

That made him laugh. He'd got the answer he had asked for.

There we were, lying in the grass, taking a peek at the mysterious old gardeners. I whispered to Dan:

'Larry Jenkins says they eat cats.'

'Who?'

'Them.'

'Bulldust,' said Dan.

'He says that, you know the Tai Tung restaurant in town?'

'No,' said Dan.

'Mum and my brother and me sometimes go into town on Friday nights to meet Dad after work and we go to the Tai Tung. Well, he says they catch the cats in the back alley and they kill them and cook them and sell it as chicken chow mein.'

'Larry Jenkins needs his head read. He's a bully, you know that?'

'Yeah, I know.'

Dan had a way of dissolving anxieties, much as Larry Jenkins had a way of creating them.

'They eat eggs,' Dan suddenly said. 'Maybe they ate those duck eggs we can't find.'

'Duck eggs? They eat duck eggs?'

'Why not?'

'I've never eaten duck eggs.'

'No reason why you shouldn't start. Mum says they make the best omelette. And the best cakes.'

We must have been talking too loud, forgetting our mission, because suddenly the old woman was at the fence, waving at us and saying things we couldn't understand, except it was obvious she didn't like us sneaking up like that. Dan stood up and said, 'Sorry' and then grabbed me and said, 'Let's go,' and we took off down the hill, but she went on shouting at us.

There was no way I could go to the tangi. It was simply that the thought passed through my head, before I dismissed it. How could I say who I was? I poured out the Lung Ching into the sweet little cup that Connie had made – a whole set of them, but only two left now – after she sold the salon and started going out to classes to learn stuff. Warm and shaped to the hand. She spent her whole life in the 'the beauty business,' training, then working for others, and, as soon as she could, getting her own business, her own place, with two girls and Stan too of course, working for her. I always liked the idea she could sell 'beauty.' And she could make it too, witness this translucent turquoise glaze, this tiny barrel of a vessel that slipped into your hand like a lover. Warm and shaped to the cradle of your palm. I crossed to the door that led onto the deck, pushed it open and stepped out. The air was dark and heavy with a brown gloom, from the Australian bush fires hanging over us. Now you really could see Australia. It had come over the hills to meet and greet.

The last time I went out over those hills to the coast, must have been three months back now, the beach was closed for the algal bloom. Closed. That was a weird feeling too, same as the light this morning as it carpeted the ground in a pale, yellow murk, as the feeble sun tried to shine through the ash particles. Those algal blooms spread out in vast swathes of bacteria, the countless billions to match the stars above, engulfing the sea; then suddenly they'd be gone, all those tiny myriad lives dead, dissolved, dispersed. I'd read all that stuff in my lunch-breaks down on the wharves. Autodidacticism 101. I think that's why I went to work, for the breaks. The work was only a way of waiting for the breaks. Though this world is called the modern world, it's not much more modern than other worlds that have ceased to be modern, because so many people still think in terms of signs and wonders, but not often in terms of actions and consequences. We were told, when I was kid, that there were seven wonders of the world, but actually it turned out there were several million wonders.

From on the deck I could see the block of flats where the old Chinese couple's cottage had stood. That old lady scared us both. I think of her now as carrying a rake as she came screaming at us. But I'm fairly certain that I'm making that up. But I do remember that the effect of her ferocity was that we kept away from that fence-line and stayed down the other end of the paddock in Dan's territory, which probably made it inevitable that such caution could only lead to disaster.

One day Dan came over his fence with his shanghai in his hand. I hadn't seen it since the day we met, but now he asked me if I knew how to use it, and because I had to say I didn't, he offered to teach me. He'd brought an old Griffins biscuit tin with a whole lot of specially chosen stones for firing, which he was carrying inside the tin. He set up the tin on one of the strainer posts at the far corner, by the gate to Dragivich's paddock. We started quite close and Dan would hit it every time, but I struggled to get the knack. Part of Dan's teaching technique was that, if you missed, then you had to go and find the stone, so it could be re-used. It was a long slow process, since finding stones in grass isn't easy, and my miss-rate exceeded my hit-rate, and Dan must have shared my brother's query about why I lacked the necessary drive to conquer the task. As your accuracy improved, so the distance from the tin was increased. I did enjoy the resounding whack that the stones made when they hit the target. So, gradually, I made progress further and further from the Griffins boy who was clutching a Griffins tin under his arm on which was pictured a Griffins boy clutching a tin under his arm, and so on, until you might have had as many boys as stars or algal bacteria, but so infinitely small they dwelt on the nano-end of detection. Tiny tiny boys. If I wanted ambition, I made up for it with absorption, and Dan was a meticulous teacher, which meant that when I heard Dan shout out, 'Look!' my mind broke out of its bubble and I wheeled round where he pointed, and there not far above us, further up the paddock, the pair of pūtangitangi were flying past. I had the shanghai in hand, the stone ready in its pouch, so nothing held me back from releasing the shot.

I missed the birds of course. Those Commie ducks were out of our class. But what I didn't miss was a glass frame covering some plants in the old Chinese couple's vegetable garden. No resounding whack this time, instead a shattering tinkle.

Dan said: 'Jesus, why did you do that?'

'I dunno,' I said.

'You don't just fire blindly. That's how you get killed. Or you kill your mates. I've been trying to teach you to identify your target first.'

'I'm sorry.'

'Yeah, well, don't be stupid next time. We'd better go up there and see them.'

'What?' I said

'You broke their glass.'

'I didn't mean to.'

'But you did.'

'That doesn't mean we have to go up there.'

But it was too late. The old lady was already coming out of the house, shouting at us. Dan looked at me and said, 'Come on,' and started walking up, but I lost my nerve and turned and ran.

I ran down into the trees and got down behind the macrocarpa and crouched down as if the Commies had me cornered. I was breathless and saying to myself, 'Bloody Dan, bloody, bloody Dan.' But I really was cornered. Not by the Commies, but by myself. I couldn't go on crouching there forever. Something in my ten-year-old brain switched on and I realized what I needed to do. I stood up, and started to walk back up the paddock, dragging my feet through the grass, but still progressing forward.

I was looking for Dan, but I couldn't see him, and I was listening for the old lady's crazy shouting, but I couldn't hear any of that. When I got to the fence I couldn't see anyone. It was as if they had disappeared. I could see the broken glass frame, which had been put in place to cover up some seedlings. The shanghai had done its work. And then a voice:

'Jack! Jack!'

I looked up. It didn't sound like Dan. On the back steps of the house, there was a man waving at me and calling out. But it wasn't the old man. It was someone I'd never seen before. It felt funny because no one had ever called me Jack except Dan. But I was Jack, I couldn't deny that.

'You're Jack, aren't you?' he called across the length of the garden. 'Come up here. Come and see us. It's okay. You don't need to worry. It's all right.'

I started climbing over the fence, using the strainer post as Dan had shown me, not wanting to make another mistake. I could feel my face growing red with embarrassment under my short blonde curls. I hated that when it happened, how I couldn't stop blushing once I started. I must have looked like the personification of guilt as I shuffled up the garden slope, red face, head down, shoulders hunched, my arms half-folded across my chest.

'My name's Samuel. Samuel Lu.'

I hadn't looked at him yet, but when I did, he had come down the steps to meet me and was holding out his hand. I had no choice but to take it and shake it.

'Did you have an accident, did you?'

I nodded.

Dan appeared at the back door of the house from inside. 'That's Jack,' he said.

'Hullo, Jack. We can get that fixed. Dan here came and told us. I'm Mr. and Mrs. Lu's grandson. I live here too, but mostly I'm not here because I work at the hospital in town.'

I still couldn't think of anything to say, but Dan prompted me.

'You better say sorry.'

'Sorry,' I said.

'Thank you,' said Samuel. 'It was an accident. My grandparents don't speak English. They come from Shanghai. I think you gave them a bit of a fright.'

'Sorry,' I said again. And added: 'I didn't mean to.'

'We won't do it again,' Dan added, graciously including himself.

'No, we won't.'

'That's good.'

'Where's Shanghai?' Dan asked

I wanted to say, because I knew, but I was still waiting for my blushing to subside.

'China,' said Samuel.

'Is that where you come from?' asked Dan.

'I was born there, yes, but I don't remember. Grandma and Grandpa took me to Hong Kong, and then when I was six I came here.'

'Was that because of the Commies?' Dan asked.

I knew that wasn't the right thing to ask, and I could feel the blushing starting up all over again. Samuel had a round smiling face, a crewcut and horn-rimmed glasses. He looked at Dan for a minute without the smile, then he smiled again.

'Yes, that was part of it. But mainly we had an uncle here in Auckland who helped us to come here.'

'What about your Mum and Dad?'

'Oh, they're dead.'

'Both of them?'

Dan wouldn't give up. It was the same with his teaching me how to use the shanghai – never give up. He was still holding the shanghai in his hands, twisting the rubber round his fingers. It went through my head that it was funny that that thing was called a shanghai and that Samuel was born in a place called Shanghai.

'Yes. Both.'

'At the same time?'

'Ah – we don't really know about that.'

'Gee, that's sad.'

'Thank you,' said Samuel, but I could see he was looking at

the ground now, hoping for no more questions.

'Hey, Dan, we better get going now.'

We walked silently together down the paddock and collected the Griffins tin and the precious cache of stones inside.

'I reckon he drives that Zephyr with the white wheels.'

'Who?'

'Him. Samuel. '

I'd seen it parked outside that house. Then we heard Dan's Mum calling him for lunch. I'd never seen his Mum, but I knew her voice. Dan hauled himself up onto the fence, and I passed the tin up to him, and then he jumped over.

'See you later, alligator.'

'In a while, crocodile.'

He fired a stone hard into the fence behind where I stood. Whack!

'Dan!' his Mum called. 'Don't be a stupid boy! Hurry up!'

I stood listening for a while. I could hear the ducks down in the swamp. The boy stood in the burning paddock. 'The boy stood on the burning deck.' My old man used to recite that when he was shaving, as if the rhythm of the poem helped him keep the strokes of his safety razor smooth and true. He could recite a range of bouncy poems he'd been made to learn at school, but this was his favourite. When I hear it in my mind's ear, it comes back in the old man's voice, as if his ghost had stepped inside me. But really, it's only me here, standing on the deck. Only me. The old man stood on his burning deck. He stood there under the darkened sky. He gazed out on the hills that had been born long ago from volcanoes. And, as he did, a pair of those ducks, pūtangitangi, flew across the valley.

ABOUT THE AUTHOR

Murray Edmond has published 16 books of poetry. Recent titles include Back Before You Know (2019), FARCE (2022) and Sandbank Sonnets (2022). His book of four novellas, Strait Men and Other Tales appeared in 2015. Noh Business (2005) was a study of the influence of Noh drama on Western theatre and Then It Was Now Again: Selected Critical Writings (2014) brought together more than 30 years of criticism. In 2021 he published a cultural history, Time to Make a Song and Dance: Cultural Revolt in Auckland in the 1960s. He has co-edited two poetry anthologies, The New Poets (1987) and Big Smoke: New Zealand Poems 1960-1975, and he was editor of the magazine Ka Mate Ka Ora: A Journal of New Zealand Poetry and Poetics from 2005 to 2020. He has been Dramaturge for Indian Ink Theatre Company from 1997 to 2023. He lives in Glen Eden in Auckland, Aotearoa/New Zealand.